BROKEN RECORD

BROKEN RECORD

Jacqueline Grandey

atmosphere press

© 2021 Jacqueline Grandey

Published by Atmosphere Press

Cover design by Senhor Tocas

No part of this book may be reproduced without permission from the author except in brief quotations and in reviews. This is a work of fiction, and any resemblance to real places, persons, or events is entirely coincidental.

Atmospherepress.com

To Tommy, Zane, and Chad...thank you.

He told me that this wasn't unconditional love—that it was based on certain conditions. I was a little hurt but I didn't care as I did anything for this man. It's amazing how you can shed your skin and gallivant around in someone else's costume of comfort. Almost a year ago this man walked into my life and changed me forever.

CHAPTER ONE

DALLAS

I was a starving graphic artist a few years post-grad from my program at the Art Institute of Dallas.

"How long does this starving artist gig last? Ahhhhh!"

I screamed as I tossed my cell phone across the room and laid back on the concrete floor of my loft, contemplating how I was going to pay my rent. Talking to my mother always revved me up. She pleads for me to call her when I need something, I call for a little financial breathing room, and she chastises my choice of living while refusing to write a check. Mother's constant nagging makes my skin crawl. Yeah, the loft sucked. It was kind of a dump hidden in the Deep Ellum district of Dallas. It sat above a bar and every Friday and Saturday evening you would hear and feel the band jamming beneath you. The rundown old building used to be a power company of some sort and was transformed into lofts to rent out cheap. Aside from the leaks in the hallway after every rainstorm and the occasional mouse you have to step over, the key word was *cheap*. Renters were musicians, artists, and the underground world of misfits. The stench of cigarettes, pot, and patchouli would linger in the hallways. Sometimes it was so strong I'd get a contact buzz just fetching my mail. There was also a never-ending band jam down the poorly lit, narrow hall. You can stop by and score any party supplies you need to get you through the next week. It has an eclectic mix of tenants, I thought to myself. I laid on my concrete floor, groaning. I could hear someone hollering in the hallway, "Five minutes man, chillax!" I laughed. There's one of the tenants now. Suddenly that voice was at my door.

"Alex, let me in! I've got neeews."

"Ugh."

I rolled over and got up to open the door. Standing at my door was this six-foot, black spiky Sid Vicious hair, thin as a rail, vinyl pant wearing best friend of mine. Tyler Black.

"Alexandria Rae," he belted out as he pushed me out of the way to jump on my bed.

It was secluded in the middle of the studio. The bed separated sleeping quarters from living quarters with white netting.

"We got a gig!" Tyler yelled as he ruffled my pillows under his head.

"Don't get that goop shit you call gel you put in your hair last week all over my pillow," I teased. Rockstars never seem to bathe. Tyler was such a rockstar for the Dallas underground scene. Lead singer of the band WHIP, some Gothic industrial I-want-to-slit-my wrist kind of music.

"My bombshell of a buddy, you HAAAVE got to go to

this gig with me." Tyler is so dramatic. "It's down at the Steel Door on Saturday night. Maybe one of your ex pretty band boys will be there, you know you need to get laid," Tyler teased as he adjusted the pillow. I did have a few in my past I'd rather not speak of. And I thought I had issues, but wait until you date a man in a band.

"Sure Ty, I'll be there."

"Bitchin'!" he yelled as he wiped his eyes, smearing last night's guyliner. "What's eatin' you? Mommy dearest reprimanding you again? I see the cell phone being flown across the floor. Are you a disappointment again?" Tyler laughed. "I've always been a drag to my mum. You're a big girl now, live your own life—I'm living mine and lovin' every fucking minute of it." Tyler let out a huff and rolled his eyes before jumping up, kissing me on the head, and jetting out my door. "Catch ya laytah Blondie, I gotta rehearse."

Of course the practice pad was just down the hall...ugh, I'm not in the mood for head-pounding live music right now. However, I do need to get laid and probably consider a move. Staring off as I held the handle to close the door, I thought of how Tyler and I made out before. The thought made me laugh to myself. He had cornered me in an elevator at an Aerosmith concert. He pushed the stop button, turned, and swooped my waist with one hand. He then pushed me against the wall and slid his wet tongue into my mouth. I felt a flush rush over me. I immediately responded to his advances. I pushed back and kissed him hard on the mouth while pulling his hair.

"Yummm, cinnamon lips," I whispered.

I was told cinnamon would conceal any nicotine taste

when you kissed a smoker. The memory made me flush again and I smiled. I would never sleep with that male slut, ew. But I'd have to admit, he was fun to play and make out with when we went clubbing. All the pretty party girls loved my rockstar Tyler. When we would flirt and show some PDA, girls would swoon and I'd just feel like a starlet. Tyler had such swagger, such a presence on and off stage, kind of like David Bowie. He had a whole set of these groupie chicks that hung around every practice and backstage at every show. I called them chicken heads. You know, their heads peck up and down when they're giving the musicians blowjobs. I chuckled again.

"Sluuuuts!" I hollered out.

I crawled back onto the cold concrete floor, where I stretched out my petite body while I decluttered my mind. Lying there, I was thinking of ways to pay these fuckin' bills since I'm cut off from my mother's payroll...ugh. Mother wants me to find a man that can provide for me. Provide? I'm not dating an ATM machine, geez! If I would take her advice and become the daughter she's trying to groom me to be, I'd be miserable. I want excitement! I want creative independence! And especially...I want love! I decided to grab my sketch pad off the floor next to me and make a list of how to earn quick cash without dating an ATM. I let out a deep breath and started my list.

*

It was Thursday—which I liked, the last workday for me. I interned at the local weekly paper *D-town*. It was made up of all the weekly music and art events going on in Dallas.

The Art Institute set me up with the gig for shit pay. I needed the exposure as well as the contacts that the paper would provide. The internship was Monday through Thursday. I was their social media gal. But I didn't need to pay that high-ass tuition at the Institute just to roll out a couple of tweets four days a week. What a crock. I have a graphic design degree. Well, the *D-town* newspaper gig was good enough for NOW, it kept me in cat food and art supplies.

Two days and counting until WHIP showcases at the Steel Door. Oh, that reminds me. I needed to notify my boss, Fat Larry, to send someone over to the Steel Door on Saturday to interview WHIP. I know Tyler would love that, such a media whore that man is. I chirped out a *#WHIP rocks it sat night at the #SteelDoor,* posting it online. I added some sweaty hot image of Ty in leather pants and no shirt. I retrieved his body art off Google Images and sent it out into the abyss. Within five minutes, every Dallas chicken head would retweet.

"Sluuuts," I murmured under my breath.

Later that night, I met up with Tyler downstairs at the Green Room, the dive bar below my loft. I sat at a small metal table with two chairs by the window. I brought in a copy of the new *D-town* to show Ty the ad of WHIP and their logo to promote Saturday's show. WHIP was already blowing up on the YouTube and social media scene. These guys were hot in this town, the next raging band from the underground scene. I liked being a part of the underground scene. I liked not fitting in. Being an artist, I guess I was a black sheep myself. An old Social Distortion song rocked on in the background. I had such a thing for music. Music always brings you back to a moment. When you hear a certain song, doesn't it always bring you to a moment? Guess that's why I space out every time I hear certain lyrics, certain old songs—I just get lost in the music.

"Yoo-hoo," said Tyler as he snatched the *D-town* paper out of my hands.

"Okay, why don't I have the cover yet?" Tyler pouted. I laughed.

"You are such a media whore, Ty. You'll get it after the show, unless you fuck up your performance," I said.

"Oh doll, I'm going to chew up this crowd and spit them out," he responded as he put out his cigarette in the beer bottle he was using as an ashtray. "I'm ready for SXSW, Blondie; this club gig is small time. I am ready to expose myself and my talents."

"You'll expose yourself all right," I laughed. "Saturday night, you'll expose yourself to a dressing room half full of chicken heads."

"Bock...bock," he replied as he motioned to the waitress for another beer. "Did you sort out your mommy dearest issues yet?" Tyler winked at me as he sipped his beer.

"You mean, did I find an ATM to mount?"

Tyler chuckled as he tried not to spit out his drink. "I'd go with the wash machine if I was going to fuck an appliance; it at least vibrates." Tyler said as he stuck out his tongue and I slapped his hand. "I'm chewing on other ways to make money." I groaned. " I should talk to the owner of this place and see if I can serve drinks to all you punks in here." I looked around in disgust. "The problem is none of you broke-ass musicians ever tip!" I scolded

Tyler as he nodded his head in agreement.

Ty and I wrapped up our evening powwow and I headed back upstairs. We had a lot of powwows when we needed face time with just each other to shoot the bull, as they say in Texas. Ty was my BF. You shouldn't always make out with your friends, but he made me feel pretty and he sure was sexy. I wasn't attached, so why not? I always did like hanging out with the boys. It's due to growing up with my older brother, Austin. He's a good egg. He's in the military now, stationed outside of San Antonio. I need to go visit him, I really miss Austin. Austin and I are from a good southern family, hence the names Austin and Alexandria Rae. We motored around quite a bit because Daddy was in the military as well. I guess that's where I get my wanderlust spirit from. He's retired now. But he devotes his time to veteran charities and volunteering at the local VA hospital. He still gets up every day before dawn and has everything in order, does not like chaos. Sounds like a bit of OCD to me, but whatever keeps him motivated. Daddy would always chant those damn military songs. I especially liked the funny ones. *Left, left, left, right, left...I don't know what you've been told...but Eskimo pussy is mighty cold...left, left, left right left.* Aw, that makes me laugh. However, I did have girlfriends, too...

Friday rolled around and one of those girlies called my cell.

"Hey hooker," I answered.

"Hey bitch," replied the sultry voice on the other end. It was a gal pal that I met at one of Ty's shows who was a local "entertainer." Nooo, not a singer, comedian, what-have-you entertainer—I mean a stripper. Yep, Ms. Party

Girl herself: Nova. She was calling me from her car on the way into work, some joint called *Vanity*. Very suiting. Nova used the stage name Mercedes at work because she said no one wants to ride a Chevy Nova, they want to ride the Mercedes Benz. The Eagles lyrics popped in my head: *she drives a Mercedes Benz...she has a lot of pretty pretty boys that she calls friends.* Isn't that true with Miss Stripper Mercedes or Nova or whatever the hell she goes by?

"So are you going to the show on Saturday?" I asked.

"Want a date?" Nova asked.

"Sure hooch, meet me at my pad on Saturday night and we'll get gussied up and walk over."

The Steel Door was only a few blocks away, as I lived in the heart of Dallas's music scene. The district was called Deep Ellum. Cool vibe, lots of music venues, and local art gratified everywhere.

"See you Saturday, dress slutty you hooker, none of that fucking cowgirl boot shit," Nova said. I laughed.

"Yeehaw," I hollered with my southern drawl.

Nova hates when I wear that country Texas shit. She's from Texas but is in pure denial. Every so often she'll call and use a different accent, wanderlust herself.

"I gotta go hunting," I replied.

Which meant, I needed to go shopping for some rocker threads for the big show. Ernie, my cat, rubbed up on my leg, purring for affection and food.

"Look, I'll catch you Saturday night, I've got a pussy rubbing on my leg that needs my attention."

Nova hissed on the phone and hung up. What sass. I love her 'I don't give a fuck' attitude.

"Come on, Ernie. I'll feed your fat ass." I love that cat.

"Friday night...what should I do?" I asked Ernie as he rolled over on my bed, displaying no interest. Just on cue, the amps were being plugged in and the guitars started strumming underneath my loft. Not sure if I'll ever get used to the music vibrating underneath my feet, but tonight seemed like blues so I didn't mind it. "Well Ernie, sounds like a blues night tonight."

Wind was rustling outside and there was a chill in the air. North Texas gets cooler in mid-October. I decided I'd stay in, listen to blues, and paint. I opened up the two big windows that swing outward toward the street New Orleans style. This was the soundtrack for my evening paint session. In light of the blues theme, I sketched a picture of B.B. King.

✱

Purrrrrrrrrrrr...I hear the motor running in my ear. I was getting my morning lovin' from Ernie. I belted out the tune *"Get your motor running, head out...to the kitchen, I need coffee!"* I crawled out of my mosquito netting and put my feet on the floor in the direction of the kitchen.

"Brrr!" I immediately withdrew them back onto the bed. "Shit, that concrete's cold!" I yelled, shivering.

It sure was a cold morning, but intending to warm up by midafternoon.

"Wow, I need hot coffee."

After a minute of rubbing the chill off my feet, I attempted the cold floor once again. Then I went looking for my Dallas Cowboy slippers that Austin sent me for Christmas last year. It's actually quite quiet in the early morning when all the loft misfits are still sleeping. No one budges 'til noon. I fed Ernie, scooped his litter box, and threw on an old Jane's Addiction tee with my skinny jeans and Converse shoes. I still had paint on my fingernails and the shoes from last night's painting session, but who gives a shit? I was thrift shopping that afternoon, what did I need a ball gown to do that? Well, if I was shopping at the North Park Mall with my mother I would—but not on my budget. *Hello, Goodwill!* I texted Tyler to see if he wanted to join me but, with no response, I assumed he was in the land of the living dead. He'll hit me up after noon. I grabbed the old ammo bag I stole from Daddy that I use as a purse—classy, eh? I headed down to my pickup truck.

Yes, we true southern gals drive pickup trucks. Mine was a red FORD that big brother Austin fixed up. He got it running 'til little sis gets a good-paying job...or meets Mr. Wonderful and starts popping out babies. You know that's what good Christian Texan women do? They get married to a wealthy man, have lots of babies, rat their hair out, and shop at the North Park Mall. Thoughts of Texas ladies and their big hair made me laugh.

"The higher the hair the closer to Jesus!" I shouted as I turned the ignition and revved him up. Yes, I call my truck 'him.' I call him Axl because it'll screech and scream like Axl Rose from the band Guns N' Roses. Luckily, my good ol' boy brother installed a decent CD player, so I can rock the tunes loud enough to drown out any noise from Axl. Love this truck, he's a beast.

I roamed around the secondhand store and picked up some cool swag. I definitely scored on the faux fur coat that I know Nova would die for. It's not Prada or anything but she'll get over it. She's such a label whore. The chill in the air got me excited to wear some autumn gear like furs and high-heeled boots. I snagged a cool pair of leather motorcycle gloves, too. I'll give them to Ty to flaunt tonight as he grips his microphone and makes all the chicken heads swoon.

"Sluuuts," I whispered to myself.

After I checked out at the register, I headed back toward Axl and decided to make one additional stop at the local Dallas Farmers' Market near home. I grabbed some goodies to eat prior to the big show at the Steel Door. I was powering up.

Chapter Two

Evening arrived and I was all dolled up for Tyler's show. I put on smoky, trashy eye makeup. I wore a shredded white tank with a black bra underneath, paired with my black faux leather leggings. I dug out my retro black ankle boots with a nice heel. I topped it all off with my new-to-me vintage white faux fur cropped jacket. I must say I looked pretty fucking hot! As I doused myself in a layer of perfume, Nova arrived at my loft.

"Hey Blondie, let me in, it stinks in this bloody hallway!"

Guess we're English tonight? I rolled my eyes. Opened the door and in strutted Miss Nova.

"Red tonight? Did you bring your British flag, eh?"

Nova had one of her notorious wigs on, flaunting around in her red disco pants and leopard fur jacket.

"Bitchin' threads, girl. Love the fur, two kittens on the prowl tonight—meow!"

Nova shimmied over to my bathroom mirror and adjusted her red wig once more.

"I hear WHIP is showcasing their new keyboardist tonight, you like him?" I hollered toward the bathroom.

"Trent, right? I'd fuck him," she said with a purr.

"Sluuuut," I teased.

Nova was a bit promiscuous; she thought if men can be male sluts and carry on with whomever they wanted, why couldn't she? Nova had issues, you could say—guess most strippers have some sort of a Daddy issue. They seem to show them by gyrating against some steel pole to bad Mötley Crüe songs. They don't think twice about taking every dollar any man will throw at them. Some revenge, eh? She'll grow out of it. I have no room to judge. I'm scraping pennies. Meanwhile, Miss Mercedes has a fat bank account, nice wheels, a condo uptown, and pure freedom. Not bad, eh? I started to pout just thinking of my sad little intern check.

"*Girls, girls, girls,*" I started singing out loud.

"What the fuck Alex—ugh—please, it's my night off!" Nova sneered at me.

"How is work?" I hollered towards the bathroom.

"I'm loving it girl, busy as usual. I have my financial plan all worked out, no need to bother yourself with worries about me."

I didn't worry too much about Nova, I just envied her confidence and ability to stand on her own two feet. I knew she secretly dated a few of the club's patrons, but that was Nova. She always defended her job by saying if you got it, flaunt it and make some money while doing it. I never harped. "I want to come see you perform one night, see how sexy and naughty you are." I teased Nova for a moment.

"Sure girl! Anytime. Would you like a private dance right now?" She giggled as she shimmied her boobs while moving towards me.

I laughed. "Come on, London, we're going to be late." I smacked her ass as she spun around and headed for the door.

"Oh, let me grab my cell and the gloves I picked up for Tyler and I'm ready to play," I said.

"Gloves, Alex? You're too good to that kid," Nova reprimanded me.

Nova and I arrived at the Steel Door venue a few blocks away from the loft. Leaves were falling outside and the scent of fire burning lingered in the air.

"Ahhh, I love that smell," I said as I inhaled deeply.

Fall has arrived. The Steel Door was part of an old warehouse gutted and made into a club. There were two huge silver metal doors at the entrance guarded by what looked like two motorcycle gang members. They were in leather get-ups checking IDs and stamping hands.

"I fucked the one on the left," whispered Nova.

"Ew," I responded.

Good thing she did, because as soon as Nova and I made our way to the front door, the guy on the left gave us a big smile.

"Hello kittens," he said while motioning us to the front of the line, stamping our hands and planting a kiss on Nova's cheek.

Thank goodness for the old flame working the door. The line forming for WHIP's show was starting to wrap around the building. There was excitement building up. Fans were wearing WHIP swag and had a few homemade signs to show their support. How cool. This Dallas crowd was a taste of what Tyler had in store for when the real record deal came knocking. My stomach got butterflies for him. We made our way into the venue. I whipped out a few backstage passes I snagged from Fat Larry at the *D-town* on Wednesday.

"Here, band slut, put this laminate around your neck." I gave Nova a pass. "All access baby, point me in the direction of WHIP."

"I need to get a drink," she hollered.

We shoved our way to the steel door to the right of the stage. This venue was pretty laid out. It had a huge stage with the carpet down littered with cords. Amps and monitors lined the front and everyone's equipment was set up in a controlled chaos manner. A dark banner hung from the lighting rig behind the drum kit. It flaunted the name WHIP with a logo of a leather whip around it. That's new, I thought as I gazed at the banner for a minute. *Whip it Good* lyrics by Devo swam in my head. I stood there admiring the crew. They worked so fiercely, wrapping cables, testing mics, and setting up the opener's gear. Poor guys had limited space in front of all WHIP's shit. I then noticed a KORG to the right of the drum kit—must be Trent's toy.

Nova grabbed my arm and pulled me toward the stage door. "Come on girl, I want to meet the new boy toy."

She smiled and soon we were backstage. Walking through a cloud of smoke, we entered the dressing room. Lights were low and candles were lit to send out a chill vibe. Road cases were stacked in the corner. A green velvet couch sat in the middle of the room with green velvet stools scattered around. Conversations seemed to melt in with the low angelic tone of music playing in the background. Must be Portishead? Nova and I walked in hand-in-hand and immediately I was swooped up by my waist, shoved against the wall, and kissed.

"Hey rockstar, ready for your set?" I asked.

Tyler set me down, pushed Nova aside, and laid another wet kiss on me.

"Come on Ty, what's going on?"

He grinned then started to purr, "You kittens look hot."

"You're wound up," I said.

"Coked up." Ty smirked.

Ugh, playing the rock god. Tyler and friends would always have a shot, pop a pill, snort a line, or smoke a joint to rehearse, play a gig, or give an interview. Does he even like playing music? Seems to me if you need to get annihilated every time you work, you need to rethink your career choice. To each his own.

"Hey Ty, I gotta pee," I said.

Ripping the leather gloves I brought him from my hands, he said, "Right through there." He pointed to a narrow hallway with gold sheers hanging from the ceiling.

More candles burned on a table at the end of the hallway. BINGO! There lay the coke out on display for Tyler. I noticed the restroom to the right and pushed open the door. In the corner sat a red velvet chair. Propped up on the chair was one of Ty's bandmates receiving a blow job from—who else?—a chicken head.

"Sorry man," I said, embarrassed by my intrusion.

I backpedaled out of the restroom and headed back to the dressing room. There, leaning against the wall sipping a glass of red wine, stood the new keyboardist, Trent. Very Gothic of him, I thought. He was tall like Tyler, heroine-sheik skinny, wearing leather pants with a hint of guyliner on. Stage gear, I presumed. Must be a prerequisite to be in a band—you have to be ultra-thin, own leather pants, and dye your hair black. His was longer, chin-length, and actually healthy looking—not stringy. It must be all the resveratrol from the grapes in the wine. I laughed to myself. Then Trent noticed me undressing him with my eyes and shot me the biggest grin. Oh God, I was busted—embarrassed and busted. I did have a thing for guyliner and leather pants. It must be the bad boy attraction. However, Trent didn't seem like a bad boy. He had a polite and calming demeanor, unlike the wound-up ass that Ty can be.

"Would you like a glass?" Trent signaled to me as I walked over to him.

"Sure," I replied, still blushing.

"I'm Trent."

"I gathered—all you WHIP boys look like a cult. There's a few dozen more of y'all downstairs hanging around the stage." I smiled at him.

"I like your drawl, dear," he mentioned.

Again, I blushed; the accent comes out when I'm nervous. Why am I nervous around this guy? Then Tyler swung by, holding a chicken head's hand in each of his hands, and smiled.

"So you've met my BF, Trent?" Tyler asked.

Trent smiled. "Oh, you are Alexandria?"

"Alex," I said. "Yes, nice to meet you."

"Glad you two are hitting it off, I'm going to get myself a little inspiration before the show starts." Tyler grinned, nodding his head toward the two Gothic-looking girls gripping his hands.

"And off he goes," Trent laughed. "I don't know how

he does it," he said.

"What do you mean, man, just say you're in a band and you're in, girls will swarm you," I said. "Give it time, once they see you wailing away on that fat KORG, they'll line up," I snickered.

"Haaaa!" Trent laughed. "That's okay; I enjoy writing and performing more than fraternizing with the groupies."

When I heard that, it made me smile. Maybe he's a little self-conscious, unsure of himself. I like that. I smiled to myself. "That'll keep your medical report clean." I said as we both laughed .

Then some stage manager dude came busting in with his long Willie Nelson braid and headset, hollering, "WHIP you're up. Stagehands are clearing the opener's gear and you're up in five!"

"That's my cue," groaned Trent.

"Don't be nervous, the first gig with a new band is always hard," I said. "Just play with your keys and enjoy it."

"Play with my keys, eh?" Trent laughed. "See you after?" he asked shyly.

"Yes," I answered. "We'll finish that bottle and celebrate you popping your cherry!" I said.

He smiled this devilish grin and I was hooked. I then went looking for Nova and headed down the stairs toward the stage. I wanted to see what this guy Trent brought. Butterflies swarmed in my belly. I was flushed.

Nova kissed my cheek and said, "You got dibs. I saw you hitting it off with the keyboard man," she teased.

"He's actually really nice," I snapped back.

I was acting predatory already. All I needed to do was pee and mark my territory and it would be done. Nova shoved me. Speaking of peeing, I never got to go. I laughed.

We made our way from the dressing room to the main floor, which was drowning in a sea of WHIP-ettes. We then pushed ourselves front and center so we wouldn't miss a moment of WHIP's opening number. Suddenly, the lights turned down and the whole crowd screamed. The huge, burgundy velvet curtains parted as an eerie sound came from the KORG displayed in the corner. Trent began his dark piano solo as his way of introducing himself. I just stood there mesmerized. His industrial-gothic vibe oozed from all the amps. The WHIP-ettes started to scream approval. Smoke machines added to the dark demise when, just then, the whole band joined in on cue. Perfection.

Ohhh, and there stood that tall drink of water, my BF, Tyler. He was gripping the mic from the stand with his new leather gloves and belting out some sex. He grabbed everyone's attention. In my head, his voice was dubbed over by Rod Stewart's voice and all I heard was *Don't ya think I'm sexy, come on sugar let me know*. I laughed. But Trent, he caught my eye. I was interested. I wanted to continue to befriend him.

Suddenly, I felt a hand grip my hair from behind. It pulled my head backward and, with hot breath, slowly licked the bottom of my neck trailing up to my ear lobe. Nova. I held my breath. She loved to tease with a bit of foreplay on any open stage which tonight's floor was the Steel Door. I responded to this temptress as I turned around, breathed out, and tugged at her hips as I pulled her closer. Nova then responded by gently tucking my hair behind my ear. She surveyed my lips with her eyes as she leaned in for a soft, slow kiss. I kissed her back, encircling my tongue with hers. Ummmm, she tasted sweet, like cherry lip gloss. We swayed a bit and then picked up our pace. We traced each other's curves with our fingertips like we were exploring for the first time, all to the soundtrack of WHIP. Touching Nova was nothing like touching a man. She was soft, pedal-like, and I wanted to keep touching gently. Oh, and her fragrance was intoxicating. That in itself heated me with desire. We continued to dance erotically with each other as the music moaned on. WHIP's music was rather erotic at times. When Tyler sang the word 'fuck' or 'sex,' all these WHIP-ettes would cream their panties. These guys had something here. I continued to dance with Nova as my body swayed with hers, but my eyes stayed on Trent. I was in awe as I listened to their set—adding Trent on keyboards was a good move on WHIP's part. He really did bring out the industrial gothic sound Tyler and the boys were searching for. I'm so excited for them! Now it's complete.

After a bit of bump-and-grinding with Nova, WHIP's music selection began to get a bit heavy. The two of us decided to head back up to the dressing room hand-in-hand so we could primp and wait for the band to finish their set. I wanted to cool down as well and slick on some more gloss to have my lips look nice and wet for Trent when he came back for their afterparty.

While chilling on the green couch, I noticed a cute

brunette. She wore glasses, a plaid skirt, and combat boots. She was pacing around the entry. She carried a laptop with a sticker on it that said *D-town*. I motioned for her to join us.

"Thanks," she said. "I'm Olivia. I work for *D-town* paper as a freelance journalist."

"Oh, you must have been sent by Fat Larry to interview WHIP?" I asked.

Oh, Ty's going to like this one. After a short interview, he'll be up that short skirt in no time. Poor thing, she's actually kind of pretty in a suicide girl punk way.

"You know Larry?" she inquired.

"I do," I said. "I intern for *D-town*—I'm the social media gal. That reminds me, I need to tweet out *#WHIP kicking ass and taking names tonight @ #SteelDoor.*"

As I finished the tweet I heard "Thank you, and good night" echoing from the hallway. Gig must be over. I looked up from my phone at Olivia.

"Put on your boxing gloves, Olivia, you'll have to fight off the WHIP-ettes—they tend to hover," I said. "I'll introduce you to Tyler. Once he hears you want an interview, he'll be putty in your hands."

She smiled girlishly and flipped open her laptop to prepare. I adjusted my tank, tossed my cell in my bag, and turned toward the door. Just then, these five beautiful men walked in looking like an ad for Leather "R" Us. The boys do know how to dress the part and put on a show. They all have it. Either you have it as showmen or you don't—and every one of them has IT. I was in awe. It was complete now with Trent. I then chucked a velvet pillow from the couch to hit Ty.

"Hey it's all about me, T!" I shouted. "Get over here

and meet Miss Olivia, who wants to learn allll about you."

Ty shoved off a few clingy WHIP-ettes and made his way to the couch. I made the introductions and scooted off toward Trent.

"Did it hurt?" I asked slyly.

"What hurt?" he asked.

"Getting your cherry popped?" I blushed.

Trent smiled with that I-Wanna-Fuck-You smile of his. "Not really," he replied. "Once I got going, it all fell into place."

I stared at him with that come-hither look and licked my wet, glossy lips. "Your solo was amazing, very erotic." I blushed once more.

"Erotic?" he asked. "Hum, let me ask you something—what's erotic to you? Can you describe it?" Trent was flirting heavily.

"I have a suggestion, how about we finish that bottle we started so I can show you what's erotic?" I asked forwardly, eliciting that I-Wanna-Fuck-You smile again.

"Yes, that sounds perfect. Here or at your place?" he asked deeply.

"Hummm." I paused to digest the abrupt offer. "I'll lead the way, I just need to say a few good-byes first." I turned toward Nova and blew her a kiss. I then turned toward Ty and flipped him the bird and said, "I'm ready."

"After you," laughed Trent as he held his arm open to guide me toward the staircase.

As we walked away from the venue, I pulled my jacket closer to my body to ward off the October night chill. In tune with my steps, Trent walked beside me. We talked the whole way back to my loft with such ease like we were old friends. I wanted to learn everything about him. I was sucking up all the information he was giving me and filing it away under the 'hot music man' file. Why do I have such a weakness for the man in the band? I pondered while Trent went on about his artistic visions. Trent seemed different. He was quite seasoned as a live musician. On our stroll home I discovered he had studied music theory. He was from Louisiana and he's written and produced music for himself as well as other popular bands. He also lit up as he raved about his newly-built in-home recording studio. Did Ty know this? This guy had a hell of a story. I was impressed with what tidbits I took in as his lips veered my thoughts toward the bedroom. Between WHIP's music, dancing with Nova, and being alone with the new keyboardist—I was wound up.

We made it back to the homestead and Ernie greeted us at the door with that loving motor of his wailing away. Trent bent down to pet him. Okay, if this guy likes cats, then he's a keeper. I don't trust anyone who doesn't like animals. I strutted over to my vinyl records, selected Nina Simone, lit a few candles, and told Trent to make himself at home. Trent obliged as he removed his jacket. He laid it on the stool by the kitchen counter. Then he moseyed over to check out my canvases leaning on the adjacent wall.

"Wow, did you paint all these? You are such a good artist," he said with true conviction.

"You want to buy one?" I chuckled as I opened a new bottle of red I picked up from the farmers' market that afternoon.

Sure glad I did, I need this sex high to hit overdrive.

"I'll give you a discount; I need to pay my rent," I teased. "I have a layaway plan."

Trent smiled as he continued to look at my work. I'd lay this man in two seconds flat if given the chance. I walked over to Trent and handed him a glass just before it slipped from my now-sweaty palms. Trent tasted the wine, set the glass down near the record player, and asked, "Can I show you my idea of erotic?"

I licked my lips in agreement. He slowly took my hand in his and pulled me toward him. Oh, fragrance intoxication again, I inhaled and—ummm—he smelled good. I breathed in as he rested his chin on my head and we started slow dancing. I was in my happy place. I felt an instant comfort with Trent, kind of like I knew him in another life. There was an instant connection. I've been in interactions where it seemed forced and awkward, filling a void. But this felt nice, honest. I continued dancing slowly, keeping rhythm with him even though my pulse had a pace all its own. I took in a few deep breaths so I could slow down and enjoy this moment without overwhelming angst. We swayed, bodies pressed as warmth filled the air in the loft.

I gazed up into those dark eyes that paired with the deep, dark voice as he whispered to me, "I want to be inside you tonight."

I exhaled. Not saying a word, I broke out of our dance stance. I ran my trembling hands through his thick, dark hair and leaned in to kiss him. I started slowly, licking the bottom lip first then the top. I then made my way into his heated mouth as the passion rose within us. Trent grabbed the back of his black tee and pulled it up over his head in one swift motion. Whoo, I felt dizzy. Ah, my eyes took in the sight of this new bare chest with yes, of course, ink. I licked my lips and dove in. I licked him from his navel up to his throat. I continued up back into his mouth, where our tongues fondled each other once more. He tasted so good, minty...Mentos? *Alex, you need to concentrate,* I reprimanded myself. He turned me around so my back was facing him. I felt his hands slither up from my hips to the bottom of my tank as he grabbed hold and pulled it over my head. He then had his hands on my bra clasp and I felt a quick tug before my breasts fell out and my nipples went hard. Trent reached around and ran his long fingers up and down my cleavage. Then he slowly drifted over to each nipple, giving them each adequate attention. He pulled on both nipples as I started to groan. Oh, that felt like heaven. He then scratched over them lightly with the tips of his fingernails. He scratched down my torso to the band of my tights. Still leaning against him, I had no power to turn around—I was in deep arousal. He slid his hand into my tights, slid my panties to one side, and inserted his middle finger into me with ease. Ohhh, was I wet. He finger-fucked me for a few minutes 'til I almost came as I pushed back hard against him with a warning to stop. I wanted HIM inside me, not his finger. He tugged at my tights, pulling them off toward the floor. I stepped out of them and turned back around to face him. With a devilish smile, I ran my hands over his cool leather pants and found out he was enjoying himself as much as I was. I let out a low laugh, happy to feel his cock getting rather hard and throbbing for a release. I unzipped his pants and pulled them down over his butt cheeks and let out his endowed dick. Very nice. Once the pants hit the floor, I pushed him onto my ruffled-up bed inside the mosquito netting. I crawled in panther-like up and over Trent until we were eye to eye.

"Do you have any protection, Alex?" he asked.

"Yes, you sit up against the wall and I'll lean toward the window sill and grab a condom," I answered.

After grabbing a condom out of my little Pandora's box next to the bed, I saddled up on top of Trent. Once again, looking into those dark I-Wanna-Fuck-You eyes, we started kissing passionately again. He tasted so good and the desire was heating up even more. He began to massage my butt cheeks and trace his nails up and down my spine. I then lifted upwards a bit as he placed the condom over his pulsating cock. I then slid back down, starting from the head, engulfing his entire shaft inside me. Oh, I could feel a slight tearing inside me as he entered deeper, slowly but deeper. He continued to kiss me—man I loved tasting him. We made love and both came so hard that I knew we both were grateful for the release. Afterward, Trent got up to use the restroom as I rolled over on my stomach and watched the candles burn on the window sill. I was grinning from ear to ear. This man looked good, tasted good, fucked good...who could ask for more? I was getting spoiled. Trent came back to bed with our two glasses of wine in his hands.

Handing me one, he said with a toast, "To a new band, new friend, and new adventures."

I smiled and sipped my wine. Entangled in sheets, we continued to talk with ease about the night's events as I laid my head on his chest. Soon we drifted into a much-needed heavy sleep.

Sunday morning arrived in its usual fashion. I rolled over to a half-empty bed. Boo. Where'd Trent go? I noticed a little note hanging from a clothespin on my bed netting and grabbed it. It read, *"Alexandria my dear, the girl with the finest rear, after a wonderful night, you inspired me to write."* I smiled. Leather pants man went off to write, cool, whatever. I leaned back and began playing the night's events over in my head with a huge grin.

"Sluuut!" I hollered.

Ernie meowed back at me and I groaned as I made my way into the kitchen for coffee and cat food. I suddenly heard a buzzing sound and scurried around, searching for my cell. I knew Ty was hunting me down; we needed a powwow. There, under my faux fur on the floor, I found the vibrating phone.

"Hello," I answered.

"Girrrrl, Green Room in ten," Ty said with a devilish tone.

"Got it," I responded, smiling at Ernie.

I headed to the closet and grabbed my flannel. Then I pulled on last night's stretch pants, brushed my teeth, and sprayed another layer of perfume. I grabbed my keys.

Walking into the Green Room on a Sunday morning was a trip. I panned the room and laughed at all the people in last night's attire. They had smudged makeup and huge grins as they recited all of Saturday's events to their friends. This is exactly where Ty and I fit in. He was tucked away at the metal table in the corner. He was smoking his cigarette and aimlessly tapping his lighter, looking a bit anxious.

"Coffee with a side of coke this morning?" I asked sarcastically as I pulled out the rusted chair and popped a squat.

"Tell me everything, girlfriend," Ty smiled. I picked up the mug in front of me and motioned to the waitress for coffee.

"You first, rockstar. Which chicken head was your pleasure?"

He smiled, rubbing his eye and smearing the guyliner a bit more. "No chicken head—you remember the cute reporter?"

"I knew it!" I shouted, "Olivia, right?" I laughed a deep, heavy laugh. "Oh, Ty, she's a cutie. What happened? Where?" I was intrigued. "Let me guess, a big red velvet chair in the bathroom of the dressing room?"

Ty stuck his tongue out at me. "No," he replied. "We went back to her pad."

"Annnnd..." I motioned, circling my hand for him to go on. "You guys slept together, right?" I was pulling teeth.

"Yes, we slept together, she's a kinky little thing." He smiled as he took another drag on his burning cigarette. "Now you, Miss Kitten." He gestured for me to get on with it.

"I don't kiss and tell," I said.

Ty slapped my hand on the table and screamed "What?" We were like two schoolgirls gabbing about our dates. "You are giving it all away with that huge grin, Miss Rae." Ty was calling me out. "I knew you would go for Trent, you southern hussy, I just knew, Mr. Dark Eyes!" he laughed at me. "You're such a sucker!" I was sensing a bit of jealousy from Mr. Front Man.

"Are you mad, Ty?" I asked.

"No girl, just be cool, he's a new band member and I'm not sure of his vibe yet." He was kind of scolding me.

"I'm sure of his vibe Ty, in fact we vibed pretty well," I barked back. "Let me get this straight, you can take Miss Suicide kinky girl home for a fuck. I take the band man home and I gotta watch myself?" I gathered up my keys and cell, pushed out the rusted chair, and stood up. "I gotta split. I got to feed Ernie still," I said in a pissy manner.

Ty looked at me while he ran his hands through his hair. I turned and walked out of the bar and headed back up to my loft.

CHAPTER THREE

It was three days and no word from Ty. What the fuck? Not cool, not like Ty. I was at the *D-town* tweeting some bullshit about some shit country band coming to play. I looked up from my cube and saw Olivia walking right toward me.

"Hey." She smiled at me, wearing bubblegum pink lipstick that made her look twelve.

"Hey." I smiled back. I should play nice. Just because Ty's a douche, there's no reason for me to be unkind to Olivia.

"Have you heard from Ty?" she asked me shyly.

"Not in three days, hun. I've been busy and I think the guys are all planning on recording and preparing for South by Southwest," I lied. "How did the interview go?" I dove in. Olivia blushed, knowing I knew damn well that she and Ty slept together. "You get a good piece?" I chuckled, knowing damn well she got a piece alright.

"It'll make the November edition," she said. "Well, if you see Ty, please tell him I'd love to see him again."

"Get in line, lady," I mumbled under my breath. "I sure will, Olivia. Take care," I responded politely.

Olivia scurried off. Ugh, that man always breaks hearts. He never lets anyone in, but who am I to blame? I keep one foot outside the door at all times myself. Shame on me. I decided to check my phone and see if either WHIP boy had reached out to me. No Ty. No Trent. Hum.

Thursday arrived. I found myself once again lying on the floor listening to Billie Holiday, moping. What happened to Trent? I bet Ty ran his mouth off to him and he's too intimidated to reach out to me. Band guys are too flighty. It's always some sort of commitment phobia. They have deep-rooted issues that only come out in lyrics cursing the heavens above for their dark depressive manner. I need a new type of man. A new breed of man. An I-give-a-fuck-about-you kind of man. An I-want-and-can-AFFORD-to-spoil-you man. Yes, I need to grow up and date a grown, intellectual, kind, wealthy, and career-driven man. Not the exciting rockstar man in a band nomad that I fall for every fucking time. But you are who you surround yourself with. I guess I need to step out of the box. Before I move on, I should text Trent to check in and keep him on the burner. I smiled and rolled over to grab my phone. I paused—was it a one-night stand? He didn't seem like the type. But am I the type? Maybe Trent thought I used him.

I texted Trent, *Hey tall, dark and handsome...still writing that inspiring song?* I hit send.

Leaning against my open window as the sun set, I inhaled that intoxicating scent of fire burning. Ahhh, I love that scent. Halloween is around the corner. I decided to go dig through a few plastic storage bins and fish out a decoration for my loft door. I found an old wooden skeleton from a previous trip to New Orleans. Ahh, Louisiana. I thought of Trent right away and sighed. My cell started to buzz while I was posting my solo Halloween decoration on the door for all to enjoy.

"Hey, Mum." My mother phoned about once a week to run tabs on me and invite me to a monthly dinner party she held.

"Hello Miss Alexandria Rae, are you joining us this Sunday?" Mother was guilting me in with her fake southern charm.

"Yes, Mother, I'll be there with bells and whistles on."

"Don't be a smart ass, Alexandria; I get enough of that from your Father."

"Yes, Mother. Did you call Austin? Can he get away and drive up?" I inquired. I actually missed my brother. We were two peas in a pod growing up. With all the traveling we endured living from military base to military base, we only had each other.

"He'll be joining us," Mom said. "Don't be fashionably late; don't come in hungover from the events from your Saturday night, either," Mother scolded. I rolled my eyes. "I wish you'd meet an upstanding gentleman and get married—"

"—and have babies," I interrupted rudely.

"Alright Miss Rae, I'll see you Sunday evening, and I love you dear."

After hanging up with my mother, I always feel a bit deflated. I have to give it to her, she does keep it together. She has the big house, Daddy, wealthy circle of friends, charities, dinner parties, and big hair. It's exhausting running over her to-do lists—where does she get the energy? I thumbed through my contacts and found Austin's number. I sent him a text. *Better not bail private, see you Sunday.*

I collapsed onto my bed and began to drift off, thinking of New Orleans and Mr. Trent. I smiled devilishly to myself as I began to explore all the places that Trent traced his tongue on me. My nipples got hard as I envisioned him licking each one with such dedication and excitement. He enjoyed pleasing me that night. I slid my hand down my abdomen and into my cotton panties towards my sex. I inserted one finger and began to thrust in and out, all while imagining Trent's breath on my skin. In my ear, he would whisper how he wanted to be inside of me. I played that over and over. I kept thrusting, making myself wet. I increased the pace until I brought myself to a heightened orgasm.

"Ahhh," I sighed. I craved that man. "Trent, thank you and good night." I smiled and drifted off into a deep sleep.

Sunday morning rolled around and I heard an obscene amount of banging on my door.

"Go away!" I hollered as I grabbed the down comforter and rolled over.

"Alex, baby."

Good God, I know that rat voice. "Go away, Ty. Bear is still in a slumber, come back later," I yelled at the door.

"Come on bombshell, open up for Daddy," Tyler ordered.

Ew. I slithered upright and out of my netting. I opened the lock with one hand and walked away toward the kitchen. I needed STRONG coffee to handle anything Rock God had to reveal.

"What the fuck, baby girl? Where have you been?" he asked as he pushed his way in and slammed my door. I wanted to chuck the coffee pot at his head.

"What time is it?" I asked as I made coffee.

"It's eleven AM, sleeping beauty," Ty said rather sweetly.

"Holy shit, I slept in." Thank you, Trent. A good orgasm will cure any sleepless night. "Ty, I thought you were upset with me and Trent."

"Girl, noise," he said as he swished his hand in front of me while grabbing a mug. "We're fine," he reassured me. "Girl, you do need new mugs, these Dallas cowboy mugs are old and nasty." I started laughing as Tyler used his hand to wipe out the inside of the mug. After the coffee brewed, I poured us each a much-needed cup of caffeine. We clanked mugs as I took a long swig.

Once alert enough, I asked, "Where's Olivia? Ya'll still talk?"

Ty smiled. "I like her, Alex; she's smart, a bit exciting, and a bit mysterious. It's all good."

"Good," I responded. "I like her too, she'll be good for you." Anyone who is actually career-driven, has her own pad, and wasn't a known chicken head was good for Ty. He needed one foot on the ground as he pursued his music career. Olivia would be level-headed, a good balance for him. "I'm heading to the monthly dinner party tonight, want to join me?" I batted my eyelashes.

"Don't bat those Manson lamps at me girl, no way am I going to crash Miss Texas's dinner party. Your mother will have me shot." Ty snorted. "Besides, you need downtime with your bro and I have to finish writing some lyrics for some sappy shit Trent wrote."

I had no control when I heard his name—I grinned from ear to ear. Tyler leaped off my counter to his feet, kissed my head, and split. I took a deep breath and knew we were okay.

*

Sunday evening arrived. I rolled up to the old stomping grounds to meet up with the family and some "friends" my Mother always invited. I usually got seated next to some prospect my mother had in mind for a future husband. Wow, if Mother ever met Trent she'd have me zip-tied at the wrists and ankles, dragged into church, and exorcised. I laughed, envisioning me dunked in holy water as I released my love for the man in the band. Wait, didn't Jesus have long hair?

"Hypocrite!" I yelled as I pulled up the drive in Axl blaring BUSH, *Breathe in, Breathe out*...which is exactly what I needed to do. I parked as Austin ran out to greet me.

"What, no date?" He smiled.

"Going stag tonight, didn't want a certain someone to get caught in her web," I teased. Austin put his arm around me as we headed toward the house. Mother was her usual frantic self.

"Hello darling, you remember the Keatons? And their son Jeb?" (Bachelor number one.) She kissed my cheek, smiling. "I seated you right next to him, he's in finance."

I walked over to Daddy and gave him a kiss. "Hi Daddy,

how are you holding up?"

"Pretty good, sweetheart, pretty good. You'd like a glass of wine?" He motioned for Austin to pass the wine. "How's your new job and the loft?" he asked.

"Everything is wonderful, Daddy," I replied, sounding like my mother with sugar rolling off my tongue. I then sat down next to Jeb.

Jeb had it all: degree in finance, nice suit, nice manners, brought up in a well-to-do family with a good name—but he was not as exciting as Trent. Jeb had stability but lack of creativity and passion. Poor thing, it must be tiresome rolling through the motions as mummy and daddy whip him from behind. Fetch the next item on their list. Degree—check, suit and tie—check, house and security—check, check—what, no WIFE? Damn you Jeb, pressure's on! At least my neurotic mother kept me on a long leash. I was out exploring all my options to the soundtrack of her sweet southern voice nagging me to find a good man. It can be exhausting replaying the tape in my brain over and over. "Alexandria, find a good man." "Alexandria, settle down already." "Alexandria, when was the last time you've attended church?" "Lord! Alexandria, fix that hair!" I have a real knack for changing the mental channel. Someday I'll find someone good enough for her standards.

"So, Jeb." I faked a smile as I turned toward him. "Getting laid lately?" Austin choked on his steak and reached for his wine. I smiled. "You sure seem like quite the catch, I figured with all your success the ladies would be dropping panties for you." I sipped my wine.

My mother gasped and burned a hole right through me with her glare, warning me to knock it off. I pushed my seat out and excused myself. Austin got up and followed me out the back door to the pool.

"Hey Alex, wait up." Austin pushed through the glass door.

I was a bit humiliated. "I'm tired of blind dates at OUR family dinner," I barked. "For once I just want to come to dinner and just BE, just be with my family. Shoot the bull where there is no intentional outside pressure. I'm not in the mood to put on another fake smile and be polite to the Keatons and to Jeb. Who, by the way, Mother had set us up before! What's the hurry to run down the aisle? I know she means well. But I'm an adult and I need time for me to find me and not strap on the veil and send me packing to produce spawn."

I was depleted. I dived into the pool, clothes and all. Who gives a fuck? I needed to cool down.

Austin laughed and said, "Fuck it," and dived in himself. We floated and the two of us talked like it should have been. Everything has to be a production with our mother. She needs to let down that hair of hers and just be.

"I need to apologize to her, don't I? My period must be coming; I'm rather emotional right now."

I felt guilty. Mother opened the glass door to the outside pool area. She stepped out in her Sunday satin gold dress, shoes to match, and scolded me.

"I'm very disappointed in you, Alexandria."

I swallowed hard. "Mother I'm sorry, I just want time with you, Daddy, and Austin without pressure from outside guests. It would have been nice to have a head's up when we spoke the other day. I wasn't in the mood for a speed date, thank you."

"You ungrateful little girl," Mother snapped. "The Keatons excused themselves and left early. I was completely appalled by your mannerism toward Jeb tonight. I brought you up to act like a lady and not some trash-mouthed streetwalker. What's going on down in that district you call Deep Ellum? I'm disgusted with you."

I rolled into a back float and tried not to shed a tear. I hate hurting her feelings. I know she means well. She doesn't want me alone.

Daddy came out to join us and see what all the fuss was about. "Alex," he said sternly, "your Mother means well. You need to apologize to her."

"Daaaad," I responded. "I did and I'm sorry, I know better." I pulled myself up the pool ladder, soaked. I headed straight into the house, leaving a trail of water streaming behind me. I caught my mother in the kitchen.

"Mother, let's not argue. I'm truly embarrassed by my behavior. I'm just tired and I did not mean any disrespect." I was trying. "Mother..." I said once more.

"I hear you Alexandria—oh my floors! You are soaked!" She scolded me like I was six.

I grabbed her and hugged her tightly, leaving an imprint of my wet silhouette on her Sunday dress. "Mother, it's okay...smile every once in a while."

She half-assedly hugged me back, then excused herself to change. I stood in the kitchen, peeled my clothes down to my bra and underwear, and mopped up the floor. I then stole a t-shirt and running shorts from my father, hopped in Axl, and took off toward downtown.

Once I hit I-35, I frantically dialed Trent.

To my surprise, he answered. "Hey beautiful, how are you?"

I grinned from ear to ear—his voice just made me melt. "Hi. I wanted to see how YOU were? I'm just leaving my parents' house and heading back downtown, where are you?"

Trent paused. "I'm with the band rehearsing, we're almost finished, would you like some company tonight?"

I'm sure he could hear my smile through the phone. "I'd love some," I responded.

As I pulled into our grungy parking lot at the loft, I parked Axl, then noticed Trent standing outside alone, leaning on the brick wall under the only working light.

"That's quite a ride you have there, Miss Alex."

I laughed, gazing back at my beat-up truck while pretending to set an alarm. Trent laughed as he walked towards me and greeted me with a big embrace. I was so relieved as he held me for a moment. I could feel the anxiety from the evening start to roll off. "I'm so happy to see you, thanks for sticking around." I said gratefully. Trent smiled as we headed into my loft.

"Hey, pick some tunes you'd like to listen to, I'm going to make some coffee, you want some?" "Sure, rehearsal kinda wiped me out so I'll need a second wind." Trent selected an album to listen to as I prepared our coffee. I then joined him on the floor while watching him thumb through my portfolio. "You are a really talented girl."

I blushed as I watched him review my sketches. "Think so?" I shrugged my shoulders. "I could sketch you?" I asked sweetly. I reached for a charcoal pencil and grabbed a nearby sketch pad.

"Really? Why?" Trent acted a bit shy as he shifted his

weight on the floor.

"Come on, rockstar, don't be shy, it'll be worth lots of money when you're famous," I egged him on.

Trent shook his head in agreement as I leaned back against the bed and started to sketch. He was so beautiful. I had such a hard time concentrating as I started to draw. Deep down, I actually loved this moment; I could stare and appreciate everything about his face.

As I continued to sketch, watching him, a strand of shiny black hair fell in his face and I just flushed. "No, leave it," I said as he tried to push the strand behind his ear. He paused then let it dangle back against his cheek. *He is so beautiful,* I said over and over in my head. His eyes were intensely fixated on me as I kept glancing up at him while I drew.

"You're enjoying this, aren't you?" He smiled as he kept watching me.

"I am, you're now one of my favorite subjects to draw. I get tired of drawing Ernie, who always seems to bathe or lick his butt when I'm trying to work." Trent laughed as I gave him a slight smile. He was so patient as I worked on the sketch. My hands started to tremble a bit as I shaded his lips while licking mine. Trent knew exactly what I was thinking about as I continued.

Once completing the piece, I signed it, kissed it, and said, "Finished!"

Trent grabbed the book out of my hand and flipped it around so he could approve my work. "I'm speechless, Alex, I mean, wow."

I sat there grinning as I chewed on my pencil. "That's a compliment, thank you." I felt pretty proud of myself.

Trent gently set the book down and crawled slowly

towards me as I leaned in for a kiss. I opened my mouth and let his warm tongue encircle mine, lingering for a bit until I nervously asked, "Hey, ummm, coffee is done—want some?"

Trent wiped his lower lip, then sat back on his heels and smiled. "Sure," he responded.

I wanted so much to sleep with him at that moment but I controlled my urge.

After I got our coffee, I sat back down next to him as we started talking. I swear a few hours can feel like a moment with Trent. The caffeine had me gabbing away as Trent just sat there listening, never interrupting, just quietly nodding as I went on and on. It felt so good to be so forthcoming about my mother with her neurotic request to find a proper man that would fit her standards. I also told him about Jeb and the fool I made of myself at dinner. He just laughed as he sipped his coffee. I opened up about how I constantly worried about Tyler and his cocaine addiction. Lastly...me. I was so lost in my direction as a graphic artist. I seem to make erratic judgments about everything. No judgment seemed to pass on Trent's part. I was thrilled to have his full attention.

He continued to listen as he put my head on his lap and gently stroked my hair. He then softly responded. "Alex, your mother seemed to have brought you up right. You have earned your degree and you do and WILL have some direction with your graphic design work—the *D-town* is only a start. You're amazing! Don't give up so easily." Trent was quickly becoming my biggest cheerleader. He continued. "As for Tyler, Tyler is being Tyler. Rockstars and partying go hand in hand."

"But you don't snort cocaine, do you?" I interjected.

"I do not. My father overdosed when I was younger so I had to take on the role of caretaker for my family at an early age. I have no desire for cocaine. Tyler is just testing his limits. He's free as a butterfly—no bills since he crashes on the pad in the rehearsal room, he sponges off you and your kitchen, and he seems to have no serious commitments. Let him be who he needs to be at this moment. I'll try to look after him when the tour starts since I'm really the only sober member. Ty has a gift and I'm supporting the musical genius by giving him a chance to see where this all takes us.

I just paused for a moment then said, "I think I've exhausted the topic with Tyler and I fear I will push him away."

Trent understood, then urged me to close my eyes and let it go as he continued to scratch my head. I relaxed on his lap and slowly drifted off to sleep.

✷

Another dreadful week moved by at a glacial pace. I was sketching and daydreaming in my cubicle at the *D-Town* when Miss Olivia popped her head in. She was looking cute as always with her hair pinned back like a '40s pin-up girl. She wore retro cat glasses and the notorious plaid skirt. She was a burst of energy.

"Hi, Alex! I was wondering if you were attending the Halloween ball this weekend?" she squealed excitedly.

"Ummm, I gotta check with Nova, sure, maybe," I replied. "Who's all going?" I was curious.

"Well, Tyler invited me and I believe some members of

WHIP as well," she squealed once more. You know where my mind went—straight to Trent. "Yeah, it sounds like fun, sure," I invited myself. I grabbed my cell and hit up Nova. *Halloween ball—we on?* I hit send.

It's on, Nova replied.

Soon enough, I grabbed the laptop and tweeted *#HalloweenBall Saturday night...who's in?* I sent a link to the event's website and posted. What shall I pretend to be? The event was called Vamps and Vampire's Ball, so what kind of vamp tramp shall I be? I got butterflies in my stomach. I was actually excited. My period would be over and I'd be on the prowl once more.

Saturday arrived in its usual fashion, Ernie purring in my ear as I was wrapped in a cocoon of sheets.

"Ahhh Ernie, go turn on the coffee," I pleaded. I had to start the caffeine drip now to get me all the way through tonight's ball. Nova was coming over early so she could dress me up and we'd head to the warehouse together. Deep Ellum does have its perks; every venue is within walking distance from the loft.

I headed to the kitchen to prepare the coffee and sign my check from the *D-Town*. I grimaced as I wrote my signature on the back. Not much money to play with. Not much of anything. I needed more cat food, a water bill was due, and I wanted more paint.

I'll deposit this today, then figure out my Plan B.

Later that evening, Nova and I were all gussied up in our finest vinyl nurses' outfits. I had the white vinyl dress which zipped up the front, leaving a tremendous amount of room for exposed cleavage. Nova wore the black one, hugging every curve she had. I must admit, we looked hot. That's the best part of having a stripper friend—slutty clothes to borrow! I was amped up and so ready to see Trent again. The other night was so much fun just talking and comfortably hanging out without the pressure of sex. But tonight, with me looking this good, I wanted to get laid. I really wanted to tell Nova all about it, but she was so caught up in her beauty routine that she wouldn't hear anything I was saying anyway.

As we walked to the ball, Nova stopped, opened a pill bottle, and handed me a pill.

"What's this, a mint?" I asked while sniffing the little oblong object resting in my palm.

Nova laughed deeply. "No, Nurse Mint, it's ecstasy, now swallow it," she demanded while lifting my palm to my mouth. I did as I was told.

"Nova, can I ask you a question?"

"Sure, I'll keep an eye on you," she replied.

"No, I know you will—I wanted to know if you think I can pull off being an entertainer, and do you think Vanity would hire me?" I immediately wanted to withdraw my question. I could feel myself turning red. "I'm having survival issues when I'm only counting on the *D-Town* check, and my Mother kicked me off her payroll. I wanted to see if I could secretly work with you and make some quick extra money? Tyler would probably say fucking go for it, I really wouldn't want Trent to know just yet, and my Mother—ugh." I felt a wave of nausea pass through me.

"I want to come see you perform, really, I'm not joking this time. I want to see what the girls do and see if it's something I can handle?"

Nova put her arm around me as we continued to walk. "That came out of nowhere, girl—of course you could handle it. I actually enjoy it but I'm very dominant and you, my little cowgirl, are a bit submissive. I love how impulsive you are, though; when you make a decision you just fucking do it, not giving a flying fuck what others think. Not a trait of your Mother's, I might add." Nova laughed and I motioned her to go on. "I'll teach you everything you need to know. First, you'll have to audition to be hired and then you'll need a stage name." She sounded rather excited about the idea.

"Oh yeah, Miss Mercedes, will you think of a stage name for me?" I asked with a bit of enthusiasm.

"Let's forget about it tonight, Alex, let's let loose and have fun," she insisted. "I'll bring you to the club soon, we'll talk to my boss, and we'll get you started right away, okay?"

I agreed. I felt instantly excited about the new adventure I was about to embark on. I wasn't sure if it was the slutty nurse costume that gave me confidence or the little pill I just swallowed, but I felt a bit relieved.

I gazed at the people in costumes heading toward the warehouse. We arrived at the Vamps and Vampire's ball and, as anticipated, it was packed. Red lights glowed from inside the venue and out the barred windows to the street. Erotic, eerie music was flowing from the speakers out to the front of the venue to entice passerby to wander in and explore. As Nova and I waited in line, I could feel the X starting to take over me. I slowly put my hand in Nova's and gently swayed with her to the intoxicating music as we shuffled in. Once inside, we still held hands as we were guided up a black iron rod staircase to the entrance of the ball. Red velvet curtains split as we entered and began exploring this underground world. Everything was a blood-red color—the curtains, the candles, the wine the patrons were drinking. All blood-red. It was definitely a vampire theme. Aerialists swung from the ceiling in nude attire and masquerade masks. There were little nooks and rooms to explore throughout the warehouse. Some had assembled furniture and candles to settle in on. Some had dungeons where anyone holding back a fetish fantasy could engage. I inhaled everything: the people, the music, the clove cigarettes—it all turned me on. The ecstasy heightened it all. Nova scoped out a vacant tent where we all could settle in and party. I made my way to the red velvet couch. As I sat down, I slowly leaned back and closed my eyes, letting the X wash over me. I kept petting the velvet and smiling to myself. I felt calm. I felt good. Then I felt the couch sink in a bit and opened my eyes to Tyler standing over me.

"Hey, Nurse Betty, are you my methadone nurse?" he asked.

I laughed. Ty was dressed up like Sid Vicious—not a long stretch for him, and his date, Olivia, was Nancy. Kind of clever, very suiting. Ty hopped down and sat next to me on the couch. He was coked up for sure. I noticed a mirror on the table in front of us. I saw Ty's party favors spread out along with a razor blade next to the line of powder. Olivia and Nova were doing lines and laughing. I decided that was my cue to escape the tent. I checked out all the other vamps and vampires swaying in erotic bliss to the sounds of New Order. I wandered from room to room, letting my inhibitions flow out the steel-barred windows. I liked the feeling of X. I continued to wander down a dark hallway lit only by a few red candles toward what I thought was a restroom. All of a sudden I felt a strong hand around my waist guiding me inside a small room. A man dressed like a Bram Stoker's vampire began to nibble on my neck from behind. I took a deep breath. I turned around and exhaled.

Trent pushed me against the wall and started kissing me with such intense passion. He forced his warm tongue into my mouth and teased my tongue, making my clit start to swell. I was hungry for this man. I accepted his mouth tease and played for a bit. I then withdrew my tongue and made my way down his inked chest and unbuttoned his pants with my teeth. I could feel his cock pulsating inside, begging to join in. I pulled out his erect cock and started circling its head with my tongue a few times. I then engulfed his whole penis with my mouth. I began stroking him alternately with one hand and my mouth.

"Ahhh," he moaned as I reciprocated my passion. He pulled me up off the floor in the secluded room, wrapping his cloak on each side of me while pushing up my nurse costume. One vampire nail caught the string of my satin pantie and pulled it down to my ankle and off my heel. He then opened my legs wide and pushed himself inside of me while pushing my back against the wooden wall. Oh my God, how I needed this. Trent pushed his tongue back in my mouth and kissed me as he thrust hard but slowly inside me. I could hear the echo of a remix of Madonna's song Erotica in the background. I was turned on. We continued to fuck—never minding if anyone could see us—until we both climaxed.

"Good to see you, my love," he whispered in my ear. "I've been watching you wander around the ball all alone and I knew I had to have you." I smiled and kissed him as I began to come down from my orgasm. "My system is compromised post-sex, you'll need to nurse me back, Nurse Alex," he teased.

"I'm so glad you're here," I whispered back. This was an intensely erotic moment for me. I was flushed. I'd fuck this man anywhere. "Should we get back to the others? I really don't want Nova to worry, I kind of wandered off while the gang was skiing," I suggested as I straightened out my costume, then adjusted Trent's vampire cloak.

"You look incredible, what a costume!" He laughed, took a bow, then said, "Lead the way, Nurse Alex," while fishing in his pockets for a clove cigarette.

As Trent and I entered the tent, I noticed the rest of WHIP had joined us in our Halloween celebration. Nova smiled at me as she pulled me down on the couch next to her and Ty.

"You little tramp," she said. "Out hunting?"

I just laughed. "Some catch, huh? I found him lurking around a dark corner." I was grinning once again.

"You had sex, I can feel it!" Nova accused me. She then licked my lip as she leaned over to talk to the drummer.

I looked up at Trent and he mouthed, "You felt so divine."

I smiled and reached for his clove to take a hit. I wasn't

sure if it was the X or just being here with Trent, but I felt amazing.

After a few hours, we all were partied out and decided to head over to the Green Room for some breakfast. I walked next to Ty as we lagged behind the group and told him how happy I was.

"Girl, I'm happy for you but..." There it was...BUT.

"But, what?" I asked Ty.

"We're looking to tour soon, so don't wrap your panties around Trent too tight. Got it?" Tyler laughed as he grabbed my head and gave me a noogie.

"Got it." I pouted as I clenched Ty's hand as we crossed the street.

CHAPTER FOUR

VANITY

I can't believe I talked myself into this. My confidence wasn't in overdrive now that the nurse costume was off and I was actually in the car with Nova driving to Vanity. What balls I've grown. I reminded myself that I needed to make some money and help fill the time while the boys were writing the rest of the material for their album. I haven't spoken to Tyler much—let alone Trent—since the Halloween ball. WHIP was working overtime trying to put this new album together and was really pushing for a tour to start any day now. What would I do without my men in black? I pouted while I stared out the window.

"Hey mama, where's your head at?" Nova asked while driving.

We were almost to the adult club and my nerves were making me have to pee.

I squirmed in the seat when Nova grabbed my leg and said, "I'll get ya in the mood, sister." Nova turned the car's CD player on and out blared NERD. We started singing as we rolled the windows down: *"You say you want me? You say you want me? Well. You can get this lapdance here for free."* I was howling. Fuck it, how harmful are a few shifts? I just wanted to meet the manager, tour the club, and get through an audition—hopefully without panicking and running for the exit! I was pumping myself up. I would make new friends, party, and have some fun while making money. My palms started to sweat. I AM GOING TO DO THIS! I repeated over and over in my head.

Nova pulled into the parking lot and I gazed at all the vehicles in awe. Limos, Hummer trucks, Mercedes, BMWs, and Porches, all lined up. The lot was loaded with money. This clientele was wealthy. I felt intimidated as a sudden flush of guilt ran through me. Ugh, my mother would die. We were in the Bible belt and there were more strip clubs in Dallas than in Las Vegas, shocker. I let Nova lead the way. I followed behind her rolling suitcase full of costumes and makeup like a lost puppy, into the club's side door. We entered the dressing room for all the 'entertainers.' I gasped as I surveyed the room. Girls were smoking. Girls were counting money. Girls were walking around topless. Girls were getting spray-tanned. Girls were EVERYWHERE!

"How many girls work here, Nova?" I inquired.

"It changes, probably a hundred or so a night."

"WOW." I gasped a second time as I scanned the room, trying not to stare. Blondes, brunettes, redheads, big boobs, little boobs, they were ALL beautiful. I noticed the one common denominator—the girls all wore clear heels. I laughed.

"What's so funny, Alex?" Nova interrupted. "Follow me, I need to introduce you to the house mom and put you on the audition list."

"There's a list?" I was shocked.

"Every Friday night—it's a revolving door in this industry," Nova schooled me.

We checked in with 'house mom,' I gave my driver's license and a $20.00 fee to audition. Scam! *I have to pay them to hire me and let me work here while I entertain their customers and sell their liquor? What a crock,* I thought as I handed over a crinkled twenty-dollar bill. Nova and I then made our way to a second non-smoking dressing room where Nova—I mean Mercedes—kept her locker.

"Here, we'll share my locker 'til something opens up for you," she said.

"You have a locker but still lug in that suitcase?" I asked.

What a production! Nova sat me down on a wooden bench facing a mirror with round light bulbs sticking out, two of which had burned out. What class? She then proceeded to get out a package of wipes and wipe down the counter where she was going to lay out all her beauty essentials.

"Day shift girls, ew—cooties," she laughed as she cleaned up the space. "Now, turn and face me, I'm going to do your makeup smoky tonight, bad girl makeup." I laughed. "I'll throw a few curls in your hair. Give you my black lace dress, a black garter to hold your money, black panties, and yes, a pair of clear heels." Nova smiled. I received the makeover and—wow—what a transformation. I may pull off the *'lady of the night'* look after all.

"Can I wear thigh-high pantyhose too?" I asked. "It'll give me a bit of comfort, I won't feel so exposed." I blushed.

"Sure, they're in my suitcase."

I grabbed a pair, slid them on, and—whoa—they do make you feel sexy! I then applied gloss, popped a mint into my mouth, and sprayed myself with perfume from head to toe. I was ready. Nova continued to groom herself as I sat on the bench and watched with amazement. "Wow, you have this down pat, you're ready in like fifteen minutes!" I was shocked. Nova didn't wear a garter. She grabbed a small silver studded clutch to help keep her earnings from the night stowed away.

"Okay, I'll give you the fifty-cent tour and then we'll settle into a table, order a glass of wine, and watch for a bit. I need to go over a few ground rules with you."

I gulped as she took my hand and led the way.

Nova and I walked hand-in-hand through a tinted glass door that led to a sidebar. Nova pushed her shoulders back, lifted her head, and walked straight to the bar. Oh, the confidence. I followed suit.

"Hey, stud muffin," Nova addressed the hot guy tending the bar.

"Hey, good looking," he responded. "Who's your arm candy tonight?" he inquired with a smile.

"This is Alexan—oh shit, girl, what's your stage name?" she asked. The bartender laughed. I flashed a smile in return and felt a flush come over my face. I was embarrassed.

"Ahh, no one pays attention to stage names anyway," the bartender said to make me feel better. "What's your name again?" he asked as he glanced over at Mercedes. "Is it Chevy? Beamer? Feels on wheels?" Nova tossed a packet of matches at him.

"We'll think of something, girl," she reassured me.

We ordered two glasses of chardonnay and panned the room in search of an open table. This place was laid out, had a very renaissance feel to it. Silver Victorian mirrors were placed on almost every wall. Chandeliers with diamonds hung above our heads and I stared up at them with amazement. Black and deep purple high back leather chairs scattered around me. I felt like royalty as I sunk into one. We arrived at the venue at the start of happy hour, just as the businessmen were starting to roll in and order their first round of drinks. Nova noticed me staring at a table of gentlemen in suits.

She elbowed me and said, "Let them settle in and finish their first drink, and then we'll pounce."

I smiled nervously as I agreed. I guess the patrons are all pretty much prey. It's good to have Nova here to break the ice. I sipped my wine slowly as I tried to settle down and settle in. Nova was flawless. Makeup, attire, her posture, her confidence—I was rather proud of her. I guess if you're going to do it—stripping, that is—then do it right. Everyone seemed to like her. The bartenders, waitresses, and even the other entertainers smiled at her. I started to relax.

"Now, here are some things to remember." Nova began schooling me. "First, always arrive early so you don't have a huge house fee. The later you arrive the more money you pay. Always tip the house mother; she'll attend to anything you need. Always tip the DJ. He will always play the music you request. Keep your lighting low to hide any blemishes you may have, not that you have any, Blondie." I smiled. "Always tip a floor man; he will introduce you to any party that is spending money. He feels out who is spending and who is here for the free show. So don't waste your time on someone who is going to decline a table dance, let alone a visit to the champagne room."

"Wow," I sighed. "When do I start to keep my own money?" I was shocked.

"I know it seems absurd to shell out to everyone. You're the one providing the entertainment and showing all your goods. Believe me, we're all in this game together. So if you want to stay and actually make some money, you have to take care of all the players."

"Gotcha." I swallowed.

"Now," she continued. "You go on stage for two songs; first one is full dress and second is topless, down to just g-string. After you rotate on all the stages, you can hit the floor. Always approach whoever tipped you on stage first. They get first dibs with your company because they got off their ass and made their way to the stage to tip you. Big tippers get your attention first, ask if they want a follow-up dance, tease it a bit but don't demand. Ask if they would like some company after the dance. If they do, then you can shoot the bull, whatever you call it, you hillbilly—" she laughed, "and continue to make money. Don't allow a customer to suck up too much of your time. Either they're paying for your company or for your entertainment. No rides are free. If you are on a roll with them and their wallet is open, then move them up into the VIP area. That's where you can have some privacy and more one-on-one dances. If they decline, move on, sister. Only thing you don't ask for is a drink, that's solicitation. You could get in trouble for that. Never solicit a drink, a date, a phone number, sex—anything, or you'll get busted. Undercover works all the clubs in the belt and they will arrest you. Then you are fucked." She took another sip of wine to refresh her palette. "Am I scaring you?" she asked, blinking with her false lashes.

"I'm okay, just digesting it all." I didn't feel as relaxed anymore.

"You'll get the hang of it after a few shifts. Okay, I'm not done," she continued. "You can touch the customer. However, they can't really touch you. It's limited. You can touch yourself except genitals and they can touch the sides of your legs. You can lean in for a tease, watch their mouths—ew, then withdraw quickly. They cannot grope, pull at your panties, touch your tits, kiss you, etcetera, or they're thrown out. No cell phone, pictures, or recordings allowed either. You can sit on their laps if you are fully dressed but watch the boners." I felt nauseous. She went on. "If and when you move into a VIP suite, the same rules apply and tip your waitress or tell your customer to take care of her. And always order a drink when asked, but recommend a bottle. Sell, sell, and sell, mama. We're all here to sell something and make money. If you run into a problem, the floor men will always handle it. When you are making money, stay and play. When it runs out, you run out, and find another victim. Got it?"

"Got it," I answered, giving her a salute.

"Let's think of a name for you so I can introduce you to management. Then we'll make a lap of the pervert premise and grab a table on the main floor where I'll dance for you. That one will be on the house so you get an idea of what TO do and what NOT to do. Main floor will also be a stage for us. Just like when you and I dance for each other at the nightclub; it's really no different. We can get an invite to join another table."

"Ahhh I see, we'll put some on display and see who wants to play, right?" I felt like a card player getting the house rules explained to me. It was actually starting to excite me. *I can do this.* Nova and I finished our wine. When I stood up, I felt a bit dizzy as we made our way over to management. After the introductions, I learned my name was Angel. The arrogant club manager shook my hand. He looked me up and down.

While licking his lips he said, "What a sweet bad angel she is, Mercedes. Where have you been hiding her?" I guess it could have been worse—could have been Buffy, Barbie, or Bubbles. I smiled at the dirty man. We all turned toward the main room and made our way to a staircase leading to the second floor. "Before I release her to the floor, I need to have her audition and sign some papers," he demanded of Nova.

We followed him up the stairs in our matching clear heels. I kept my head down and eyes on the carpeted stairs, wondering if they had ever been cleaned as I followed behind them. There on the second floor stood a tall metal birdcage that must have been ten feet high with black metal bars. *What the fuck? Am I an animal? Do I have to audition in a metal cage? What sick fetish shit is this?* I pinched Nova's side.

She smacked my hand away as she continued to flirt with the manager. "Two songs, Angel, and we'll get on with our night," she reassured me. I lifted my lace dress up to expose my heel as I grabbed a hold of a metal bar to thrust myself inside the cage. I turned red panning around the contraption.

"Okay, Texas Angel, you have two songs. First one is fully dressed; I want to see if you CAN shimmy. The second is topless, I want to see what you're actually shimming with, got it, doll?"

The dirty little manager barked at me while I nodded, and then I turned to Nova and rolled my eyes. The first song began and I gulped. Every song in this establishment sounded like one continuous techno song. They pulled you into an erotic trance. I could see the main floor below from my cage as I started to sway, mimicking the entertainer on stage. The girls really didn't portray much talent as actual dancers. They were more like a runway model as they strutted around their platform. Each girl was awaiting a crumb of hope rolled into a dollar bill to grace their stage. It gave them encouragement to go on. Ugh, I felt a little depressed. Suddenly a rolled ten-dollar bill ball hit me on the side of the head and startled me. I turned with a scowl, noticing Nova standing behind the manager, signaling me to get on with it. I smiled, deeply, then paused and released. I actually thought the song was rather sexy—a lot of *oohs* and *ahhs*. I grabbed a metal bar, swung my head around in a circular motion, and flipped my hair back. It's showtime, mama. I pushed off the barred cage into the center and bent over. I flipped my hair upwards once again. I started tracing my ankle with my hand, up my thigh-high, across my panties, and over to the opposite side of my waist. I kept the pace slow. I continued to trace my waist with my fingers 'til I reached the side of my breast. I grazed it as I moved my fingers up my throat, tilted my head back, and swung my head around again to finish the tease. I saw Mr. Manager Man gulp and shift his weight as he watched me. I felt like I was in a bad Mötley

Crüe video, some hot model teasing the boys. Soon, the first song rolled into the second song. I reached for the ties at the back of my neck, underneath my hair. I untied my dress, letting each satin strand fall loosely. I grabbed the ties in each of my hands and pulled my costume down, exposing my breasts. Wow, there they were, all out there. I swayed my hips and began to strut around the small box of shame with some fake confidence. This is Angel, NOT Alexandria—I can play this role. I shimmied out of the dress and kicked it aside with my heel. For the rest of the song I just gyrated and pulsated 'til Mr. Manager Man's heart was content. By the song's end, he walked up to my holding cell, handed me a hundred-dollar bill, and held out his hand. I accepted the tip and took his sweaty hand in mine as he led me out of the cage.

Turning to me, he said, "Welcome to Vanity Angel, you're hired."

I let out a sigh and smiled at Nova as I gathered up my attire. The nerves were gone and I was amped to work the room and make some money. I couldn't believe he gave me a hundred-dollar bill. I imagined all the paint supplies I could buy with just this little bill.

"Whew, girl, I knew there was a big slut in there somewhere. You did good, Alex; we'll make some money tonight." Nova was proud of me.

A few hours into the shift, I started to settle in. Most of the entertainers were friendly. However, there's always a clique or two of girls who see you as a threat. I also learned that many of the girls had their own "customers" so I was warned to steer clear of a few club patrons. If only these men—blinded by beauty, attention, and a great pair of tits—knew they were getting taken for a ride. Maybe some do, maybe some don't. We're all in here for our own selfish reasons, I guess. It is unbelievable how many men walk into this venue with candy under one arm. They carry jewelry under another and pockets full of cash. All for that one select entertainer. All with the hopes of a date or a lay. Lucky bitches. And they all lay it on you. How they would take care of you, lavish you, and take you away from all this. It's sad, really. Then there are men who come in here with girlfriends or wives at home. They seek the attention they're not receiving at home. Some are a part of a bachelor party and some come in as part of a couple looking to spice up their sex life. Good visual foreplay.

For me, I'm not seeking a date or a lay, but cold hard CASH. I just need some breathing room and continue to maintain my independence. I cannot and will not move back home.

Nova seems to have found an old "friend" at the bar. I decided I wasn't going to play shadow any longer and began my solo lap around the room. As I strolled past a table of four, one man reached out and grabbed my hand. Going with my initial reaction, I pulled back and gave him a dirty look. The gentleman laughed and stood up.

"Sorry doll face, I didn't mean to startle you. Would you like to join us?" He gestured for me to sit down next to him as he pulled out a chair for me. I obliged, smiled, and sat down. "Would you like a drink, doll?" he asked while waving the cocktail waitress over.

"Sure, glass of chardonnay please." I smiled at the buxom brunette taking my order. I then turned toward the table and asked, "So are y'all from around here?"

The three other strippers at the table who were on the other three customers' laps rolled their eyes. They continued groping their men.

"So you are from here? I love that drawl," the kind man said. "We're from Chicago, we're down here for a convention."

I smiled and continued to make mindless chit-chat while watching a girl on stage strut her stuff. As a new song started, I leaned over to Chicago Man and requested that I dance for him. He nodded his head yes, grabbed my hand, and helped me to my feet. I began the little routine I had assembled after dancing for a few other patrons earlier that evening. When I got to the part of removing my dress and exposing my breasts, it just brought this big smile to Mr. Chicago's face. He must be a boob man. I continued to sway, lick my lips, and tease with my black panties, knowing he was enjoying himself. When the song ended, he motioned me to continue and I obliged once more and made another twenty bucks. Soon after, the DJ announced last call. I gave the DJ a slight smile as I looked up to his booth. If he only knew how he was my saving grace at that moment. I was spent. I've had more introductions of customers' names in my head than I could ever remember. I was starving and my feet were burning from all the entertaining. I thanked the table for the lovely evening, excused myself, and headed for the dressing room door. Once inside, I spotted Mercedes.

"Girl, food and my cowboy slippers pronto," I pouted as I sat down on the bench and began to gather my things.

I felt exhausted but excited to count all the money I made throughout the shift. I knew I'd be able to handle this gig for a while. I'd be okay.

*

Saturday morning came too fast. I groaned as I rolled over and started to pet Ernie. I awoke with smudged eyeliner on the pillowcase and smoke-drenched hair. Ah, I needed a shower. I stepped off the bed and nearly lost my balance, my feet still burning like crazy as I made my way to the coffee machine. As soon as I pushed the start button, there was a tap on the door. I shifted my weight.

"Man, my dogs are barking—hold on," I hollered as I searched for my slippers. I then opened the door, and there stood Tyler.

"Holy hell, woman, what happened to you? Were you attacked or something?"

"Perks of a new job," I groaned as I took two coffee mugs out of the dishwasher. "You don't look so fresh yourself, what's going on?"

"On studio duty, killing this album," Tyler replied.

"Oh yeah, how's it going?" I was curious.

"Girlfriend, I—I mean WHIP—would love for you to do our album art. Is that cool?" Ty inquired as he pulled on a piece of my stringy, smoke-drenched hair.

"What does it pay? And how soon is it needed?" I smiled and dumped another scoop of sugar into my coffee. I needed to wake up a bit before I could digest any requests from the frontman. "I'd love to comp something for you, what did you have in mind?" I was caving.

"Tattoo art, no title—just art." Tyler smiled with excitement.

"Deep, dude," I said while rolling my eyes. "I'll work

on some sketches and meet up with you guys soon."

"Thanks beauti—well, you need a shower first. Appreciate it, girl," Ty laughed while erotically eating one of my bananas.

I slapped him. "You PIG."

Tyler went on. "Now tell me all about this little adventure Nova dragged you into."

"You know about this?" I was shocked. "Wouldn't call it much of an adventure. I'm desperate; I need some financial room to breathe. It'll be for just a little while, Ty. I'm being careful," I explained shamefully.

Ty responded, "Look Blondie, if you got it, flaunt it. Make some paper, girlfriend. Who am I to judge? We're all selling something, Alex."

Tyler was always comforting to me. I didn't have to sell the idea of me working at Vanity—he just understood. "Thank you for not giving me a speech," I thanked Ty.

"Just be careful, girl. Working clubs, drinking, and bad decisions all go hand in hand. Believe me, I'm the king of bad decisions." Tyler smiled, reassuring me he was cool with it. "Your mother did a real number on you, huh? I do love you, Alex."

I gave Tyler a half-ass smile and said, "I'll swing by rehearsal in a few days with the album cover sketches. I do love the whip as your logo, though," I said with excitement as the caffeine started to kick in.

"Cool, well, I gotta jet, we're recording vocals today. I'll tell your loverboy you said 'hello,'" Ty teased as he grabbed his keys off the counter and took off out the door.

I had no time to answer. I'll just finish my coffee and head straight for the shower.

Few days have passed and I've been distracted with *D-Town* as well as sketching out WHIP's album cover art. I had butterflies swarming in my stomach as I hid in my cubicle. I couldn't wait to show the band the art, see Trent again, and prepare for Friday's shift at Vanity. Wow, my dance card was getting pretty full! However, Tyler's comment about telling "loverboy" I said "hello" was still lingering with me. Is Trent my loverboy? A booty call of some sort? Am I now a chicken head? I laughed. Do I need to get intertwined and caught up with some rockstar? One that was about to release his album and hit the ground running on a WHIP rock tour? AM I CRAZY?

I shook my head as I noticed Fat Larry heading my way—ugh, another project. I smiled as I stowed away my cover art and any thought of Trent until later.

Thursday arrived and I had the afternoon to myself. I figured I would head uptown to see Nova and join her for a spa day. A little mani-pedi with some lunch afterward? I could then possibly drag Nova to WHIP's rehearsal with me as I presented my album cover designs to the band that evening. Scurrying around, I threw on my old CLASH t-shirt, my favorite pair of shredded jeans, and cowboy boots. I headed out to my truck. I had to park in some lot down the street from Nova's condo. I was a bit embarrassed asking the valet to park my beast Axl for me. As I headed toward Nova's place, I took my time walking. I enjoyed all the holiday decorations that were being hung all over uptown. I just grinned from ear to ear. I love this time of the year!

When I reached Nova's, she was standing outside chatting it up with the doorman, flirting as usual. She stuck her tongue out at me as I approached them.

"The CLASH? Ugh, girl, we need to take you shopping," she scolded me.

"I need to save money, Nova, not spend it on a new wardrobe," I barked back.

"Well," she sighed, "we're heading to the Za-Za hotel spa. We're having a late lunch at Dragonfly, you should have dressed more appropriately. Come on."

She grabbed my hand and we crossed the street together, heading toward the hotel.

Lying there with cucumbers on my eyes, I decided to be open with Nova. "Hey girl, what do you think about Trent?" I was fishing. "Do you like him?"

Nova huffed as she rolled over for the masseuse to rub on her backside. "Question is, do you like him? I wouldn't tie yourself down—unless you're having kinky sex—to just one man. You've just started making real money, the band's about to hit the road, girl you have pure freedom right now. Why are you so afraid to be alone? What's the rush? I mean, if 'Mr. Right,' with all the right goods like money, fame, car, etcetera came along—I'm not stopping that, but a starving musician? Not my bag, girl. Your life. Your decision."

I tossed a cucumber at her. "That didn't help. Do you like Trent as a person? I don't care about the money and all that other stuff." I huffed, awaiting her approval.

"I do, I guess." She pursed her lips at me then said, "Girl, please quietly marinate over there with your salad and stop trying to figure it all out today." She then tossed the veggie back at me.

After our spa treatment, we made our way to the DragonFly restaurant and immediately ordered a bottle of wine. I just let Nova carry on about the girls at work, the patrons she dated, and all the loot she was making. I had a feeling she didn't really want to discuss WHIP after I brought up Trent during her massage and then pleaded for her to join me at the band's rehearsal tonight during dinner.

Finishing our overpriced meal, Nova agreed she would accompany me to WHIP's rehearsal. I was relieved. We gathered our things, overtipped the waiter (completely understanding what working for tips was like), and made our way back downtown. I was beaming internally with excitement to see Trent again.

Nova and I walked into the smoke-clouded rehearsal room. It was nearly a hop, skip, and jump away from my sleeping quarters.

"Girl, you need a new pad. These hormone raging boys are waaaay too close for comfort to you," she said while gazing around the room. She was unsure where to step next amongst the ashtrays, cables, and papers with half-written lyrics littered everywhere.

"I know, you snob," I bit back. "This is on budget for me and I actually kind of like being in the center of the creative circus that's going on here. It inspires me," I lied as I took a deep breath.

"Well, cigarette buds and leather pants don't inspire me. Money does, Alex." Nova smiled and kissed my cheek. "You deserve sooo much more than irrational, 'I'm so misunderstood' ego-maniacs like WHIP."

"Easy there tiger," I scolded Nova.

The leather god I've come to adore flipped his hair back, fastened it with some dude clip to get it out of his eyes, and started to approach me. I got butterflies.

"Hi Alex," he said with that devilish grin.

"Hey Trent," I responded as my butterflies kicked it up a notch by doing somersaults.

"What's in the portfolio case?" he inquired.

"The case, oh, ummm—" I stumbled, "the sketches Ty asked me to create for your album cover, wanna see?"

"Sure babe." He took the brown leather case from my hand and sat down on the closest amp to review them. He was excited as he took each piece out and studied it with those dark, dreamy eyes. I smiled to myself, sort of proud of my work.

"Nothing is set. These are just the first drafts so please make as many notes on them as you wish and I'll give it another go until I get it right." I swallowed hard, feeling a lump of embarrassment in my throat.

"These are perfect, Alex," he gloated, not taking his eyes off my work. "Very dark and Gothic. I appreciate you capturing our vibe so well. Can I hang on to these and present them to the band during our meeting with our manager tomorrow?" He smiled. "I'll take good care of them, and I'll see to it that I return them myself."

I smiled back, giving my permission. Nova interrupted our moment as she said her goodbyes and split. I hung around the band jam for a bit. Olivia was there with a few of her suicide punk girlfriends. They were occupying all the chairs as they giggled and whispered to one another. I leaned against the doorway until Ty noticed I was there. He walked over to me during a guitar solo, kissed my head and winked, then went back to belting his lonely ballad. I watched with amazement. These boys will be on the road soon, pedaling their album, and I'll be making new friends at Vanity. Wow—I wondered if Ty told Trent I was picking up the weekend shifts there yet. Should I care what he thinks? Well, we're not an item and I'm unsure what my future holds as these dudes are about to blow up. I'll let each day unfold. The song ended and the WHIP-ettes cheered and squealed. They jumped off their chairs and mauled the boys. Trent wrapped up a quick convo with WHIP-ette #3 and headed back toward me.

"I got to get my pedal outta my truck, wanna walk with me? We're taking a quick break." He hesitated a bit.

"Sure." I smiled and grabbed the doorknob. "I'll walk you to your truck then I'm heading back to my place to feed Ernie."

"Hey, how's my buddy doing?" he asked politely.

"Ern is good, happy, thanks for asking," I laughed.

As we approached the truck, I stepped aside so he could open the door. He turned around and I grabbed his arm and pushed him against the vehicle. I slipped my tongue right in his mouth. He smiled. I licked a bit of teeth by accident. Trent laughed then he gave me a deep heavy, I-long-for-you return kiss. We made out for quite some time leaning against his truck. We couldn't get enough of each other. My wet lips smothered his wet lips as my tongue teased his tongue. This man is intoxicating to me. I love those moments where you just make out like hungry teenagers and that's all you do. After a while, I decided to withdraw and give him some of his own air back.

"Yummmm," he purred as he hugged me and kissed my neck tenderly.

"Ernie," I said.

"WHIP," he replied.

We knew we each had to get back to our respective places.

CHAPTER FIVE

Friday night I was at Vanity once again. I was starting to get the hang of this. After the panic passed, I usually sucked it up and got started. Nova already had a customer waiting for her in the VIP area; she would be set for a while, so I was flying solo. I walked on the main floor and checked in with the DJ, who put me in rotation to work the stages. Then I headed straight for the bar. I snagged a seat next to this beautiful, exotic girl sipping a glass of wine. She swiveled her chair toward me and smiled.

"Mercedes' friend, right?" she asked with a Spanish accent.

"Alex—ngel," I replied. It was so strange to call myself by another name. It was hard not to stumble as I formally introduced myself. "Angel." I smiled as I shook her hand.

"I'm Skylar. Girl, it's going to be busy tonight," she dreaded as she sipped.

"Convention and some football thing?" I laughed. Yep, Dallas Cowboys are playing at home where I should be, instead of this smoky joint. "Good for us," I responded and decided to sit back and watch the girls strut the room and work their magic.

Moments later, two men in dark Hugo Boss suits approached the bar and asked if we would like to join them. We obliged, stood up, and straightened our dresses as we made our introductions.

"VIP?" one man offered. Skylar immediately grabbed his hand and headed toward the staircase. The other man smiled.

"Shall we?" he asked, and I smiled as we followed the other couple up the stairs.

In the upstairs VIP area, purple velvet chairs leaned up against Victorian mirrors, and candles reflected light everywhere. It had a sexy ambiance, for sure. Skylar and I found our suite and spent a few hours in VIP. She was a pro for sure. I let her do all the negotiating. While I excused myself to freshen up, Skylar fetched a waitress. She ordered a bottle and got half our money up front. When I returned, she already had her dress off and was gyrating slowly for her gentleman friend. I blushed as I entered and slowly removed my dress. After a few songs of exotic dancing, my gentleman friend offered me a chair to join him in conversation. I obliged, dressed, and sat next to him. He reached for my hand, startling me as he began to lightly kiss and caress it. I smiled, feeling rather annoyed, and sipped my wine with the other hand. He continued to lightly kiss my cheek and neck where a few days ago Trent had been purring. I felt sick. I closed my eyes briefly, took a deep breath, and reminded myself that I could do this. This is Angel, NOT Alex, I repeated over in my head. The club would be open a little while longer so I had to play along—it was guaranteed money. I pulled away and tried to converse with my new "friend." He seemed rather annoyed.

"Baby, there's not much time. See how hard you made me? I want to make out with you—" He tried to put my hand on his hardening dick under those Boss pants.

I gulped and responded. "I am enjoying your company and love dancing for you; can I please start entertaining you again?" I asked shyly as I began to stand up. This man let out a sigh and tugged on my dress to hurry me along.

"Well, tease and show me what I can't have." He groaned as he continued to drink.

I let out a deep breath, feeling super self-conscious and vulnerable. I glanced over at Skylar, who was sitting on her customer's lap, kissing him. I was ashamed of her. This VIP has too much of a brothel vibe to it. I'm completely comfortable with the dancing element...but when you start to make out here, you begin to turn down a different road. I continued to dance as my short-tempered man started to roll his eyes and motioned for me to get on with it. I did. Then he grabbed my ass and pulled me into him, trying to lick my breast and squeeze my cheek at the same time. I was mortified. I pushed him away as Skylar started to laugh. She warned him to be on his best behavior. He laughed while slurring his words.

"She's driving me crazy, I paid for this, and I want ALL of this," he said while pulling at my g-string.

"Would you like me to leave?" I was humiliated. "You can pay me what you owe for the dances and I can be on my way."

Skylar gave me a dirty look and gestured for me to sit down. I returned the dirty look but agreed. As I continued to fake my drinking, Skylar was rather intoxicated. Her gentleman friend kept whispering in her ear as they would laugh and carry on. I wanted to recluse and disappear.

Moments later, my man excused himself for a bathroom break and cigarette run. I contemplated ditching him so I could head straight to the dressing room, grab my shit, and go home. I sighed, then leaned back, closed my eyes, and listened to the erotic foreplay music carry on. I then heard a slight moan and opened my eyes to take in Skylar giving her client a handjob. I froze. She had this man's throbbing dick out of his pants and engulfed in her spit-saturated hand as she worked him up and down. I was stunned. That was my cue: cut my losses and bail, fuck it. I stood up, ditched my drink, and headed out of the suite so fast that I ran right into Mr. Wrong.

"Hey baby, you're not bailing, are you? We're not quite finished," he said while grasping my hand so tightly that it hurt.

I said the first thing that men hate to hear: "I started my period."

He released me and I motored out of there, down the stairs, and into the dressing room. I passed a few doormen along the way but chose not to rat on Skylar—can't afford enemies here. Once I made it to my locker, I started to cry. I heard the DJ call out, "Last call for alcohol!" and I took a deep breath. I already took care of my tip-out process so I did not need to stand in that line of loud, obnoxious, drunk party girls. Whoa, bypassed that one. I got dressed rather quickly, avoiding any conversation about the evening's events. I slammed my metal locker door shut. Nova startled me as she pinched my side while strutting by.

"Hey Miss Thing, how was YOUR evening? I noticed you were tucked away in a suite. I'm a jealous girl. You banked, right?" she teased as she flipped off her clear heels to let her aching feet breathe. "I'm starving, breakfast?" she asked.

"There's gotta be a story about tonight, eh?" I sighed. "Yes, but I'll pass on the breakfast...rain check? I'm heading home for bed. I'm beat."

Nova pouted a bit then was occupied by another girl's tale about her night. I was off the hook.

"Catch ya later, Nova. I'm out." I waved as I headed out of the dressing room and straight for the exit. I held my breath until I hit Interstate 35.

After getting on the on-ramp, I started to cry again. I was exhausted and I did not have any fun tonight. This gig is harder than I thought. It started to rain. When I reached the loft, I sat in my truck for an extra minute, letting the depression wash off me with the rain. I leaned my head on Axl's cold steering wheel and took in a few deep breaths. "What am I doing?" I asked myself.

Suddenly there was a banging on my driver's side window and I jumped. It was Trent. I paused for a second then rolled my window down.

"What on earth are you doing here, Trent?" I asked. I felt the butterflies kick up again. I half-smiled.

"I had practice tonight and just decided to stick around to see if I would catch you. Ty told me you were out with Nova so I bummed it with the boys. You okay, Alex? You seem sad." His eyes were so endearing. I gave him another half-smile. "Do I want to know?" Trent smiled. Then he opened my door and held out his hand. "Come on, kitten, let's get you out of the rain."

I laughed, grabbed my bag, and tucked myself under Trent's coat as we hurried through the cold rain. When we entered the loft, I turned on a small, dim light and dropped my bag and keys on the floor. Trent turned me around and removed my jacket.

"You're all wet, can I run you a bath?"

I smiled, not saying a word. Trent guided me to my bathroom, pulled a lighter out of his pocket, and lit a few candles. I stood there watching with amazement. He's really sweet. He then ran the bath water, adding a few drops of eucalyptus oil, and tested the water with his hand.

"Feels good. Now let's get you out of those clothes."

He removed every item of smoke-scented clothing I had clung to my body. I tried not to cry. I felt exhausted. I then stepped into the bathtub with no insecurity whatsoever. Trent gazed at my nude body with such appreciation. As I settled in, Trent scotched up on a wooden stool next to the tub, rolled up his sleeves, and wet a washcloth. I smiled. He proceeded to wipe every inch of my body slowly. I released any bad thoughts the evening had cast over me. He leaned my head back and began to wash my hair. Goosebumps took over my body and my mood shifted. He scratched my head and brushed out my hair. He then leaned over me as my head still lay back on the tub and kissed me so softly. He licked my lips, then slid his soft, warm tongue in my mouth as I responded with a heavier kiss. His hands started to trail down my neck and over each breast, giving each nipple a tender squeeze. I closed my eyes. He continued to trail down toward my sex that was soaking underwater. He gently inserted a finger. He began to finger me as I opened my soapy legs wider and moaned. I laid back and let him take over my pussy. He stroked in and out and in and out as I continued to moan. He then pulled out his wet finger and began to pull on my clit and inserted once more to bring me over the top. In and out, in and out. I came so hard on his finger. I then opened my eyes, giving a slight grin. I was whipped. Trent turned and grabbed a towel off the rack and opened it up, motioning for me to get out. I obliged. He then led me over to the bed and had me lie on my stomach as he grabbed something for me to drink. I obeyed. I was spent. The bath and the orgasm both relaxed me. When Trent returned, he handed me juice. As I sipped, he showed me a small bottle of oil.

"Ahh, you brought gifts," I said. He smiled back.

"Yes, kitten, stay put. I'm rubbing the rest of the stress away."

He began to massage my neck, down my spine, over my buttocks, and down to my feet. Wow, I needed this. I let out a slight groan every once in a while to let him in on how good this slice of affection from him felt. When he wrapped up the feet, he rolled me over and began to repeat the same massage on my front side. He started at my neck and down each arm, over each breast, down my abdomen and legs. Oh, his hands on me felt like heaven. He rubbed every inch of skin on my body. I continued to groan and take in the moment. This is nice—being spoiled. As my thoughts drifted, they came right back to Trent as he lifted my arms over my head and held them there. I obeyed. He then opened each leg and backed himself up off the bed. He removed his tattered jeans and tossed them aside. He then crawled back into bed toward me, placed a condom on his throbbing cock, and slipped into me.

"Ohhhh." I closed my eyes once more as Trent began making love to me.

*

The next morning, I felt a bit achy from the club and Trent's massage. However, I felt revived. I laid there with a grin, staring out the window. I turned my head and noticed that tousled black hair lying across my other pillow. I smiled. He slept as soundly as I did. I could wake up every morning like this. Suddenly I felt a pounce on my bed and—yep—Ernie was there to greet us and remind us that it was breakfast time. I reached out to pet Ern as I felt another hand pounce me—Trent's.

"Good morning, kittens." Trent smiled sleepily. He reached for me and Ernie.

"I'll make some coffee and feed Ernie here, you stay and rest." I kissed his head and ran my fingers through his hair.

Cat fed. Filled two cups of coffee and headed back to my masseur. I smiled remembering those strong hands stroking me last night.

"Hey babe, thanks for the coffee," Trent said as he sat up and took the steaming Cowboys cup from my hand.

"I wanted..." I paused. "I wanted to thank you for last night. I kind of had a rough night. I actually wanted to talk to you about something." I felt like a child confessing to her father. I felt ashamed. Trent didn't say a word. I continued, "I wanted to know if you knew where I was last night." I paused, thinking of Tyler's big mouth. WHIP and everyone in Dallas sure would know every one of my indiscretions. Trent looked curious. I was stunned. "Ty didn't tell you anything?" I was shocked. Hum, he might be a good friend after all.

Trent replied, "Were you on a date?" I laughed and looked back down to the concrete floor. "It's okay if you were, I would understand. I mean babe, we haven't declared ourselves an item and I have no place to say anything if you are seeing other people. I mean, I know the band and I are all hitting the road and we shouldn't tie each other down and..." Trent paused. "Am I on the right track?"

Wham, what the fuck hit me? I had a hundred scenarios swirling in my head. I shook my head to settle all the chaos and concentrated on one.

"Tour?" I focused my attention back on him.

"We have a record release party coming up. By the way, your sketches were a hit with all my bandmates. We've selected one for the CD cover." I half-assed a smile. "Then a few gigs down in Austin, then we're hitting the road for a tour after the holiday. I don't want to tie you down, Alex. You deserve better. I mean, someone who will be there for you every day. I'm sure you don't want to be a roadie. No wives or girlfriends are tagging along. We'll be pulled in every direction." He paused once more. "You okay, Alex?"

I swallowed. "It's a lot to digest. I understand. Commitments and the road are a bit much to handle, plus the temptation." I stopped myself before I sounded like a catty bitch. I didn't want to be selfish. This was his dream, not mine. We were having fun, that's all.

Trent got out of bed and pulled on the tattered jeans that had been lying on the floor. They had been there since he tossed them there before making love to me. We were so close last night and now everything seems so far apart.

"Trent, I don't want you to go," I said shyly.

"Alex, I adore you, maybe a little too much. Every time I see you or talk to you, I feel like a teenager all over again. I need to shelve those feelings for the time being and not get distracted. You did nothing wrong. I don't want to hurt you when I'm physically not going to be here. I hope you understand. Plus, you'll finish your internship, land a great gig at some ad agency, or something. Meet someone who CAN be there for you. Someone who can love you and experience all life is offering you something that I'm unable to do right now." He stopped to take a breath.

"You're bailing," I let out. "Many people travel for work and still maintain relationships and commitments. You're just bailing." I was sad. I let him off the hook.

He gave me a dirty look and pulled his jacket on. He then leaned on the bed and kissed my head. "I adore you. I don't want to lose you but I have to let you go so I'm not distracted when I'm out there...there on the road. Distracted in a good way."

He gave me that beautiful grin of his and I melted. This sucks. I locked the door after Trent left and crawled back into bed.

*

"Oh for fuck's sake, would that fucking phone stop beeping!" I woke depressed and now fucking agitated as my cell was blowing up. I hung off the bed and grabbed it off the floor. "What?!" I hollered into the phone, startling Nova.

"Alex, girl, you okay?" She was checking in on me.

"No!" I let her have it. "Work sucked. Some hooker

Skylar was giving some customer a handjob. I was getting molested by my customer. Kind of broke up with Trent, and I wanna go back to fucking bed." Whoa, I felt better. "I let him off the hook, Nova. I adore Trent. But he's heading out on tour. I'm alone again in this shit loft with my shit internship while getting fondled by shit men." I could feel myself begin to sweat.

"Oh, girl," Nova shushed me like she always did and took over the conversation. "Girl, Trent is sweet and all, but the band man needs to pedal his music. You are NOT going to be a fellow chicken head and follow WHIP around. You deserve better. You need to ride out your shit internship or fucking quit the drag already and bust your ass at the club. You need to make your own money and feel good about yourself. Fuck those convention pricks that come in to let loose from their ordinary lives. Made you feel worthless. You are beautiful, talented, and can run circles around their boring wives. Take a deep breath and let it go. Mr. Right will waltz in soon or—"

I cut her off. "I let him off the hook, Nova; I should fight harder for Trent. I really like him." I stopped myself.

"Trent was exciting, creative, and a little different from the other WHIP guys, like Ty. But he's not for you."

I fell silent.

"You okay?" Nova chimed.

"I'm good. I'll let it go. I gotta go. I have holiday plans to do with my mother. Love you girl, thanks for listening."

"Anytime. Next weekend you'll pair up with me and not hand-job central Miss Skylar."

I laughed and we both hollered "Sluuut!" I hung up and headed for the shower, ready to wash away Vanity and Trent.

CHAPTER SIX

This week was moving at a snail's pace. I wanted these holidays to be over. Did you know the suicide rate increases over the holidays due to loneliness? I twirled my hair with one hand. I was too distracted to focus on this social media bullshit. I sank down in my chair and hid in my tiny cubicle smeared with band posters, ticket stubs, and backstage passes. How can I focus when a poster of WHIP is taped to my fucking cube wall? I groaned. I then took a dart off of a dartboard in the cubicle next to me and threw it at Trent.

"Fuck him."

I smiled, flipped my laptop open, and got back to work.

*

A few weeks have passed and it's almost Christmas. Man, I sure would like Trent wrapped in a big red bow under my tree. I paced the loft. I hated waiting on Nova; she was always fashionably late. Tonight is the big record release / holiday party for WHIP and their new label. I took extra time getting ready, knowing damn well that I wanted to knock Trent's socks off and make him regret our last conversation weeks ago. It was strange not seeing or talking to him or Tyler. Maybe my boys are slipping away from me. They are caught up in a whirlwind and floating on air as they promote their gift of music. I paced a bit more, then glanced back into the mirror, checking my dress. It was a silver sequined mini number that I had splurged on recently for this affair tonight. I wanted to treat myself. I felt I deserved it since I've been busting my ass at Vanity lately. I've really come into this Angel character. I'm a better actress than I thought. The club has been super busy with all the holiday excitement. While the wives were shopping, the husbands were playing at Vanity. Money has been quite free-flowing and I was taking every damn dollar they threw at me. I smiled as I looked at my purchase in the mirror—worth every penny. Soon there was a bang at the door.

"Hey hooker, let me in!"

Startled, I let Nova in.

"You look stunning, girl!" she squealed as she made her way over to the mirror for one last glance at herself. "Like the red? I'm feeling rather festive." Nova smiled while applying her red lipstick.

"You always look stunning, you ho ho ho," I teased. I strapped on my silver heels and checked my lipstick once more as I grabbed Nova's hand. "I can do this," I said sternly. "I've let Trent go, I had a few weeks to get used to the idea of being alone, so we'll see what adventure will unfold tonight." I smiled confidently.

Nova squeezed my hand back and grabbed her clutch. "We got this," she reassured me once more as we headed out to the car.

Arriving at the party, we were stunned to see how laid out it was.

"This label went all out," I gulped, looking at Nova as we entered the event.

We were shocked. Christmas trees were lit up at the entry doors, where a cardboard cut-out of the album's cover was on display. My design was parked next to the tree. I smiled. I stopped to have Nova take a picture of me in front of the display. A gold runner led us into the ballroom. Soothing music came from the live band. Tables were set up with candles. White strings of light hung from everything, giving the room a beautiful holiday ambiance. Record executives, recording studio personnel, and *D-Town* staff were at this party, along with an eclectic mix of WHIP's family and friends.

"Wow, I'm truly impressed," I said as I swallowed, surveying the room. "I figured we'd be walking into a dungeon of some sort in someone's basement."

Nova snickered. "I'm impressed. These boys are going big time, babe. Tyler ready for this?" she questioned as she scanned the room, looking for the bar.

"We're long overdue on a powwow—Ty and I—so I'm not sure where his head is at." I sighed. I noticed Olivia breaking free from her clan of chicken heads and starting to prance over toward me. No girlfriends tagging along, huh? Go fuck yourself, Trent. I huffed. I then faked a smile. "Hi, Olivia. Wow, what a setup, huh?"

I began to engage in trivial bullshit. She looked beautiful. No glasses tonight. Fucking Tyler has done her some good. He's a handful but he's the lead singer, which every woman wants, so Olivia is on a real high right now.

Nova pinched my side. "Bar...business suits...see ya."

She snubbed Olivia and headed right for the bar. She was on a mission. Nova had no qualms about playing up the Mercedes card and reeling in some potential clients. I kind of wondered to myself if she slept with some of these men outside of Vanity. My woman's intuition told me "yes," but I dismissed the thought. I returned my focus to Olivia, who hadn't stopped chatting since she reached me.

I waited for her to take a breath then asked, "Where's Tyler, Olivia? I do miss him. We haven't seen each other in a while."

She pointed toward the opposite corner of the room, taking a sip of her drink. There was a small gathering of people all gawking and an assembly of photographers taking pictures of the band. WHIP stood against a backdrop banner, like the ones you see on red carpets, where once again was my design. I smiled, giving myself a moment to be proud of the artwork I'd created. The boys looked gorgeous, every one of them dressed in black. Swoons of lyrics by ACDC's *Back in Black* swirled in my head. These boys looked gorgeous, all in black velvet jackets, hair sprayed up and out. Guyliner smeared on, WHIP to perfection. As I moved closer, I gave each one a good look-over, memorizing each member as a sense of pride washed over me. I love these guys. Soon enough, I got busted. Tyler jumped up from the group photo and raced toward me.

"Alex! You came!" He threw his arms around me. "Whatcha think? Hell of a setup, huh? Did you see your album cover design?" Tyler grabbed my hand and dragged me over to the photographers. I smiled shyly as Tyler started his introductions. "Alex designed the art for our album cover." Immediately flashbulbs went off. I smiled once more, looked over at Trent, and rolled my eyes. There, I got a smile out of him.

I turned to Ty. "Hey man, I need a drink. You do the paparazzi thing and I'll meet you at the bar?"

He kissed me on the cheek then whispered in my ear, "It's so fun being a rockstar." Ty then let go of my hand and rejoined the band.

Hanging at the bar, I felt like a third wheel with Miss Mercedes and her adoring new fans. Can't I ever endure an activity that doesn't revolve around a damn bar? I smiled to myself.

"What are you smiling about with that devilish grin?" a startling voice asked from my right side. I glanced over and smiled. "Hi, I'm Gage," he said as he gestured for me to shake his hand.

"I'm Alexandria, nice to meet you." I smiled back.

"Enjoying the party?" He smiled once more. What a grin—am I a sucker for a nice smile or what?

"Yes, I am," I replied.

"How do you know these men?" Gage inquired.

"Oh boy, long story but Cliff's Notes version: I'm best friends with Tyler Black." I smiled, still so proud of him.

"Ahh, the infamous lead singer. That guy has got a hell of a range on him," Gage replied.

"I also created the artwork for the cover," I said.

"That dark creation came out of you? The guys love your work," he said. What was that? I was instantly putting up my wall.

"Yes, there's a dark side to each and every one of us," I responded, sort of biting back.

"I didn't mean to offend you, you're very good. Have I seen your work anywhere else?" He sounded sincere, so I slowly began to shed my armor. This Vanity trip had me second-guessing every man I met. I put up this protective shield to ward off any intrusion. I needed to stop and settle down. This is a beautiful man who is genuinely interested in my work, so I need to shut the fuck up and play nice.

"No, just art for a few local bands and a few local gallery shows. My background is in graphic design. I'm just getting started," I replied shyly. I get embarrassed talking about my goals and such. Everyone always seemed to have an opinion. Nova noticed me conversing with this gorgeous man.

She walked by, stopping long enough to whisper in my ear, "Now that's more like it, money baby."

"A friend?" Gage inquired.

"A nuisance." I grinned and stuck my tongue out at her as she walked away.

Gage then straightened his tie and smoothed out his jacket. He said, "Well, Alexandria, it was a pleasure meeting you. Here's my card." He reached into his suit jacket pocket, took out a slim business card, and handed it to me. "I have connections with music artists. You should keep in touch. I can throw some projects your way." He smiled that intoxicating grin as I accepted his card.

Blushing, I smiled back, hoping I didn't come off as a bitch. "I'll do that."

Gage took a final sip of his drink. "By the way, beautiful accent." He tipped the bartender and walked away.

I blushed. Soon enough, Nova was in my space, casting a shadow over the business card I studied in my hand.

"Gage Heston, huh?" she purred.

I glanced at Trent across the room, then back down at

the business card in my hand, and felt a flush of guilt wash over me. I shouldn't feel guilty, I shamed myself. I discreetly tucked the card into my purse and took another sip of my drink.

Tyler finally broke free from all the photographers and met me at the bar as promised. "Hi, beautiful." He clutched my hand. "How about a dance?" Tyler asked.

"Won't Olivia be upset?"

"Nonsense." Tyler waved his hand in my face as he dragged me off my barstool.

I squeezed Tyler's hand as he led me to the dance floor. I wrapped my arms around him and we started swaying. Tyler squeezed me tighter, knowing I needed the comfort of my best friend right now. He could sense a sadness smothering me but neither of us needed to address it.

We just danced, holding each other tightly.

*

The next morning, I woke up thinking about Gage. Should I call him? Is it too soon? I rolled onto my back, staring at the ceiling. Or should I reach out to Trent? Letting out a long sigh, I was confused. I miss Trent. Tyler sensed it last night as we held each other. This was Trent's decision not to let us get too close because he wanted to play rockstar, not mine.

Plus, he only smiled at me at the party and pretty much steered clear of me the entire evening. Gage, on the other hand, made innocent conversation and invited me into his world.

"That's it," I hollered to Ernie as he stood up and

rearranged his sleeping position. "I'm calling Gage." I reached for my purse to hunt for my cell and his business card. "Found it!" I squealed. I dialed his number and immediately got a voicemail. I almost hung up when the beep went off. "Ugh," I stuttered. "Hi Gage, it's Alex from the record release party last night. I wanted to say hi and say it was so nice to meet you. Um, keep me in mind if any potential projects come across your desk. Thanks. Oh, my number should show up on your phone, call or text whenever. Bye." I hung up and fell back onto my pillow, feeling like I was sixteen again and calling a boy I liked for the first time. "New day, Ern...new day." I smiled to myself. Suddenly there was a knock at the door.

"Alex baby, let me in." It was Tyler. I groaned, rolled off the bed, and headed toward the door. There stood Tyler in last night's attire and smudged eyeliner. He reeked of cigarette smoke. "Hello, doll." He smiled as he leaned against my door frame.

"Hello, sticky rockstar," I replied.

He laughed and made his way into my loft. "Coffee on?" he asked.

"I'm on it," I said as I made my way over to the kitchen counter. "Where'd you sleep last night?" I asked curiously.

He laughed while rubbing his smudged eyeliner. He took a seat at my counter where we've had endless conversations. "I was with Olivia and another chicken head. Girl, those bitches are freaky."

"Ew," I responded and smiled at Ty while I started the coffee. "This is only the beginning, rock god. You better be using protection," I disciplined him and handed him a coffee mug.

"What happened to you, where did you end up?" He

was digging. "Trent went home alone," he said.

"Now, why did you feel the need to tell me that?" I gave him a dirty look. "I'm glad he went home alone, but it's none of my business. I did, however, meet a nice guy." I didn't look up at Ty as I poured my coffee.

"Reeeeally?" Ty remarked slyly. "Give...come on, we never keep secrets between us. By the way, I think Olivia has a bit of jealousy toward you and our relationship." He threw a sugar packet at me.

I looked up from my coffee. "Really, jealous? Of me? Good, it's good for her. I met Gage Heston." There it was, said out loud. "Please don't tell Trent. He doesn't need to know what I'm up to. He walked, remember?"

"I know, baby girl. Gage, huh?" He sipped his coffee.

"What's wrong with Gage? Do you know him? God, is nobody good enough for me by Tyler's standards?" I pouted a bit.

"He's a label executive douche, Alex; he's fuckin' loaded and can be a prick. Be careful," Tyler warned.

I stared at the counter. "I need to step out of my misfit world and be open to relationships with other types of people. I haven't even gone out with him. He gave me his card and said he might be able to throw some design work my way. What's wrong with that? Seems innocent enough?" Ahh...I let out a sigh. "God, I always feel like I'm defending who I let into my life."

"Easy, baby girl. He's got a bit of a rep, but who doesn't in Dallas, huh? Do me a solid, just be careful and don't fuck him over or lead him on since he's dealing with WHIP. Plus, I don't want the guys to get screwed 'cause he's trying to get back at you for something. Got it?"

"Wow," I responded. "Got it, Ty—it was just a

conversation, not a marriage proposal." I was spent. My cell buzzed, notifying me of a new text.

"Are you going to grab that, sugar?" Tyler asked.

I headed to my bed where the phone was lying on my pillow. I picked it up and read a text from Gage.

Hey, southern beauty, got a few possible bites for you, dinner tonight?

I blushed. "It's Gage, Ty. He wants to have dinner." My hands started to tremble with excitement. "I have to respond."

Tyler moaned, "Do it, girl, if you feel you need to. You'll get spoiled and believe me, that would be the man who can do it right."

I smiled. "Thanks."

I then replied, *I'm available, what time? And where?* I texted him my address and he said he'd send a car around seven. I threw my cell back on the bed and headed into the kitchen. I was beaming.

"I take it you accepted his invitation?" Tyler pryed.

"Yes, I'm just having dinner. By the way, you'll be busy with rehearsal so why do you give a shit what I do?"

Tyler finished his coffee. "I don't. Fuck it. I'll be on tour soon enough so you'll be free to lollygag around with whoever you fucking want." Tyler chugged the rest of his coffee without saying much more.

"You will be gone soon enough, Ty, and I'm going to fucking miss you." My eyes started to well up as I wiped the tears with the back of my hand.

"I love you Alex, be FREE. I asked you not to get too serious with Trent so now I need to shut the fuck up and let you make your own decisions. We both have a lot of changes going on in our lives, let's embrace it." Tyler then stood up and said, "Speaking of embrace, come give me a hug." Tyler opened his arms wide.

"Even though you're sticky, I'll still hug you." I laughed as I let Tyler wrap his arms around me.

*

Evening arrived and I decided to blow off Vanity. I texted Nova that I was ditching work and going out with Gage. Soon enough I got a response: *Sluuuut. Good. I like him. Details later?* I laughed. I was ready to go by 6:30 PM. I did my last-minute touch-ups with my outfit, waiting for seven to arrive. I was nervous, and for what? I felt a tad insecure about my appearance since I wore the only expensive dress I had to the record release party. This guy was in the major leagues and I was in the minors with this second-hand pencil skirt and tight sweater. Fuck it, it wasn't an interview or anything—or was it? He said he had prospects for me, or was he bullshitting me just to get me to go out with him? I was making myself nervous. I think not—that takes too much time and energy, and a man who is this busy and important has better things to do. I sprayed my perfume once more, grabbed my keys, and then headed out the door to the front of the bar. I'd wait for my car service to pick me up.

Right on time, this shiny black town car pulled up in front and parked. Out stepped a gentleman. He was younger, shaved head, probably ex-military, and asked if I was Alexandria. I smiled as he opened the car door for me and I slid onto the cold, black leather seats. I looked outside the window and noticed all the punk rockers standing out in front of the Green Room, staring at me. I felt like a celebrity. I couldn't relax. I was excited.

When the driver got into the car, I asked, "Where are we going?"

He glanced into the rearview mirror and replied, "Mr. Heston wants you to join him at a restaurant uptown in the Crescent hotel."

I smiled. "Fancy," I mumbled under my breath as I leaned back and tried to enjoy the ride uptown.

When we arrived at the Crescent, the driver got out, walked around the car to my side, and opened the door for me. I felt foolish as I giggled to myself. "Thank you," I said and smiled as I got out of the car and adjusted my skirt.

Another man stood at the hotel door and opened them for me as well. I couldn't stop giggling. I approached the restaurant and told the hostess with the big boobs who I was meeting. She gave me a once-over and, with slight attitude, ordered me to follow her. I obliged and let that snooty bitch roll off my back as I looked around in awe. Lights were dimmed. White linen tablecloths draped every table. Soft music played as the most beautiful people in Dallas enjoyed their meals. I walked with my shoulders back and acted like I was a part of the club. We finally reached the table in the far corner. As Miss Attitude and I approached the table, Gage stood up and met us with his beautiful grin.

"Hello, ladies." He smiled. "Thank you, Ivana," he said to the hostess. He then turned to me. "Hello, Alexandria. Car ride okay for you?"

I blushed as I stood there. "It was perfect, thank you.

It was nice not having to find a place to park up here this time of night." I was rambling. I felt nervous with this guy. Trent seemed like one of us, one of the gang, no weirdness. But this Gage guy made me a bit edgy. Gage motioned for me to sit down as the waiter arrived to fetch my order.

"She'll have a glass of chardonnay and I'll have a refill, please." He handed the waiter an empty glass, which must have been something on the rocks with all that ice. I was flattered and a bit annoyed that he ordered for me. Then again, it was a sweet gesture and I needed to relax. "Chardonnay, right?" He interrupted my train of thought. "You had wine at the party the other night, right?"

"Right, good memory." I smiled.

"You look beautiful."

I blushed once more. "Thank you, Gage." I felt beautiful sitting at this man's table. Everyone knew who he was. Everyone was looking at me, wondering if we were on an actual date, or who the hell I was. "Everyone's looking at us wondering who your mystery date is?" I laughed.

"Good," he responded. "Let's get drunk and rowdy and have the place throw us out. Then they'll all want to know who you really are."

I started to laugh. The waiter arrived and handed me my glass. I saluted Gage once he had a hold of his glass. Our glasses clinked together.

I shouted, "To getting drunk and rowdy—yeehaw!"

I laughed and sipped my wine as Gage did the same. I started to feel a bit more at ease. Throughout our supper, we talked about his company. We talked about WHIP, my internship, his upcoming projects with other bands that were about to be signed, and so on. I never experienced an uncomfortable pause until his cell phone went off. He excused himself and stepped away from the table. I sat there, pushing my food with my fork and glancing around the restaurant. I was having a good time. I was happy. When Gage returned to the table, he had a hard look on his face.

"Intense look, everything okay?" I asked.

"Ah, yeah, but hey, Alexandria, I need to send you on your way. I have some business to attend to."

I gulped. "Okay, dinner was delicious and I enjoyed your company," I said to him as we both stood up from the table.

Gage walked me to the front of the hotel. Upon reaching the town car, he leaned in, smelling incredible, and kissed my cheek. We said our goodbyes and I waved to him as the driver shut my door. As soon as we pulled out of the hotel, I fumbled for my phone and texted Nova. *Evening ended early. I'm heading up to Vanity. Why waste all this good hair and makeup?* I laughed as I finished the text. I then asked the driver to take me to the club.

*

I woke up Sunday exhausted. It's going to be one of those lazy days. I needed to regroup and digest the weekend. Quite the socialite, I must say. Apple didn't fall too far from Mother's tree. Hanging with the boys in the band, dinner with the executive, and making a fat wad Saturday night. I was spent but feeling good.

It's almost Christmas and my internship is up by the end of the year. I needed to go holiday shopping and make some future plans. Wow, what do I do now without the *D-Town*? Without WHIP?

I texted Tyler: *I'm gonna really miss you when you hit the road. Had dinner with executive dude and I kind of liked him. He's very interesting but a bit intense. I also busted my butt at Vanity. When is our last hoorah before the bus pulls out?* I hit 'send.' I went over to my window and swung it open. Breathing in the cool morning air was refreshing. Deep Ellum is quiet this time of morning. I then selected a cool vinyl and put on some mellow tunes as I got out my sketchbook.

*

My cell started to buzz around the concrete floor. Wow, I must have crashed out. My body needed a good nap. I was facedown on my sketchbook and it was dinner time. I reached for my cell.

Wow, three missed texts.

First one was from Mother. Oh yeah, holiday party plans were in order.

Second, Tyler. The text read: *Aw, I'll miss you too Blondie, last hooray on New Year's...you're in right?*

Third was from Gage. I gulped as I read: *Sorry for the abrupt ending to our dinner. I enjoyed you very much. Dinner again soon?* I smiled.

I responded *Yes* to Mom for holiday planning. *Yes* to Ty, that I was in for New Year's. And *Yes* to Gage, *Dinner anytime*.

CHAPTER SEVEN

These last few weeks of December are going to be hectic. Fat Larry had me on overtime with social media. I've been posting all the holiday music events around town. Vanity was busy with all the holiday shoppers spending a little extra on their favorite girl. I had a few fans by now that helped keep my earnings consistent. I had to remind Nova that she was my date for the New Year's Eve party WHIP was attending. Unsure if Gage was showing up or not. Really doesn't seem like his thing. I believe he said he had a prior commitment in Miami. He sure spent a lot of time there. I'm going for Tyler; I need a few more of our powwows before he's off like a gypsy. Christmas was here. I love this time of year! Everyone is so happy and giving.

It was the week before Christmas and Vanity was having its 'private members only' holiday party. It was Mercedes and Angel's last attempt at cleaning up financially for the year. Every client that held a VIP card was on the esteemed private list of attendees. The venue was all decked out in holiday bling. Christmas trees were decorated in silver and gold on each side of the main stage as well as up in the VIP suite area. Silver and gold candles burned on every table. White lights were displayed above every bar and stage in the house. Entertainers strutted around with holiday-colored gowns. Some had angel wings, and some even displayed Santa hats. Everyone was in good cheer. I was dolled up in a form-fitting, Christmas-red floor-length gown. It had a "come hither" slit up the side to show off my red fishnet stockings. I also applied my glossiest red lipstick to match my holiday panties and felt ready for the event. Nova had on her white floor-length gown. It had diamond-like beading all over, very glamorous. We took each other's hands as we walked through the glass doors. We entered the club from the dressing room and headed straight for the bar.

"You look hot, mama." Nova smiled at me as she ordered us each a glass of champagne. I smiled back as I fidgeted with my gown. "Are you nervous? What's your deal, Alex?" Nova asked as she sipped her champagne.

"I am. I still get anxious before the night gets started. I can't help it." I blushed as I reached for my glass.

"Look, I'll get up and do a dance for you on the house to get you more in the mood, okay?" Nova licked her lips to tease me.

"You are such a hussy, girl. I'll take one 'on the house,'" I teased as I pulled on her g-string and snapped it against her hip.

"Owww!" Nova moaned as she slid off the barstool, stood in front of me, and spread open my legs. "Hot fishnets, babe," she teased as she stroked my inner thigh. She then started to sway seductively as she ran her hands up and down my fishnets. She paused to sip her champagne, leaned in, and dripped a small amount into my mouth as I swallowed the rest of her sip. She then traced my lips with her champagne tongue as I squirmed in my seat. Nova is such an erotic dancer. She turned around and leaned against me. She instructed my hands with her hands to graze up and down her chest. She then loosened the ties behind her neck and let her dress fall, exposing her breasts. She ran her nails over each nipple as she moaned while continuing her dance. I reached my hands around to help her shimmy out of the rest of her dress as it dropped to the floor. Nova stepped out and kicked it to the side as she continued to sway against me. She never took her eyes off of me. She teased as she pulled on her g-string and ran her fingers up my dress and pulled on my g-string. What a flirt. I couldn't say a word. I was mesmerized by her. She continued to dance, swaying and exposing every part of her with no shame. I could sense the other girls watching nearby with a hint of jealousy. The song finally came to a close as I smiled and took in a deep breath.

"Ahhh, thank you gorgeous. I believe I'm ready for my night. However, I might have to change my panties cause you made me a little wet, girl." I smiled. I reached for her dress on the floor, kissed her lips as I handed it to her, and said, "Thank you, you're fuckin' hot."

The DJ called both our names with the rotation coming up and I groaned as I slid off the barstool and headed backstage. After a few cheesy holiday songs and strippers in Santa's helper outfits, I was on deck. Nine Inch Nails was my usual soundtrack for stage, not very holiday but very erotic. As the DJ introduced Angel, I rolled my eyes and smoothed my dress over once more as I stepped out on the main stage. Wow, the venue was filling up for the holiday party. The more crowded the place was, the more nervous I got as I strutted around the circular stage. I tried to look above everyone's head so A) I won't lose my balance and, B) I won't lose my nerve. My heart felt like it was going to leap out of my spandex dress. I sang the lyrics along with Trent Reznor under my breath as I moved about the stage. Oh God, did I just think about Trent? I wish I could dance for him tonight and show him how much he turns me on. As the second song started, I started to remove my dress. This is when men actually watch the stage—removing your garment and showing what you have on display. If they like it, they tip; if they don't, they continue to drink. I made a few circles around the stage, then hit the floor for some ground work. I laid on my back, opened my fishnet-covered legs into a V, and scissor-crossed them to tease my audience. I then rolled over onto my stomach and ever so slightly raised my ass into the air. I flipped my hair back and sat up on my toes as a few pieces of green started to shower onto the stage. I was appreciated. My song was coming to an end so I gathered the money, smiled at the patrons, and headed for the steps backstage. Reaching backstage, I collided with the next entertainer on deck.

"Sorry girl! Oh, Skylar, it's getting busy out there."

She half-smiled. She stepped on a few of the bills I dropped during our collision and headed on stage. I let out an "ugh" as I bent down and collected my money.

After putting myself back together in the dressing room, I sprayed a bit more perfume, applied gloss, and straightened my money in my garter. I headed back out onto the floor and straight over to Nova's stage. She smiled as I approached her. She bent down so I could tip her the twenty in my hand. I smiled as I gently tucked the bill into her g-string.

I whispered, "Thanks for the erotic dance, lady." She laughed.

A gentleman nearby noticed and waved for me to come over and join him. My holiday party was about to start.

It was midnight and I was taking a much-needed breather in the smoke-free dressing room. I sat on the bench, kicked off the clear heels as I made circles with my feet, and read my text messages. Oow, Gage. I immediately opened the message.

Hey Alexandria, I'm wrapping up a meeting, too late for a drink?

I smiled. Wow, he literally sent the text two minutes ago. Without pondering, I replied: *At a Christmas gala, I would love to meet you, as long as you don't mind my holiday attire?* I waited a few moments for a response and—ding—there it was.

Bring you and your holiday attire over to my penthouse, say half hour?

I smiled as I looked up into the mirror in the dressing room and glanced over my slutty red dress. *Perfect*, I responded, *text over the address and I'd be on my way.* I quickly jumped up and headed out to the club floor, searching for Nova. I found her perched on some expensive pair of pants. As I approached, I bent down and whispered in her ear.

"Mr. Heston requests my presence at his penthouse, can I pleeeease borrow your car? I'll return it tomorrow with a romantic holiday tale to share with you." I kissed her cheek while I batted my lashes at her.

"Oh lord, I'm stuck with old Axl, when the fuck are you going to dump that truck?" She laughed at me while gesturing for me to go away before she changed her mind.

I quickly scurried off the main floor and back to the dressing room. I swapped keys and my flannel for Nova's long faux mink to cover up Gage's holiday surprise. I paid my dues at Vanity so bailing wouldn't get me fired. I took a deep breath, then raced toward Nova's car and set the GPS to the penthouse.

*

When I reached Gage's penthouse, I chose to valet Nova's car. I walked in through the decadent lobby. I found myself at the glass elevator doors looking at my reflection. I don't feel like Alex—more like Angel. I looked like a Christmas bulb, all red and shiny and ready to break at any moment. *Stick to the Angel character*, I had to remind myself. I'm completely out of his league as artist Alex. The elevator doors opened and I stepped in and hit the PH button. I got goosebumps. I knocked on the big wood door. I shifted weight between the heels I found in Nova's car. Thank goodness I found extra shoes. Clear heels would completely give my extracurricular activities away. Gage would lose any respect he had for me by glancing down at my shoes. A close call on that one. The heavy wooden door opened gently and there stood Mr. Heston, gazing down at me with that beautiful grin.

"Santa must have received my letter." He smiled again, giving me a once-over with his dark eyes.

I returned the smile and replied, "Happy Holidays, Mr.

Heston," as I stepped into his home. What trust he must have inviting me into his home so soon after we've just met. I guess there is no Mrs. Heston? I glanced around his pad as Gage started to remove my coat.

"Wow, Merry Christmas to me," Gage smiled as he took a look at my dress.

"Too dressy?" I asked as I smiled back.

"Never, no dress codes in this establishment." He gestured for me to come inside. Doubt that, every place this man frequents had a damn dress code. Money and dress codes go hand in hand. "Something to drink, Miss Alexandria?" he inquired. This man was so charming and proper.

"'Alex,' please, and yes, I'd love one."

"I can put on some holiday music to keep you in the mood. By the way, how was the holiday party? Anyone I know at the gala?"

I know he was fishing for a tidbit of WHIP but calmly I replied, "Just Miss Nova." I swallowed.

"Oh, the 'nuisance'?" he asked. He laughed a bit as he hit 'play' on the CD player. Some instrumental holiday music started seeping out the speakers. There was my cue—I walked slowly over to Gage as he handed me a glass of wine in front of a set of glass balcony doors. I sure had confidence in this little red number.

"Lovely home." I was engaging in meaningless conversation.

"Thank you," he responded.

"Love the city view from here. I'm that little dot waaaaay down in the district," I laughed as I pointed toward Deep Ellum. "You're the big eagle up here watching all of us chickens pecking around down there in the city below you," I giggled. I needed to slow down. I had wine at Vanity and now I was drinking wine nervously here, which can get me into trouble.

He smiled at me. "How's the internship going? Are you making any headway with it?" He was prying; he had a way of making me feel a little insecure, like I needed to explain myself. Maybe I was being paranoid. Whichever it was, I needed to quit dissecting every comment and enjoy the trivial banter. I took a deep breath.

"*D-Town* is great, very busy due to all the holiday events. Do you have any holiday plans?" I was curious as I shifted the conversation back to him. "Label commitments? Family commitments?" I was fishing this time.

"No plans for Christmas," he responded. Kind of sad. "New Year's I'll be in Miami." He took another sip of his little concoction on the rocks.

"Never been to Miami, beautiful beaches and beautiful people, huh?" I hiccupped. Embarrassed, I continued to sip my wine.

"You'd love the art scene there. I'll need to get you involved," he suggested. This man sure had connections and knew what was going on everywhere. "Speaking of beautiful people, you in that dress, now that's beautiful."

My cheeks flushed and I smiled as I made my way over to Gage. He set his drink down on the large wooden conference room-like table behind him as I approached. He then held out his hand and took my hand in his as he pulled me closer. I held my breath for a moment and then let out a slow breath to calm me down as I looked up into his eyes. He smiled as he reached for the satin dress strap and gently pulled it down on one side. I swallowed. He then took hold of the opposite strap and let that one fall as well. Gazing back up to my eyes, he leaned in and kissed me. My weight shifted to the back of my heels. Not wasting a moment now, is he? I didn't stop the advancements due to wine and a secret motive to get back at Trent. I began to enjoy Gage's advancements. I kissed him back. It was sexy, yes, but different. Gage then ran both his hands up the sides of my Christmas-themed thigh-highs 'til he reached my waist. I slowly dropped my head back in ecstasy. Gage feverishly leaned me back onto the wooden table and pulled my holiday panties down. I went with it. He pulled on my satin straps once more until my breasts were exposed and then he began to devour them. Standing between my spread legs, he grabbed his belt and began to undo the buckle and unzip his jeans. I laid back in awe. He was taking control. He's not much for kissing or any foreplay; he was craving my pussy. Gage then pulled his endowed cock out of his jeans, slapped on a condom, and began to fuck me while I leaned back on the cold wooden table. After a few pumps, surprising even myself, I came rather quickly. The wine, maybe? Or was it the pure size of his cock that did the trick? He fucked hard. He fucked fast. Gage then pulled out, pulled off the condom, and came all over my dress. After our moment of passion, he zipped up his jeans. I laid there, still spread-eagled, glowing in the aftermath of what the fuck just happened.

I slowly sat up and, as cold as the table, Gage said, "Hey, my holiday angel, early start tomorrow, let's call it a night. You are everything I could ask for and more this Christmas."

He gestured for my hand and dragged me off the table like a rag doll.

Moments later, I pulled up to the valet stand at Nova's condo to drop off her car and pick up Axl. I gave the keys to the concierge and retrieved mine in exchange. I had a lot to mull over; I really did not want to involve Nova at this point. She's a cheerleader for Gage and not Trent. I sighed, thinking about Trent. He was more passionate. Gage seemed a bit robotic and rushed—however, it could be my imagination. I was spent; I needed to head home and wash off Vanity and Gage and get a good night's rest.

CHAPTER EIGHT

The next day, I woke up to Ernie nestling my ear. Rolling over, I grabbed him and smooched his belly 'til he pawed at me and dove off the bed.

"Ahhh, what a fucked-up evening!" I hollered, startling Ernie as he hovered over his bowl, waiting for breakfast. Groaning, I rolled off the bed and headed toward the kitchen. As I poured the kibble into his bowl, I noticed my phone blinking. "Hummm?" I grabbed the cell as I tried to focus. I saw it was a text from Gage. *Thanks for the holiday surprise, when can I unwrap you again?* I smiled and let out a deep breath as I tossed the phone back on the counter. "Ha!" I laughed. I needed to hold off for a moment and shelf this man and my emotions for the time being. I had plans to head out to Mockingbird Station today to finish some Christmas shopping.

*

As I was sifting through some bargain bin, my cell rang. "Hello?" I answered as I mulled over the sale item.

"Greetings my holiday surprise, would you like to have dinner with me tonight? I have a few potential projects to discuss with you."

I got goosebumps. "Well, hello stranger, how was your morning?" I inquired.

"I've been busy putting out fires and making people famous. Should I make a reservation for two at café ol' Penthouse?" Gage questioned as he invited me back to the penthouse. Smiling, I caved in.

"Sure, what time is the reservation for?" I checked my watch and saw it was close to five already.

"Eight o'clock sound good? I'll reserve a quiet wooden table for two." I could hear the smirk through the phone.

"Eight it is, holiday attire?" I smirked too.

"Attire optional," Gage teased.

"See you at eight with holiday bells on." I smiled once more as I hung up with Gage.

I headed to the register with my final purchases. Holiday shopping was complete.

Eight o'clock sharp, I selected the PH button on the elevator and headed up to see Gage. Wow, two nights in a row. I surprised myself with the thought. I still was a bit nervous about seeing him again. Twice now we've had plans together and I haven't heard about one potential project. I rolled my eyes and stepped off the elevator.

"A reservation for two?" I was startled by Gage standing there to greet me. There's that gorgeous man standing in the doorway awaiting my arrival. I smiled.

"What's on the menu?" I teased as I handed him a local bottle of wine I had picked up at the farmers' market.

"I grilled some steak, sliced zucchini with mushrooms on a bed of wild rice. You Texas girls like a good slab of meat, don't you?" He smiled as he headed toward the balcony door to flip the steaks on the grill. "Dessert is optional," I heard him holler over his shoulder toward me.

"Dessert is my favorite part, let's start with that," I replied as I glanced around.

The cold wooden table I had my legs spread out on last night looked a bit warmer this evening. Gage had set the table ahead of time with some art deco dishware and added a few candles for ambiance. Kind of sweet. I noticed he put up a Christmas tree decorated with white lights. Instrumental holiday music was playing as well.

"I like the tree!" I hollered toward the balcony.

"I was put into a festive mood last night so I decided to have it set up today. Christmas is right around the corner already. Are you on the naughty or nice list, Alexandria?"

"Alex, please," I corrected him once more. "Naughty for sure," I responded. You have nooo idea, Mr. Heston.

Gage walked in from the balcony. "Dinner is served, ALLLLLEX," he said, teasing me. "Have a seat and I'll get you a glass of wine. Thank you for the local wine, is it good?"

"Delicious," I responded. I needed a glass to settle me a bit. As we sat at the set table, we chatted all through dinner. We talked about WHIP. Gage filled me in on his business, which seemed like all he had time for. I was rather impressed. He was so focused and driven. I respected that. Not like the misfits in my building. Guess that's how he can afford this fat penthouse as well as the property in Miami.

"So, Mr. Heston, what do you do for fun?" I was much

more relaxed and I was intrigued. "You seem to work your ass off, how do you blow off steam?"

Gage lit up with his beautiful grin. "Well, doll, you led me astray from projects with that red holiday dress last night. I like to blow off steam with you." He smiled and began scooting his chair toward me. I smiled and felt my skin flush. "How about blowing something right now?" he teased.

I laughed and then obliged. I wanted to please this man for some odd reason. I wanted to fit in with him; I felt a little intimidated by him. I liked the attention, so I slid off my chair and knelt on the floor between his legs. Looking up at him with desire radiating from me, I started to unbuckle his belt and unzip his pants. His hardened cock pushed its way to the surface as I pulled the fabric to his ankles. Giving him a smile, I engulfed his throbbing cock into my mouth. I had a rather small mouth so I tried not to allow my teeth to scrape as I pleasured him. I pulled his cock in and out of my mouth at an even pace, then began to suck on the head as I stroked it up and down. Gage closed his eyes and leaned back in ecstasy. I could feel him pulsating in my mouth and I knew it wouldn't be long 'til he came. I continued to stroke as my moans vibrated on his erection.

Within a few minutes Gage cried out, "Oh Alexandria, I'm going to cum!"

I pulled up and let his excitement take over all over my chest. Smiling with a sense of accomplishment, I wiped my mouth and cleavage with my dinner napkin.

"Thanks for dessert, it was delicious," I laughed while getting back on my feet. I began to collect the dinner dishes as Gage reprimanded me.

"Don't touch those, babe; I'll have the maid attend to them."

"Okay." I set the dishware back on the table. "Now what?" I asked shyly.

"Well, I have to call it a night, doll; I have an early conference call. Thank you for joining me for dinner. I enjoyed the conversation and the dessert." He smiled while leaning in to kiss my cheek.

"Thank you, Gage, the meal was good but the company was better."

I bent down to grab my bag as we both headed toward the elevator.

*

Christmas is this week. I still needed to wrap everything and check in with Mother. I searched for my phone through a pile of paints and brushes, then dialed Mother's number.

"Hello, Alexandria," Mother answered in a high pitch.

"Good morning, Mother, I wanted to check in on the holiday plans."

"Good," she responded, a bit frazzled while scolding her staff. "No, put the ornaments over by the fireplace. Sorry dear, you were saying?"

I huffed, pouting like I was six. "Mama, when should I arrive for the party, and what should I bring?"

Mother let out a breath. "Same as always dear, eight PM sharp. Don't bring anything except your overnight bag." It was tradition to stay at the family house after the party to wake up with everyone Christmas morning. "Are you bringing a date?" Mother interrupted my train of thought. I sensed a bit of attitude and concern at the same time from her. "You're not sauntering into my holiday event with some tattooed, leather-pants-wearing man, are you?"

I rolled my eyes. "No Mother, Jed refused to wear leather," I laughed.

"You're not funny, Alexandria," she barked.

"No date thus far." Though it was tempting to show up with a musician on my arm to keep the party guests on their toes, I'd hate to embarrass Mother any more than I already do. I would love to waltz in with Trent; he would surprise everyone for sure. He is a brilliant man and can run with the best of them. I wonder what his holiday plans are? I wouldn't see anyone from WHIP until New Year's. Mother would LOVE Gage, though. Money, a businessman, a big penthouse in the sky, everything she dreamed up for me.

"Okay hun, wear a lovely holiday dress and be in a good mood for your Father, okay? I need to get back to directing the staff," she huffed.

"Yes Mother, see you in a few days."

I hung up the phone and let out a long sigh. Holidays are draining. I sat there on the cold concrete floor, mulling over our conversation. Maybe I should show up with Gage? Mother would be pleased and would not worry so much about me if I was dating a proper man. I hadn't heard from Trent. He must be back in Louisiana for the holidays. All the WHIP boys were with their families or significant others during this break. I was elated with my idea.

I texted Mr. Heston; he'd be the perfect date for this

event for sure. *Holiday party plans? Want to be arm candy?* I hit 'send.'

*

Christmas Eve rolled around and I was all dolled up, ready for Mother's yearly soirée. Must say, I felt beautiful. I borrowed one of Nova's sequin numbers in emerald green to match my eyes. Just short enough to tease but long enough for Mother not to roll her eyes when I made my entrance. I slicked on some gloss, gathered my bag of gifts and my roll-away. I was ready for holiday happiness with the family.

After loading up Axl, I started him up with a roar. With my high heels on the gas pedal, I headed toward the interstate, leaving the city in my rearview mirror.

As I arrived, snowflakes began to litter the driveway, which was full of town cars and limousines. I smiled: it's Christmas and I'm home. I parked Axl on the far drive next to Daddy's workshop so as not to block all the drivers letting off Mother's party guests. As I stepped out of Axl, my heel gave way and I started slipping on the damp driveway. At that moment, I felt a hand grip my arm to halt my fall. I looked up and saw Gage smiling at me. He was dressed to the nines with his black tuxedo on, hugging every muscle on his body. He was looking very sharp and very handsome. I flashed a smile, pleased.

"What are you—how'd you—" I stumbled for the right words.

"I received your text message the other day. My plans didn't pan out so I thought I would join you," he said while flashing that sexy grin. "I couldn't leave you to attend this event stag now, could I?" I laughed. "There are lots of eligible bachelors attending tonight. Your Mother has some rich friends, you know." He rubbed it in while I slammed the truck's door. "What a beast you got here." He laughed as he slid his hand along the truck's bed.

"Do not hate Axl, my chariot is in the shop, you know." I laughed, feeling a little bit embarrassed about my truck. All the women Gage ran with probably had drivers—there might be a few of them here tonight. Smiling at him, I put my arm around his arm. "Shall we make our grand entrance?" I asked.

He smiled back. I took a deep breath and thought Mother would love this.

Gage and I walked through the two grand front doors, which were trimmed with green garland and white shimmering Christmas lights. I heard the piano player quietly playing carols. Mother doesn't leave any stone unturned. I gazed around the room in awe. Suddenly I heard a squeal.

"Alexandria Rae, you look stunning!" Turning, I saw Mother approaching.

"Thanks, Mama," I replied as I leaned in to give her a fake kiss on each cheek. Mother looked stunning in her silver wrap dress, heels, and her rock to match. She always did. Style came naturally to her, whereas I had to work at it.

"And who's this handsome fellow?" She lit up with joy as she reached in to give a fake kiss to Gage as well. Mother's voice always went up an octave when she was entertaining and trying to be polite.

"Mother, this is my friend Gage." I started with the introductions as Austin walked up to us and handed me a glass of champagne.

"Hey sis, need this?" He laughed while handing me the glass. He then leaned in and whispered, "Mother's in rare form tonight."

I laughed and agreed. "Oh, she's just happy I didn't walk in with leather on and a date that looked like Marilyn Manson," I whispered back. We both started to crack up when Gage joined us. "Oh, Gage—this is my brother, Austin. He's up from San Antonio where he's stationed." Gage reached out to shake Austin's hand. "Nice to meet you, soldier."

Austin replied, "Looks like you could use a drink, Gage. Here, let me lead you to the bar. It's this way."

While Austin directed Gage toward the bar, I stood there downing my champagne. What is Gage doing here? I was happily surprised.

A few hours into the party, I was tipsy and exhausted. Mother introduced me to a plethora of people, all of whom I had to let my representative shine. I wasn't so surprised to notice how Gage actually knew many of the guests. He was a very successful businessman. He had to attend a lot of charitable events in the Dallas and Houston areas. Mother continually acted fake as she laughed at petty jokes. She ordered her staff around like she was Scarlett Fucking O'Hara. Gag. I gulped down my third glass of champagne. Daddy walked into the room. He noticed me leaning against the window, staring outside and watching the snow fall.

"Merry Christmas, sugar, are you having a good time?" Daddy inquired as he joined me.

"Yep, Dad. Nice party, just a little intoxicating with all the guests in my face," I said.

"And champagne in your face as well," Daddy added as he took the empty glass away from me.

"Sorry Dad, I just needed a moment to hide and take a breather."

Daddy laughed. "I understand, sugar, I feel the same way. Where's that nice fella you showed up with? I wouldn't leave him alone for too long, you know. The cougars get very lonely during the holidays," Daddy chuckled. "You better find Mr. Heston, Miss Alexandria, now that's an order."

"Yes, sir," I laughed as I tried to straighten my stance and give him a salute. I kissed Daddy on the cheek and made my way out of the main room for a breather. There, over by the grand tree, was Gage holding an empty glass. As I strutted toward him, I ripped a piece of mistletoe off the archway and held it over my head.

"Hey there, handsome, a kiss for the devil in green tonight?"

Gage smiled.

"Are there many women waiting to kidnap you and put you under their tree?" I laughed, looking down and noticing Daddy had taken my glass away. "Hey, let's ditch the bar route and let me give you a tour of the wine cellar. I'm sure I can find more champagne down there and refill whatever it was that you were drinking as well."

Gage threw me a perverted look. "It was old fashion." He licked his lips while he started to undress me with his eyes. As he leaned into me, he grabbed the mistletoe from my hand and whispered, "Show me the way, devil in green. There is something I do want to kiss."

He shook his empty glass, then set it on a passing server's tray. He grabbed my hand and gestured for me to lead the way. I proceeded toward the wine cellar. As we made our way through the crowd, I could feel cougars' stares burn right through me. I kept my head up high and gripped Gage's hand a bit tighter as I made my way down the narrow corridor and away from the party. It led us to a softly lit room with wooden flooring and stoned walls. There was a musty odor coming from my Father's collection of vintage bottles and barrels. Gage seemed impressed with the collection. He smiled, reading label after label of the bottles on display.

"So Mr. Heston, where is that mistletoe?" I flashed a devilish grin as I licked my lips, flirting with my date. He reached into his pocket and pulled out the mistletoe, waving it he grinned back. He then glided a few steps toward me as I purred. "Hey tiger," I teased.

Gage rubbed the mistletoe under his nose, sniffed, and purred back. He gazed at me like I was something to eat. He tapped the mistletoe on a wooden barrel next to us and asked, "Can I kiss you, Alexandria?"

I replied softly, "Anywhere."

He smirked at me. He pushed me back against a barrel and began to reach up under my sequin dress. He grabbed ahold of my satin panties and pulled them down until they hit the wooden floor. I gasped. He lifted me up on the barrel and spread my trembling legs open. I swallowed hard, hoping none of the party guests would interrupt. Gage then dove in, claiming his kiss. He licked my pussy up the right side and down the left. He began licking my clit with conviction. He was horny and he really wanted me. I smiled as I leaned my head back against the wall. Gage continued to suck on my swollen clit over and over as I lost my breath. I was dripping for this man. He made me so hot with desire that I started to come all over his tongue. Gage kept at it until I pushed him back and reached for his tie to pull him into my mouth. I kissed his sweet, hot mouth as I came down from my orgasm. He then retracted and pulled me off the barrel.

"You don't get off that easy, Alexandria. I want to come as well."

I let out another breath. He flipped me around so I was bending over the wooden barrel, legs spread. He unzipped his black tuxedo pants and began to enter me from behind. He was throbbing so hard as he kept forcing himself deeper and deeper. I actually had a tear escape from the corner of my eye, which pissed me off. I continued to get fucked against the rocking barrel until he pulled out and came all over the back of my dress. Fuck, where will I get a rag down here? Gage reached into his pocket and pulled out a red cloth handkerchief. He began wiping his mouth, his cock, then me.

"Oh, love the holidays, especially the mistletoe," Gage interrupted my train of thought. "Alexandria, you okay?" He stared at me as he adjusted his tie.

I suddenly felt a wave of panic wash over me as I fixed my dress. "I'm good, we better get back to the party before someone finds out what we've been up to," I sighed.

Gage huffed as he grabbed a bottle of wine, took my hand, and led us back down the corridor to rejoin the festivities. Once rejoining the party, Gage made sure he made his way to my parents and thanked the hosts for a lovely evening. He then kissed my head and whispered, "Merry Christmas, doll. I've got to run. It's been a pleasure." I was shocked but a bit relieved that he wanted to take off. I wanted to peel out of this sticky sequin dress, shower, and hit the guest bed.

"Bye Gage, thanks for showing up and being my date tonight," I hollered. He was walking down the snow-covered driveway toward his driver. "You made Mother happy," I laughed. He grinned back at me as he got into the car and shut the door.

*

The next morning I heard the stereo downstairs playing *We wish you a Merry Christmas, we wish you a Merry Christmas and a Happy New Year—* "Ugh," I moaned as I rolled over. Dad must be up making breakfast.

"Knock...knock...you up, sis?" I heard heavy boots enter the room.

"Ugh...champagne," I responded.

"Yeah, you were pretty blasted last night, Alex. Here, I brought you some Tylenol and coffee." Austin tried not to laugh at me as he set the coffee mug next to the bed and tossed the Tylenol tabs at my head.

"Thanks, dude." I pulled the tabs out of my hair, rolled over, and looked at Austin, trying to focus.

"You look like shit. Did you have fun last night?"

Flashing him a dirty look, I popped the two pills and took a heaping swig of the coffee. "Thanks, this is good. I had fun last night. Shocker Gage showed up. You like him?" I asked Austin.

"I do, he seems all right. It doesn't matter if I like him or if Mother loves him, the thing is do you like him? He doesn't seem your type at all, Alex, you know?"

"I have a type?" I was curious.

"Yeah, creative dudes, not uptight business dudes." He laughed.

"Yeah but creative isn't paying the rent, dude, I need to step it up a notch." I laughed as I sipped more coffee. I was starting to come around a bit.

"Okay," Austin responded. "Business CAN pay the rent but it won't make you happy. You deserve to be happy, that's all."

"I know, Austin, thank you. I am happy at the moment."

He paused then huffed, "Well, we better make our way to breakfast and get this holiday on the ball. Otherwise Mom will be pissed if we don't get our butts downstairs."

I laughed while throwing the sheets off me and started crawling out of bed. "I'm on my way…and Austin…thanks for the coffee and tabs." I raised my mug to him as he left the room.

*

Christmas night I packed up the truck with gifts from the family and drove back home to feed Ernie. When I entered the building, there was an oversized box leaning against my door. "Huh, what the hell is this?" I glanced at the label that read 'Louisiana.' I quickly opened my door, pulled the box inside, and dropped my bags. Ernie was there to greet me. I leaned down and scooped him up to smother him with kisses. "I missed you, Ernie," I said as I kissed and kissed his furry little head. Of course he responded with the drawn-out meow to let me know I needed to check his food bowl and attend to his box. I removed my coat and lit the string of Christmas lights hanging over my two large windows. I then put on a holiday record and made some hot tea.

Once settled in, I sat down to check my voicemails and return text messages I had received over the past few days. Nova was the first message confirming our date for New Year's. Tyler was another, short but sweet, missing me over Christmas. Third was a message from Gage, thanking me for the mistletoe. And lastly...Trent. My heart always sank when I heard his voice. He phoned to let me know he was thinking of me. He was in the studio and was admiring the artwork I created for the album cover and just had to phone me. I kinda missed him. I then glanced over at the box I dragged in and decided to open it. Inside was a little note: *I wanted to send this gift and say thank you for the sketch, I hope you like it—you are truly gifted Alex.*

Merry Christmas. Trent. I started pulling out all the paper stuffing. I was so excited! I then pulled out a wooden artist easel stand. It was beautiful. I sat there admiring it for a moment. Gage gave me sex, and Trent sent this easel. Who knew me better? I was so tempted to return his call that moment but hesitated. I'll wait 'til tomorrow to call back. Christmas evening seemed too desperate. I didn't want him to know I was back at the loft...alone.

CHAPTER NINE

A few days passed and I've done nothing but putter around the place. I was avoiding Tyler, Trent, Vanity, and Gage. Felt good to sort of shut down and reboot. New Year's Eve was this weekend and I needed to square away my date. I picked up my cell and phoned Nova.

"Hey babe, where ya been hiding?" She sounded groggy and throaty. "Club has been pretty lame; holidays seem to slow everything down. Family shit. I've only made money off my regular, Jim. Thank God he's a lonely motherfucker or my clutch would be light." She laughed a little. Nova always had a few men on the back burner to help her float through the slow times. I, on the other hand, didn't date outside the walls of Vanity. That seemed to dampen my relationship with the regulars.

"Well Mercedes, wanted to check in and confirm our date for New Year's." I was smiling.

Nova replied, "You always have a date with me, Blondie, but what happened with Money Man? Thought he'd be dropping his pants for you while the ball dropped?"

I laughed. "More like a ball gag in the mouth." I

laughed to myself. "He made the perfect date that Mother was over the moon for, but I feel like I'm just his fuck buddy—it's all pretty much sex, girl." I laughed again to cover up my sadness.

"You little minx, you need to see where this takes you. He seems to me that he's the distraction from Trent you were looking for. You don't love Gage. You're not sure you even love Trent. Take some time to think about it, but if you're asking me, my radar is up for Gage."

I didn't want to tell Nova about the gift from Trent. It was between me and Trent. "I haven't even spoken to Gage since Christmas Eve. Girl, I'm trying to figure this out. I honestly think Gage can fill the loneliness I'm going to go through once Tyler and Trent leave."

"Bet he is." Nova chuckled. "Bet he is indeed...meow." Dismissing my agony and confusion, Nova wrapped up our call with, "I'll scan my closet for some sexy threads and head over around seven on New Year's Eve?"

"Sounds good, luv." I let out a breath of frustration as I clicked off.

I then texted Tyler about my date with Nova for New Year's Eve, assuming he was bringing Olivia. She seemed to be keeping him out of trouble thus far into their relationship. I'm sure he'll pass the word along to WHIP—and, of course, Trent—that I'll be making an appearance at their gig. I smiled thinking about Trent. Oh, how I craved that man. *Bing*—a message appeared on my phone.

Devil in green, my holiday doll...you have plans this weekend? Love to ring in the New Year with you. Needing some arm candy for a gala I need to make an appearance at. Are you up for it? It was Mr. Heston. His ears must have been burning like the brush burns he left on my knees.

I hit 'reply': *sorry sugar I've got a date with Miss Nova, no Miami?* Feeling a bit guilty, I groaned and flopped back onto my bed. Arm candy? Prick. I would like to be wined and dined, though. I responded quickly back to Gage. *Pre festivities drink?*

Perfect Doll, my house at eight? Leave your date behind; have her pick you up here instead.

I agreed and texted Nova the new plan.

Again, her response was: *sluuuuut.*

I don't know why, but I continue to let Mr. Heston squirm his way into my plans. Was that a shitty thing to do to Nova? I bet if the shoe was on the other foot, she wouldn't think twice about bailing on me. Money always trumps her friendships. I let that pass. I headed to my closet to see if I had any threads of my own to assemble to look hot enough for Gage and tease Trent. Hey, his decision to sideline a relationship with me for the old "band bros before hos" bullshit. His loss—focus on Gage, girl. Don't let this one slip away. At least he's making the effort, unlike the man in the band. It was eight o'clock on the dot when I arrived by cab to the Penthouse. Stepping out of the car, I pulled down my little leopard ensemble. It was a black, white, and silver snow leopard print dress. I paired it with sexy, shiny, silver mid-calf high-heeled boots to match. I felt sexy for sure. Minutes later I was greeted at the front door by Mr. Gage.

"Purrrrr," he teased as he let me in. "You look incredibly sexy, Alexandria. I should kidnap you and keep you all to myself."

Smiling, I looked him up and down with appreciation.

He had on a designer suit—dark, of course, to match those dark eyes. His shirt was unbuttoned and untucked with his tie dangling loosely from his neck. I reached up, pulled him toward me by the tie, and went in with a lick across the lips, then gave him a passionate kiss. When I withdrew, Gage licked his lips and purred once more.

"You're tempting me...I can kidnap you, kitty kitty." He groaned and pulled away. "Care for a drink?" he asked while heading over to his bar.

"Yes," I replied as I made my way inside and over to the balcony. I looked out from the balcony with awe. What a beautiful city. Within minutes a glass of wine appeared in front of me.

"Hey, pretty kitty, whatcha thinkin' about?"

I smiled, accepted the glass, and turned around to face Gage. "Just admiring your view of the city." I shivered a bit from the balcony breeze.

"You seem chilly," he said as he set his drink down on the metal outdoor table. "I can warm you up a bit." He grinned as he wrapped his strong arms around me. I felt safe for a moment in those arms. He then turned me back around to face the city and whispered in my ear. "I'm not going to warm you up. I'm going to make you hot."

I began to laugh until he pulled my hair back with his left hand. With his right, he reached up my dress and pulled down my panties. I was shocked and breathless. He kept a firm grip on my hair so I was unable to move my neck. His right hand removed my panties and he kicked open my legs. I was startled as I was positioned in a hair grip, legs spread, leaning over the balcony to the bustling city below. Gage unzipped his dress pants and pulled out his throbbing cock. Licking his index and middle finger, he made them wet enough to slide into me. I groaned with a bit of shock and a bit of pleasure. He worked his fingers a bit, then pulled them out and slid himself in. He began thrusting in and out and it was quite hard. I had a hard time catching my breath. I stood there, spread open as he fucked me then pulled out in just enough time to cum on the bottom of my dress and down my leg.

"Now are you warm, kitty? Because I'm fuckin' hot, myself." He laughed and then took a sip of his drink as he handed me his cocktail napkin, laughing. "Man, you make me so fuckin' horny, Alexandria. Sorry about your dress."

I took the napkin from him and wiped my inner thigh. I had barely caught my breath and he had fucked me, came on my leg, and had a sip of his damn drink. After wiping up his excitement, I excused myself. I grabbed my clutch and made my way to the bathroom to salvage my dress. Gage hollered up to me as I cleaned frantically.

"Sure you don't want to tag along with me?" he asked.

I rolled my eyes. "No sugar, I promised Nova."

Responding sarcastically, he asked while acting a little drunk, "You girls going to tag along with the baaaaand?"

I laughed. "We're meeting friends and, yes, the baaaand will be there." That's how we met, through the band, and now he gives me shit every time I want to hang with WHIP. WTF? "They are my friends, you know," I hollered out of the bathroom. I guess the lack of response was his way of saying this conversation was over. I freshened up a bit; the flush of my skin from the romp sure made me look sexy, I must say. I gathered my things back into my clutch and went back to Gage. "So what about your evening plans, Mr. Heston? Should I be worried about anything?" I giggled as I stood on my toes to kiss him once more before I had to split to meet Nova. My cell buzzed with a text message from Miss Nova, letting me know she was downstairs waiting for me.

"There is your cat call," he sneered, a little drunk, rolling his eyes.

"Happy New Year," I responded with another kiss before I jumped in the elevator. I pushed 'lobby' and blew him another kiss as the elevator door shut. I let out a long sigh. As I walked out into the brisk Texas air, I noticed Nova's Mercedes parked in front. I immediately got butterflies. I was excited for tonight. I dealt with Gage. I fucked him to shut him up, and now I was ready to see my friends. I needed this. Gage can be so fuckin' intense at times. I opened the door and jumped in.

"You just fucked that man, didn't you?" Nova pried. "Sluuuut!"

I bit my lip and laughed. "That man can be so damn intense, girl. I'm a little unsure about this. I'm assuming it's heading into some sort of relationship mode where no protection has been used lately."

Nova rolled her eyes. "Girl, you have such a good thing going with this man. He doesn't play in the band or peddle around with the band. He practically owns the band! Intense or not, girl, you are sowing some security seeds. Get tested, have a chat with Gage, and enjoy the no-fuss mode he seems to like. Straight shooter girl, he likes sex, he likes you—he loves the sex WITH you!" Nova set me straight as she lit her clove cigarette and turned up the tunes in the car. "This is going to be a blast tonight, don't worry about Gage. Have some fun with your friends. You already let your panties down, now let your hair down, girl." Nova laughed as she headed toward the parking garage for the downtown clubs.

"He ripped my panties, girl. I'm pantie-less. Ugh."

Well, she's right. Gage is a little intimidating, but he's good for me. I keep ignoring that intuitive voice that says "run." Who I'd really love to run to is Trent. I feel much more at ease with him. I feel myself. He lets me express who I am without any label-stamping like Gage. Gage is a label whore like Nova. Money and labels go hand in hand.

"Girl, hello—we're here. Now wake the fuck up." Nova pulled my hair to shake my thoughts.

"Okay, I'm ready for the night." I smiled to myself.

We arrived at this small intimate club called LUST. It was a black building with gold-plated doors, hidden down some side street. It was an invitation-only party. WHIP, promoters, photographers, and anyone high up in the Dallas art scene were on the guest list. I was excited and proud to be on the list. I was an artist; I did design the band's album cover, after all. That holds some weight in this town. WHIP is one of the newest, biggest bands to come out of Texas in quite some time. I grabbed hold of Nova's hand. We entered through the plated doors, down a dark hallway lit by candlelight. I let go of her hand when we reached a beautiful woman in a gold dress accepting the guest's invitations. She smiled as she accepted mine and—straight out of The Price is Right—gestured toward the door. I smiled back, feeling the excitement build as we entered LUST.

"I heard we have a table roped off in some VIP section dedicated to the band," Nova said. She licked her lips and took a look around. I heard a whistle from the far left corner of the club. I looked up and saw Ty waving us over.

"There." I pointed him out to Nova. "There's the frontman," I laughed as I pulled her over to the table.

"Hi, my southern beauty," Ty said as he kissed me straight on the lips. "That is some fucking good tasting lip-gloss, Alex." Ty licked his lips.

"It's from fucking, all right," Nova laughed.

"Were you guys fucking around in the car before you got here? Who went down on whom? I need details, you hot bitches," Ty teased as Olivia rolled her eyes and lit her cigarette.

I took a look around the table and smiled at the other bandmates—however, I didn't spot Trent. Was he here tonight? Of course he was at this party—it was for WHIP, after all. They are hitting the road soon. I quietly pouted and took a seat next to Nova as she handed me a glass of champagne. The DJ booked for this gig was hidden up in a loft space of his own as the speakers belted out sexy sultry music. A sex vibe was going on inside LUST tonight. I already had sex during the pre-party but somehow I'm a little revved up once more. Tyler jumped between Nova and me on the couch. He must be coked up. He never has this much energy unless it's snowy weather.

"Come on girls, let's dry hump on the dance floor," Ty laughed as he wiped his nose and licked his teeth. Yep, snow season.

"As appealing as that sounds, I'll pass, you hormone." Nova squeezed out from underneath Ty. She finished off her glass of champagne and headed toward some friends she knew.

"Okay then Blondie, it's you and me." Ty looked at me and extended his hand. I accepted his hand as he led me to the dance floor. The music was slow and grinding. Very good sex music. Ty stopped on the floor, turned to me, licked my neck from base to ear, and whispered, "You look good, kitty." I blushed and threw my head back as he moaned in my ear a bit more and gyrated his leather pants on me. I closed my eyes and swayed with Ty. This felt good. Free. Ty moved with me while leaving little kisses on my neck.

"Ummmm," I purred to Ty. I was enjoying this moment when I got all of Ty's attention before he took off for the road. I swayed and suddenly felt another warm body embrace me from behind while joining the swaying rhythm Ty and I started. I smiled. I felt a hand slide up the right side of me. It went under my dress and lightly passed over my pussy a few times then back out and up to my hip. Ty's eyes were closed. He turned me around so I could face the body behind me. It was Trent. I stopped moving for a minute as he smiled at me. I swallowed hard and restarted my rhythm with both Tyler and Trent. I then took Trent's hand in mine as I leaned back on Ty. Gyrating with two beautiful men in leather. I laughed. Ty then pushed me toward Trent and followed in behind as I rested my head on Trent's shoulder. Ty leaned in and licked Trent's lips. I was hot. Trent grabbed Tyler's hair and pulled him in for a deeper kiss. OMG, was this happening? Were these two beautiful men kissing as I was smack in the middle witnessing it? I lifted my head and turned towards Tyler, kissing him deeply as Trent leaned against my back. I was so turned on. Kissing both Tyler and Trent—a WHIP-ette's dream. Tyler looked down at me and smiled as I wiped his lips with my fingertips. Trent then slightly pulled my fingers away from Ty's mouth and put them into his mouth. For the second time tonight, I was wet. As the music groaned sounds of "uh-uh-uh" through the speakers, I suddenly felt a chill from behind me as Ty was pulled away by Olivia and into her arms. I stayed breathless, swaying with Trent. We didn't even speak one word to each other but I still could sense passion between us. I dragged my hand up the side of his leather pants and up the back of his shirt, using my nails to drag back down to his waist. Trent moaned. We danced so erotically that I was still wet. Trent slid his hand once more up the front of my dress and passed his finger along my glistening pussy once more, then inserted it inside me. He slid it in then out, in then out. I moaned and bit his neck. I was so turned on. This club is intimate and it was dark. I could barely see who was next to me. I felt alone at that moment, only Trent and I. He let out a sigh as I bit his neck then reached up and pulled my hair back. He returned the lust with a bite of his own. Then he kissed me so deeply, so passionately, that my knees almost buckled. His tongue engulfed mine as he rotated it around a few times before he withdrew.

"I'm going to miss you, Alex. I still want to be a part of your life. I want to keep this open between you and I?" Trent whispered as he let go of my hand and stepped away from me.

I stood there and tried to catch my breath. I was shocked. I needed a moment to myself, so I decided to head toward the bathroom. I found an open stall and walked in, locked the door, and let out a stream of tears. I'm confused. My heart beats so heavy for Trent but I like this lifestyle with Gage, who is making room for me in his life with no nonsense. Trent is only offering me moments and that's not enough. It's not fair to me. I stood in the stall for a little while longer, trying to process it all.

"Hey Blondie, whatcha doing in there? I can recognize those shoes anywhere." Nova laughed as she banged on the stall door, obviously intoxicated. I wiped my eyes and opened the door. "That waterworks shit better not be for any man, girl, neither one of them deserves your tears. What happened? You looked all chummy on the dance floor with the leather twins." Nova was concerned as she patted my hair into place and wiped my smudged liner. "Come on girl, we'll head back to the VIP, have another drink, and try to let it go and have fun. Okay?" Nova took my hand and pulled me out of the restroom.

"I love you, Nova, I'm all right, I'm just—"

Nova interrupted, "You just fall in love too easily hun, it'll work itself out. Mr. Band Man is heading on tour; you really need to focus on Gage. Now I know Trent is a 'creative, sexy rockstar—'" she made air quotes with her hands, "but Gage owns that 'creative, sexy rock star,' you know." She laughed as she overemphasized her second pair of quotes. "If I were you, I'd have fun with both of them. Let it play itself out."

She kissed me on the head. Then she became distracted as some fly boy walking by caught her attention and she took off after him. I headed over to the VIP area and noticed a man in a suit whose back was to the crowd. I stopped instantly in my tracks as my stomach turned. What the hell is Gage doing here? Checking up on me? This man seems to have an underlying trust issue that he sugarcoats with fucking me prior to my party. Yes, MY party with MY friends. Why is he sniffing around?

"Hey Alex, look who showed up, Olivia yelled

sarcastically. She was giving me a jab because I was getting all the attention from her boyfriend earlier.

"Bitch," I mumbled under my breath as I let myself in through the red velvet VIP rope. "Hi Gage, um, what are you doing here slumming with WHIP? Did you bail on your event?" I was a bit cold to him.

Gage chuckled, then grabbed me by the waist and pulled me into his side. "I just missed you, Alexandria. Wanted to ring in the New Year with you. Aren't you happy to see me?" he asked with a slight attitude.

"I'm very happy, I just thought I'd enjoy my friends for the evening and we'd meet up tomorrow? You want something to drink?" My hand started to shake as I reached for the champagne bottle.

Gage grabbed the bottle and shoved it back into the ice bucket. "I think you've reached your limit. You seem overly flirtatious when you drink," Gage scolded me.

I rolled my eyes. Shit—has he been here the whole time? Did he watch me with Trent and Tyler? Ugh. What the fuck? "Do you want to sit down?" I asked very kitten-like as I rubbed on his arm to chill him out.

"Sure, it's almost midnight. Can we ring in the New Year with your friends then head back to the penthouse?" He flashed me that controlling grin. I was butter.

"Sure." I smiled as the DJ announced the New Year was upon us and everyone hollered "Yay!!!!"

Everyone in the VIP started kissing and hugging each other. Gage leaned in and gave a light kiss on the lips and hugged me. I held him for a second and noticed Trent over Gage's shoulder. My heart sank. He reached out his hand and shook Gage's hand, wishing him a Happy New Year. Then he turned, stepped over the velvet rope, and walked out. Ty immediately distracted me by kissing me on the cheek.

He whispered in my ear, "Green Room tomorrow, I know Money Man is going to steal you away for the rest of the night. The Green Room at noon?"

I smiled as Ty turned around and jumped on one of the couches, screaming, "Happy New Year!" He began toasting all his bandmates. I felt pushed out of the circle. I looked around for Nova to let her know I wouldn't need a ride home, but she was nowhere to be found. I reached in my clutch and fished for my cell to text her goodbye. Gage and I left LUST hand in hand—well, more like an owner and pet dog. He pulled my arm as I dragged behind as we headed toward his car. He opened the Mercedes passenger door. I slipped in while looking around at the leather interior. I realized then that I hadn't been in his personal car. There was usually a driver who picked me up or chauffeured the two of us around.

"Nice ride."

Gage smiled as I complimented him. Any compliment fed his ego. I leaned back in the seat and smiled. Gage started the car as he fussed with the radio until he tuned in to a public news station.

"Talk radio? How romantic," I teased. Gage ignored me as he headed toward the penthouse. Arriving back at the penthouse, Gage headed straight for the fridge.

"Snack, Alexandria?" he asked as he sifted through the shelves. "I'll make us some eggs," he suggested.

"Umm, that sounds good." I licked my lips as I lifted myself up onto the steel barstool. I watched in amusement as this beautiful man prepared me eggs. He flashed that grin every few minutes, knowing I was admiring him from my seat.

"Having fun, Alexandria?"

I chuckled. "You need to get out of that penguin suit of yours and get more comfortable. You're home. This is where you should be yourself, comfortable." I smiled.

"Oh yeah? Well, you butter the toast and I'll slip into something comfortable." He smiled back. He made his way to the master bedroom, peeling each piece of his suit off until he disappeared into his room. Yum, he sure is sexy in that healthy build, proper businessman way. Different from those misfits I always seem attracted to. This is good—this relationship is more adult. I buttered our toast, grinning as I recalled our adult moment on the balcony earlier that evening. I suddenly felt my hair being pushed aside as Gage kissed the back of my neck.

"What were you fantasizing about?" He kissed me a few more times along my neck.

"You, and what was under that penguin suit you left on the floor." I laughed, setting the butter knife down on the counter.

Gage reached over me and grabbed his toast. "You need to eat your eggs then head to my bathroom and wash all that WHIP off of you before you climb into my bed." I rolled my eyes as I poked my egg with my slice of toast. "Don't pout beautiful, I don't share well." Gage was making a statement.

"I understand." I just shut my mouth and ate my damn eggs.

∗

The next morning, I rolled over and gazed out the window. I could smell coffee brewing from the other room. I can't believe he's up already. Does this man ever rest? Suddenly Gage was at the bedroom door.

"Good morning, Alexandria." He smiled as he handed me a mug of coffee. I sat up in bed and happily accepted the mug. "Here's some Tylenol. Sit here and enjoy your coffee." He handed me two tablets. "I really love waking up next to you, Alexandria, you fit in nice with my décor." He bent over the bed and kissed my head, then turned to walk out of the room.

"Wait a minute, Gage." I go with his décor? Okay. I mulled over that for a minute as I sipped the coffee. Gage turned around and gave me his full attention. "Are we exclusive? I'm trying to read this rapidly developing relationship we have between us that I'm starting to get whiplash putting all the pieces together. Plus, you haven't used protection when we were in the heat of the moment and I want to know where you stand? I do adore you, Gage. I'm not dating anyone exclusively right now. Are you?"

Gage replied, "I'm not, dear; I'm so busy with work that I haven't had time for an exclusive relationship in quite some time. I do like you—in fact, I would love for you to be more a part of my life than a dinner date every once in a while."

I was pleased at what I was hearing. "Good." But I was confused. "I do have another question: do you understand how important WHIP is to me?"

Gage interrupted. "Trent?"

"No...Tyler, that's my best friend. I do not want to give him up. They will be out on the road but I do not want them out of the picture."

Gage nodded and responded, "I do not share well, Alexandria, but I'll be a little more lenient with you."

"Thank you, that's all I want. There is room for you both in my life." I smiled. Suddenly I panicked— "What time is it?" Gage stepped back. "I made plans to meet with Ty at the Green Room at noon."'

"And it starts," Gage mumbled under his breath as he left the bedroom. I ignored him and reached for my cell next to the bed to check the time. I quickly texted Ty that I would be there in half an hour. I needed to get the coffee down, pee, and say goodbye to Gage.

I have a feeling Gage is going to be quite relieved once the tour bus moves out of Texas.

I walked into the Green Room and headed for our favorite table in the corner. As I settled in, I sang along to the Pretenders playing from the speaker above our table. Gazing out of the window, I stared at the confetti-covered street of Deep Ellum. I then spotted Ty. He was standing at the crosswalk lighting a smoke. I smiled. He looked pretty fucking good for an unwashed rockstar that hasn't yet been to bed. As he strolled across the street toward the window, he noticed me. He stuck out his tongue while flipping me devil horns. I returned the gesture. I'm completely myself around Tyler. I'm sure going to miss him when they hit the road. As flighty as he seems to others, he always comes through for me. Smiling, I turned toward the Green Room entrance and watched Ty make his way to our table.

"Ty, I'm sorry I bailed last night." I was embarrassed as I pleaded. "I should have stood my ground. Should have told the pretty boy to go home and let me have the evening with my friends. I can't believe he just showed up!"

Ty shook his head while he shimmied out of his leather jacket. He grabbed his smoke and put it out in the ashtray on the table. Blowing his mouthful of smoke away from us, he smiled. "I understand, Alex, you're lining up another body to lie next to while all your friends are gone. Kitten, you're smitten. I know you're in awe of Money Man. Go ahead, just be careful with him." He reached over the table and placed his hand in mine.

"I'm gonna miss you, Ty," I said as I squeezed his hand in return. My eyes started tearing up.

"I know, doll. I'm gonna miss you too. I'm going to have fucking fun though. I will play like the darkest, sexiest rock god you've ever known," Ty responded as he howled aloud.

I laughed.

"You're going to kill it out there, just be sure not to kill yourself. I'm super worried about you, Tyler." I stopped myself, remembering Trent stating that he would look after Tyler for me.

"Doll, listen...none of my mates are going to let anything happen to me. You know Trent is at least the responsible one of WHIP." I nodded in agreement. "I'll be semi-good. Plus, Olivia will be at some of the dates, so I'm on a short leash." He grinned, gesturing for the waitress to fill his coffee.

I took a deep breath. "Be sure to call me from every city you're in. I want to hear all about it. I'll try to make the Austin or Houston show. I'll drag Nova with me." I swallowed hard.

"Well, when Money Man shows his fucking face to check on his investment, I'll try to be nice. Just don't run off marrying this egomaniac." Ty smiled.

"I won't marry him!" I pouted.

Ty let go of my hand, got up off his seat, and knelt on the floor in front of me. I laughed while my cheeks flushed.

"Alex, my love, my best friend, I'm going to miss the hell out of you. But, I'm going to make you so fucking proud. I'm following my dream and you're supporting that. For that, I love you. Plus for loving me no matter what I say, wear, do, or smoke." Laughing, Tyler put his head in my lap and I embraced him as tears streamed down my face. I was then startled when the table full of punk rockers next to us all clapped for Tyler. I laughed again and wiped my face as I helped Tyler to his feet.

Tyler walked me up to the loft after our powwow. As we reached my door, I noticed a box from the florist leaning against it.

"Ooo flowers, girl. You hussie. Is Gage being romantic?" Tyler teased as he pinched my waist. "Hardly, unsure that man knows the definition of romance—it's more like *wham bam thank you ma'am.*" I paused, looking at the box. "Kinda sweet though, right?" I scooped up the box and brought it into my place. Tyler kissed my cheek then took off down the hall.

I just smiled to myself as I took the roses out of the box and placed them into a vase. Ernie jumped up and smelled them. "Beautiful, huh, Ernie?" I read the card. Gage was apologizing for how he overreacted yesterday at the club. He promised me I still can have WHIP and have him too. I was relieved. I was not going to choose. I love those guys, especially Tyler, and did not want to choose. It was an unfair request.

I then searched my pockets for my cell and sent a thank-you text to Gage.

That evening, I knew Gage was busy so I decided to sneak off and work at Vanity. I was flying solo. Nova had a big date with a wealthy customer so I knew I'd roll through the evening alone. I needed a distraction. My band friends, my best friend, and my ex-lover were all leaving town and I had never felt so alone.

"You're awfully quiet, sugar." Some random stripper smiled at me as we applied our makeup next to each other. "Where's your sidekick Miss Mercedes, hun?" she inquired.

Not really feeling like conversing, I smiled as I told her Nova was on extended holiday. She smiled then butted into someone else's business as I let out a deep breath. It'll be fine. It'll be okay—you're a big girl and you have to let other people live their lives and make decisions for what's good for them, not me. I stared off for a minute. I felt sorry for myself. Then I got nudged back into reality when the house mom poked her head in the dressing room. She let me know I needed to get my butt out on the floor.

I began to pace through the smoke-infested room, searching for a lonely face. I like one-on-ones. Group tables are usually obnoxious and I didn't have the energy to deal with that tonight. I spotted the out-of-town business suit customer in the corner sipping a scotch, and I decided to make my move. The gentleman turned out to be surprisingly very kind. He was relaxed and not pushy. We had a generic conversation to start the evening as I proceeded to knock out a few table dances for him. We never spoke about our private lives. He never gestured to move our private party of two upstairs. I felt comfortable. I was slightly distracted. At about eleven PM, the gentleman wrapped up our table dances by letting me know he was heading back to his hotel. He was grateful that I entertained him as he handed me twelve hundred dollars. I was shocked. It had only been a few hours of table dances and minimal conversation. He stood up, drank the last of his scotch, and wished me a Happy New Year. I smiled with relief. I had some money in my garter so I didn't have to take any shit from the cheap customers. I could pick and choose who I wanted to spend my time with. I then sat back down at our corner table for a moment as I watched the man leave the club. I sighed and sat back to finish my wine. I caught myself daydreaming once more as I listened to techno music blare a little too loud for my taste. I watched the girls gyrating on the pole. I studied each one as they worked the room. I watched the waitress scurry across the carpeted floor delivering drinks. She received pats on the ass from tipsy customers. It was all quite amusing to me. Then, from the corner of my eye, I watched five beautiful, leather-wearing men walk through the front door of the club. Oh my God—WHIP was here. I swallowed hard in shock. What the fuck? I thought they hit the road this afternoon. I jumped to my feet and walked straight over to Tyler.

"What are you doing here?" The guys had no idea I worked here, aside from Tyler.

Tyler smiled and said, "Babe, I wanted one more goodbye hug." He picked me up and twirled me around. I was dizzy. Even with Ty's past approval of me dancing, I was still somewhat embarrassed. "Babe, we're just going to have a drink, get a dance or two from the girls, and roll outta Dallas in style."

I smiled as I searched the room for a table toward which to direct my friends. Joining the band, I sat down in the velvet chair and felt a little uncomfortable.

"You're a knockout, Alex." The drummer smiled as he scanned the room.

"I like your getup," the guitarist chimed in.

"I feel silly, rather gaudy for my taste," I responded while I looked over at Trent. He gave me the warmest smile as he stood up and claimed the seat right next to me. I smiled and leaned into him.

"I like your thigh-highs, Alexandria," he said, licking his lips.

"It's Angel...shhhh...I'm incognito," I scolded him. We both laughed. I missed Trent. Gage would not accept me being here.

"Hey babe, you gotta do what you gotta do to survive. I get it." Trent smiled as he took a sip from his wine glass. I love watching this man drink his wine—so elegant, so smooth. He was not judging me and seemed to accept me no matter what the fuck I get myself into. It turns me on. He looked ravishing, too. Of all the bandmates, he was by far the sexiest and most confident. I smiled to myself.

"What are you smiling about?" Trent inquired.

"Ahhh, nothing. I'm glad y'all stopped in. I'm going to miss y'all so much it hurts." I leaned in toward him again and we brushed shoulders. He sure does smell good—intoxicating, really. I inhaled deeply, knowing it was going to be a while until I would see him again. "You're going to kill it out there," I said to Trent, ignoring the vultures on heels swarming the table. I put my hand on Trent's leg, claiming him. The girls all selected their prey as they sat on their laps to get the party started.

"We all will, girl, we're ready. I'm super grateful to the label and all they've done for us." He took another sip of his wine. I felt my stomach churn.

"Are you upset that I'm seeing Gage? It's nothing serious. He's a nice guy, Trent. Just straying for a bit while you guys head out and take on the world." I smiled.

"Hardly the world, Alexandreee—Angel," he corrected himself with a grin. "Let's not talk about Gage. I'm in a good mood. Let's get you up in front of me so you can show me what the hell it is you do in here," Trent said.

Soon Bijork's *Army of Me* started and I stood up, squeezed between Trent's legs, a bit wobbly, and began my routine. At this moment, no one in the room existed but us two. I wanted to seduce him in the best way I could to give him something to think about on those empty nights on the tour bus. I stared right into his dark eyes as I swayed my hips. Reaching up to my mouth, I licked my index finger. I began tracing my bottom lip, down my throat, and up and down my cleavage. I then leaned into him, pressing my breasts into his face, and slid down his body until I was on the floor between his legs. I flipped my hair into his lap and let my hair graze his leather pants a few times. I felt that familiar hardening of his cock as he shifted his weight to his right. I slowly flipped my hair back, smiled, and pressed my body all the way up until we were face-to-face once more. He breathed heavily into my ear.

"You are turning me on, Angel."

I smiled. I then reached for the straps of my black lace dress, untying them, letting each breast out one at a time.

He smiled. Squeezing my breasts together, I made insatiable cleavage for him to adore. Then I let my lacy ensemble shimmy off my hips and land on the floor. As I stepped out of the dress, I placed one leg at a time on his lap and began slowly gyrating to Bijork.

"You're killing me, doll. I want you so bad," Trent sighed.

I leaned in and licked his lower lip. As I pulled back I felt a tap on my shoulder.

"Both feet on the floor. House rules, Angel," the bouncer said firmly.

I giggled. "Rules." I rolled my eyes and grabbed my dress to suit up again. When my garment was back on and in order, I sat down next to Trent. "I want you so bad," I whispered.

"We have the tour bus out front, beautiful," Trent teased.

I checked Trent's watch for the time, smiled, and said, "Give me five, okay?"

Trent laughed and asked Ty for the bus key.

I scurried about the smoky dressing room gathering my things. I tossed a mint in my mouth, sprayed another shot of perfume, then headed for the back door. As I breathed in the brisk, fresh night air, I made my way around the building toward the parked silver tour bus.

I leaned against the monstrosity of a vehicle. Trent greeted me with that weak-in-the-knees smile of his as he shook the bus key. "Hey." He grinned as he unlocked the bus. I followed him inside. Cozy, I thought to myself.

"Not bad, Trent, if you're a sardine," I said as I glanced around WHIP's future living quarters. We could still hear the music blaring from the club inside the bus.

Trent laughed as he turned around and took my hand. "Now where did we leave off? I prefer the private party for two over you being on display in the club," he said softly.

I smiled. "I believe I was straddled on your lap, sir," I responded, voice cracking a bit.

He laughed. I removed my jacket and ditched the street clothes, fully nude in thirty seconds flat. "Wow. You're in a hurry!" Trent laughed as he sat on one of the cold red vinyl benches and leaned against the bus window.

I stepped right back into his lap, this time not holding back. I was very wet from the foreplay of the previous dance. I let Trent unbuckle his pants, pull out his cock, and passionately enter me. I moaned aloud, knowing the club music outside would drown out our affection for one other. I tried to catch my breath as his swollen cock pushed deeper inside me. I licked his lips and took in every inch. I was in heaven. So much had built up between the two of us since our dance at LUST that we just thrusted and came together so hard and so fast.

After my heightened orgasm, I stuck my tongue in his mouth, thrusting against his tongue. He gladly accepted the deepest kiss I've ever given him. I pushed his hair behind his ears, pressed my forehead against his, and said, "Let's stay open for one another, like you said. I'm here. Call me anytime, Trent, to talk about anything. Enjoy this tour, live your dream, we'll meet up again along the way. You told me let's stay open—I'm open to you, Trent."

Suddenly, there was a bang on the tour bus door and I jumped up and feverishly got dressed. Trent pulled up his pants and unlocked the door. He glanced back at me and said, "Here we go, the band's back, I guess we're taking off." I sat back on the vinyl bench and started pulling on my cowboy boots as the tears started to surface. Tyler stepped onto the bus singing, *"They say that the road ain't no place to start a family, right down the line. It's been you and me, and lovin' a music man ain't always what it's supposed to be..."* Then the whole band joined in—*"Oh girl you stand by me, I'm forever yours, faithfully."* I started to cry as I stood up and hugged each member of WHIP one by one. "I love y'all," I muttered, then stepped off the bus.

The next morning I laid in bed mulling over the dance, the fuck, and my last goodbyes to WHIP. This sucked. I stared at the ceiling. I kept wishing Trent was lying next to me and that Ty would bang on my door, begging me for coffee once more. But no such luck. I was alone. Well, not completely alone. I do have Gage, which confuses me, and yes...I have Ernie. Just then he lifted his head, meowed, gracefully walked up to me, and licked my nose.

A few days of hibernation had passed. I needed a few days to digest it all. I cleaned. I donated clothing. I painted. I wanted to start the new year fresh. Just as I was about to haul the last bag of clothing to my truck to donate, my cell beeped with a text. This actually startled me. I had the ringer off for a few days to be alone in my principles. However, this morning I decided to switch the ringer back on and move on. I dropped my trash bag next to the door and exhaled. I walked over to the counter to check the cell.
Hey Alexandria, how about dinner tonight?

I gulped. Gage wanted to have dinner. Fuck it. Nova was nowhere to be found. The boys were out of town. Gag if I wanted to go to my parents for dinner.

I replied, *Sounds perfect.*

A few hours later, Gage pulled up in front of the Green Room as I gazed down the empty streets of Deep Ellum. I turned, grabbed my faux fur coat, purse, and keys, and headed towards the door. I only stopped for a second to quickly glance in the mirror and pat Ernie's head.

"See ya later, Ern." I smiled and shut the door behind me.

Gage and I went to dinner in uptown at the Crescent hotel once again. The ambiance was to die for. The subtle piano was a nice touch to drown out lovers' conversations. I glanced around in awe as the hostess guided us to our table. Gage slowly helped me out of my coat, pulled out my chair, and kissed me on the cheek as I sat.

I became flushed as the hostess handed me a menu. Gage settled in across from me and smiled at the hostess while she retrieved the menu for him.

"I'm so happy you could join me tonight, Alexandria," Gage said to break the silence.

"Thank you for the invite. It's good to get out of the house and away from my thoughts for a moment," I sighed.

"Well, WHIP is doing fantastic. They're having the time of their lives and you'll see them soon," Gage reassured me, even though I never mentioned the band.

"That is good to hear." I continued to look over the piano player and not make direct eye contact. Gage made me a bit uncomfortable, knowing he had his hand in WHIP's future. I'm just being protective of my friends, even though if it wasn't for WHIP I wouldn't have even met Gage in the first place. It's kind of nice to roll at a fancy restaurant uptown with Gage while the boys are eating BBQ from a truck stop. I smiled to myself.

"What are you thinking about?" Gage inquired as he sipped his Old-Fashioned.

"I'm just happy to be here with you, Gage. Thank you again for the company."

"Well," Gage went on, "I don't mean to sound selfish but it sure is nice to have you all to myself."

I rolled my eyes.

"It is, Alexandria. Those boys sure can distract you."

I interrupted him. "Those so-called boys are my friends, that's what they're supposed to do. They're supposed to distract me," I defended WHIP, especially Tyler.

"I didn't mean to upset you, Alexandria. I'm just stating that I am glad you and I get some alone time. I like you in my life. Now let us have a quiet dinner and then head back to my place for dessert." Gage firmly picked up his fork and attended to his steak. I sat back and quietly enjoyed my salmon until the hostess returned to offer more wine. Gage waited until 'Miss Hostess with the Mostess' finished refilling our glasses. "Would you like a drink, dear?" Gage proposed to the woman pouring the wine. She blushed, leaning over to expose a little bit more cleavage, whispering something into Gage's ear. She set the bottle down and walked away.

"Um, did I miss something? Do you know her?" I interrogated Gage.

He laughed and said, "Come on, let's get out of here." He sifted through his pockets for the valet ticket and a hefty tip to leave behind. I brushed it off and headed for the valet.

Walking into Gage's penthouse, I looked around the master's living quarters and rolled my eyes. "You need to warm up this place a bit," I suggested.

He smiled as he removed my coat and his as well. "Warm up how? I could turn on the fireplace?"

"That's a start," I responded. Gage tended to the fire as I made myself comfortable on the cold leather couch. What home has cold leather to park their ass on? "I thought we were having dessert. Are you making s'mores by the fire?" I chuckled. If this was my house I would have had s'mores with extra chocolate sauce to smear all over his fine ass. "You have chocolate syrup?" I teased.

"Umm, matter of fact I do." He looked like a kid as he hopped to his feet and made his way into the kitchen. He returned in ten seconds flat with the chocolate syrup and a smile. Still a bit tipsy from the wine, I grabbed the syrup from his hand and pulled him onto the couch next to me. He laughed. "I like where this s'mores thing is going," he announced.

I slid off the couch and over towards Gage, parking myself right between his legs. I reached up to unzip his pinstripe pants and slowly pulled them to the floor. Tossing them aside with one hand, I flipped the syrup cap open with the other hand. Greedily, I took his hard cock into my hand while I began dripping chocolate all over the shaft. I then tossed the bottle and started to lick the syrup off his erect cock, giving him the best head he's ever had. Even better than 'Miss Hostess with the Mostess,' I was sure of it. I put on a hell of a performance. Men in power need to feel powerful. I stroked his cock up and down with my chocolate-covered hands. Gage's head went back and he ejaculated all over my hand and his stomach.

I smiled. "Bet you didn't know I was such a chocoholic, did you? I love this stuff." He laughed adoringly. He suggested I grab a towel before his leather got stained. Nothing screams "I'm turned on" like fetching cleaning supplies. I went for the towel.

*

The next day I woke to an empty bed. Gage got up early and ran off to some meeting. I was alone in his penthouse. I stretched and rolled over on his California king mattress.

"Ahh, luxury!" I reached for my hobo bag on the floor and rustled through it, searching for my cell. I longed for a text from the guys. All I received was a text from Gage stating he was out for the morning and one from Nova. I immediately pushed the call.

"Hey, girl," her raspy voice answered.

"Morning, sunshine," I laughed. "Wanna come downtown for some coffee?"

"You lonely, girl? Am I going to get all your attention now that studs in leather are out of the picture?"

"They are not totally out of the picture." I suddenly felt saddened.

Nova apologized and said she was on her way.

I slithered out of bed, groaning. I brushed my teeth,

peed, and headed towards the kitchen to start some much-needed coffee. Moments later, there was a knock at the door.

"Come on slut, let me in," Nova hollered from the hallway. I ran to the door and unlocked it quickly. There stood Miss Nova in faux fur, big gold sunglasses, and what looked like last night's attire.

"Is this the walk of shame?" I laughed at her as she pushed past me, heading for the kitchen.

"Good to see you, too. You've been missing in action, Miss Mercedes." I chastised her about missing her shifts at Vanity.

"Don't you worry, girl. I've been making plenty of money outside those walls of Vanity." She smirked as she leaned over the stainless steel countertop. "Shit." She perked back upwards, rolling her eyes. "This counter's fucking freezing. Is everything in the penthouse sterile and cold?" She glanced around the place. I grabbed us some mugs and pulled up a barstool, waiting for the coffee to finish brewing.

"It is rather cold, huh? Gage likes it clean and in order."

"Is that how he likes his sex?" Nova teased.

"Kinda," I responded, blushing. "Girl, everything has to be cleaned up afterward. I mean, he wants to shower prior and post-sex. It's strange."

Nova started to laugh. "He wants to clean his slate after sex. Probably feels guilty after a good fuck then wants to shower it away. Guilty of something I suppose. Gage is a strange bird." She let out a deep breath as she motioned like she was wiping the countertop down. "Bet you never fucked on this cold ass countertop, have you?" She laughed.

"Well," I chimed in. "Last night, I gave good head with some chocolate sauce for dessert, but we didn't linger too long in the sweet stuff." I got up from the barstool and went to fetch the soy milk.

"You are kidding me, right?" Nova howled.

"I had to grab cleaning supplies and attend to our mess."

Nova couldn't stop laughing. "Well, Molly Maid, have you fucked on this countertop? Smearing sauce all over it?"

I stopped her. "No, he would die. We'd have to bleach the whole damn thing. Too much work." I laughed at the thought of it.

"Well, Alex, I have an idea. Let's rub chocolate sauce all over your ass and roll you around on the counter, he'll never know. It'll be our secret, our inside joke." Nova was serious. I stood at the fridge, opened it back up, and pulled out the chocolate sauce. "That's my girl!" Nova screamed. She jumped off her barstool and removed her faux fur, tossing it on the cold concrete floor. "We need to turn the heat up around here!" She reached out and grabbed the chocolate from my hand and pulled me towards her. "Okay, beautiful, out of these sweatpants and tee." She tugged at the clothing I'd borrowed from Gage and threw it all to the side.

I laughed. "It is fucking freezing, girl!" I shivered, standing naked in Gage's kitchen.

"Hop up on the counter," Nova ordered. I obeyed and hopped up. Nova then opened the sauce and poured it all over my breasts and down my thighs as I laughed hysterically. "Now roll on your side, girl, I'm icing the cake." She smeared chocolate on her hands and rubbed it all over my ass, smacking it a few times for good measure. I rolled all over the countertop and bar. "Take that, Mr. Clean. I need to serve dinner at this counter bar tonight. Wait, Alex, I need a pic of this." Nova bent down and grabbed her cell. I was laying on my back then, legs spread open with sauce dripping down my thighs. I laughed. I gazed at the stainless steel pendant lights above my head and smiled. Nova took some good racy shots of me, Miss Chocolate Queen.

I didn't even feel guilty; Gage can be a tightwad sometimes. We laughed as we sat on the chocolate-smeared counter drinking coffee.

"I love you, Nova," I said. She smiled as she took her finger and swiped some chocolate off of my shoulder.

"Good breakfast." She licked the chocolate off her finger as she snapped another picture.

After Nova took off, I decided to linger around Gage's pad for the day. I cleaned up the photoshoot remains and headed for the shower. I wanted everything (including me) to be crisp and clean when he came home that afternoon.

A few hours later, I tossed aside the boring novel that Gage was reading and got up off the couch. I roamed around a bit as I searched for a sweater. I was being lazy. It felt good, but I wasn't a hundred percent comfortable in his home yet. The sun was going down as I gazed out the picture window, admiring the buildings of downtown. A few snowflakes fell from the sky. I rubbed my shoulders warm. Hated this time of year in Dallas. I wanted to gaze out of this window and see a palm tree. I lingered in my thoughts until I heard a door close.

"Hey Alexandria, you're still here?" Gage appeared in the living room.

"I am. I hope you don't mind. I played hooky from my life for the day."

He flashed that beautiful grin. "I love coming home to you," Gage said.

I smiled. That felt good to me.

"How about you get dressed and we head out for some dinner?" he offered.

"Ah, it's kind of chilly out, why don't we order in?" I suggested.

"That sounds perfect. You set the counter with dinner plates and wine glasses. I'll shower and call something in."

I obliged and headed toward the kitchen to get started. I grabbed a bottle of wine and set it on the counter as I searched for an opener. Pouring myself a glass, I sat on the stool and relaxed while I waited for Gage. I could get used to this. I glanced around at the expensive furnishings, the cold but modern kitchen. I admired the height of the ceilings. I then noticed smeared chocolate on the hanging stainless steel pendant light. I grabbed my napkin. I started to wipe feverishly until Gage walked in and broke my concentration.

"What are you doing?" he asked.

"I was wiping some prints off the pendant. Stainless shows everything."

"Thanks. Never liked the cleaning company the HOA recommended."

Of course he didn't. "Wine?" I offered.

"Sure." He handed me his glass.

We ate our takeout dinner and drank wine. The more

Gage drank, the more he loved to talk about himself and how fabulous he was. I just listened in awe. This man has a vast amount of friends, and successful business that has him traveling the world. And he has a second home in Miami, Florida. I guess I have to get Gage drunk to get the goods on 'Money Man.'

"I love having you here, Alexandria." He slurred his words a bit.

"Oh, do you?" I smiled back as I sipped my wine.

"Now that the boy—I mean boys—are out of the way chasing their teenage dreams of becoming rockstars, I'll get you all to myself." He grinned as he reached for the bottle of wine to refill. He went on. "I like that. I'd love to move to the next level with you, Alexandria. I started thinking after our last conversation in the bedroom when you were wondering if we were exclusive."

I swallowed hard, taken a bit back by his openness. "Next level, huh?" I inquired.

"Yes. You are a big girl now. You graduated from your program. You are starting a new career of becoming a graphic artist of some sort." He rolled his eyes as he stated, "You need to get out of that dump in Deep Ellum. You are not safe there. The party boys are no longer in the same building. I don't like you there alone. Why don't you and that cat of yours come live with me? Here at the penthouse? Top floor, best view, best accommodations, and just about the best of everything. Most of all, you get me!" He smiled and took another sip of his wine. "Now, one thing I am adamant about is that this is not unconditional love. It's based on certain conditions. If you would like to live with me and be my exclusive girlfriend, there are conditions."

"Conditions?" I repeated.

"Yes, conditions," Gage said sternly.

"Oh, did I say that out loud? Where's the romance in that, Gage?" I swallowed to help digest these conditions.

"I mean, I have a company to run and I need a woman, not a girl on my side. I need someone who can walk the walk and talk the talk at galas and events. Especially in front of friends and colleagues. We'll get you to update that wardrobe of yours. That beast you drive will need to be parked at a parking garage, not at the penthouse."

"What, Axl?" I interrupted. "I love Axl. What's wrong with Axl?" I was confused.

"Axl, my dear, does not fit into my image. He will not be seen on the property. I'll pay to have it parked down the street."

I was bummed, but I understood. Oh well, it's just a truck. I would love to bail on Deep Ellum. Too many memories, too many struggling bands rehearsing all night for their big break. "I do sleep better here." Gage smiled at the thought of that. "I will need some more graphic design gigs, though. You can throw me a bone every once in a while?"

Gage agreed. "I'll even let you see Tyler when you need to. I know he's your friend."

"A friend. Yes. Need I remind you that you would have never met me unless it was for the band," I intervened.

"You are right, Alexandria."

"Alex, please," I corrected once more.

"Then it's on!" Gage held up his glass to celebrate us moving in together. I clinked my glass with his and took a deep breath, wondering what I had gotten myself into. Then I thought of Trent. Trent asked me if we could keep things open and I obliged. Open to me means the *possibility* of a future relationship but one never spoke of the present. I made my decision then and there to date Gage and stick with it.

CHAPTER TEN

A few days later, I called Nova with the news. I convinced her to come over and help me pack. We packed all my canvases, boxed my vinyl records, loaded my clothes into trash bags, and packed the kitchen. After sealing the last box, Nova collapsed on my bed.

"You sure are lucky, girl. Gage can give you everything. You're growing up. I'm jealous and happy for you. Just be sure to keep the Clorox nearby."

Laughing, I threw some old tees at her. "You want any old rock shirts, girl? There's a dress code where I'm going. It seems a bit sudden, huh? Gage didn't ask me, he kind of suggested it and made the decision like that." I snapped my fingers.

"Alex, keep your tees, this is a trial. Go for it. Let down your hair. No more stinky loft. No more stoner neighbors. No more Vanity. See where it takes you. Maybe his guard will come down a bit once you settle in. Maybe there is a romantic inside, waiting to burst out and surprise you." Nova always seemed to talk me off the ledge.

"I know he's a good guy, it's just he's always so negative about Tyler."

"Who isn't, girl?" Nova bit back. "Tyler is a fucked-up rockstar who will never grow up. When was the last time he called you?"

I huffed. "I know. I miss him, though."

"Grow up, girl. Rockstars are never prince charmings. It's the men who own the rockstars who are. You are hurdling over the rock god to your secure prince charming. It'll be okay." Nova rolled off the bed and gave me a hug. "I gotta jet, Mrs. Heston; I have a date with Vanity tonight. When you want to get away from all the galas and go slumming, call Mercedes! We'll play at Vanity and you can stash some emergency cash for a quick bail out if need be. Okay?" She kissed my cheek.

"Okay." I felt like everyone was slipping away as Nova left. I deadbolted my dumpy loft door and returned to taping the last few boxes. Am I sure? I am alone down here, with no band. I should move on up and see what life is like in the penthouse. I sat on the cardboard box, reached for my cell, and yes...dialed my mother.

After the third ring, I almost hung up, then heard: "Alexandria Rae? Where have you been?"

"Hi, Mama!" I was playing the doting daughter. "How are you?"

"I'm fine dear, sorry to hear that your band friends left town, Austin told me everything. I do, however, want to know if you're still seeing the Mr. Heston you brought home at Christmas?"

I let the band thing roll off my shoulders and just honed in on Gage. "He's good, Mama. We go to fancy restaurants, he has business contacts for me and my design work, and...Mama, he asked me to stay at his penthouse for a while."

"Thank you, Jesus!" Mother shouted. "You're getting married! Get yourself out of that dungeon you call home and start acting like a Christian lady. You got yourself a good, successful man there, Alexandria—I'm so happy for you."

"Wait a minute, Mother, I'm NOT getting married. I'm just going to stay for a while," I interrupted her celebration. "Yes, my dungeon is a bit scary at times, but it was all I could afford to claim my independence from the family. Now with Tyler not being around, I'd feel safer staying with Gage. Okay?"

Mother fell silent.

"Mother?" I waited patiently.

"Alexandria, I brought you up better than that. You need to get back to church, young lady, and marry that man already!" I never seem to do anything right. I always somehow seem to disappoint. "I'm not going to say anything to your Father about this move you're considering, Alexandria. Nothing. You work this out between you and Jesus, hun. Now, I need to run, I have a luncheon to attend to." Mother was flustered. And so was I.

*

It took me a few weeks to settle into Gage's penthouse. Parking was down the street. I learned all the doormans' names. I had keys to the elevator and keys to the penthouse. He gave me my own credit card for clothing to store in an empty penthouse.

Gage traveled a lot. I felt like a doll inside his glass house where he kept me. When he traveled, I felt locked up. When he returned, he took me out, played with me a little, then set me back on the shelf for display.

Tonight was a good night, though. Gage was coming back from his New York trip. I was preparing to pick him up from DFW airport in a few hours. When he called to check in on me, he told me that he felt tired and a bit sore. So I decided to dip into my costume box down in storage and wear my vinyl nurse Halloween costume to greet him. I could then bring him home, massage him, and have amazing sex. We haven't had sex since before he left for his trip a few weeks ago. I got all gussied up and looked slutty as hell. Gage would approve even if the costume didn't have a Dior tag hanging from it. I smiled at myself in the mirror, then called downstairs to have Gage's car pulled around. Gage would die if I showed up in a costume and my truck. I grabbed all the sets of keys (the car, the pad, the elevator) and my coat and headed downstairs.

Arriving at the DFW arrivals terminal, I pulled the car up to the curb and turned on my flashers. I grabbed my cell off the passenger seat and read Gage's text. He had arrived and would be down shortly. Within moments, Gage knocked on the driver's side door window. Startled, I opened the door and let Gage drive. He kissed me when I stepped out of the vehicle, walked me around to the passenger side, and let me in. When he got back into the driver's seat, he smiled at me.

"Ready?" he asked.

"Wait a minute. I know you were feeling run down and sore. So we need to make one stop to fill this prescription." I smiled, handing him a prescription saying, "One Free Rub Down."

Gage laughed. "Who gave you this prescription?"

I smiled as I opened my jacket to show off my nurse's outfit and fake stethoscope.

Gage laughed. "You spoil me, Nurse Alexandria. I will fill this right away." I laughed and was so excited when he didn't make fun of the costume.

Arriving back at the penthouse, Gage dropped his suitcase and went straight to the liquor cabinet. He made his favorite drink, an Old-Fashioned. He seemed to always need a drink before getting naked. Then he headed for the shower. "I'll be back in a minute my little nurse, get yourself a drink."

"Would you like a sponge bath?" I invited myself to join him.

"No, Alexandria, I bathe alone."

Okay, your loss, mister, I thought to myself as I pouted my lips, contemplating my decision to continue to play nurse with him. I had been picking up on these little quirks ever since I decided to stay with him. Nova was right in describing him as a strange bird. I guess I'm okay with the drink, as long as he relaxes.

I removed my jacket and walked toward the liquor cabinet, pouring him a second drink—fuck it, I wanted him to relax tonight. I scurried around to make the room as romantic as I could for him. When Gage returned from his shower, I took his hand and led him to the bedroom. I had all the candles lit and soft, erotic music by Enigma playing in the background. I turned toward Gage. I unbuttoned his black dress shirt, peeling it off his solid, strong arms and tossing it to the ground. I then unbuttoned his slacks, removing and tossing them onto the pile as well.

He stood there, naked, finishing his drink. "Where do you want me, Nurse Alexandria?"

I smiled and pointed to the bed. Gage got comfortable on the bed as I grabbed the massage oil and climbed in with him. I straddled his back in my vinyl dress, dripping oil all over Gage's muscular back. I love when a man takes care of himself. He's so metro. It's such a turn-on.

I began my massage from his shoulders, down his back, and over his butt cheeks. At first I received a giggle, then a sigh as I rubbed harder. I massaged both his legs and feet, then flipped him over. I started on his front side. I provided a good facial massage, then moved on to the manual lymphatic drain technique on his neck. He was purring with joy. I worked his arms and chest. I finally made my way to a throbbing cock that had continued to grow as I massaged every other area.

I lubed up extra good as I started on the cock. I rubbed his shaft up, around his head, and back down for a few rotations as Gage breathed heavily. I continued to be a good nurse and added a few licks to the top. I sucked the head a few times while his cock pulsated. I felt it getting harder and harder within my grasp. I then returned to the slow motion of jerking him off. Within seconds, Gage released a vast amount of cum all over my hard-working hand. I smiled. He groaned, then immediately rolled off the bed and headed for the bathroom. I sat there with cum dripping from my hands.

"It's okay," I said to myself. "I'll grab a rag."

Gage emerged from the bathroom, "You spoil me, nurse. Thank you."

I let out a deep breath. "Well, Mr. Heston. Get some

rest and we'll talk about your trip in the morning."

I wiped my hand and headed to the laundry room to dispose of the rag. When I was walking back, I noticed Gage's suitcase half-unzipped. I looked up and there was no sign of Gage. Snores were coming from the bedroom. I sat on the floor and unzipped his bag. I took his shaving kit out and rustled through it with curiosity. A toothbrush, paste, razors, all the essentials. Then I felt a foil packet. My heart stopped. I pulled out a condom. I shuffled through the bag, removing more packets of condoms.

"What the fuck?" I whispered. Why would he need travel condoms for a New York trip? My heart sank. What did I get myself into? Are we NOT exclusive? Why would this man invite me into his home, into his world, if he had no intention of being faithful? Shit. I sat back on my heels, looked around, then discreetly zipped the bag closed.

*

The next morning. I woke up early. I wanted to surprise Gage with breakfast. I dressed, called a cab, and headed out the door to the downtown farmers' market. This outdoor market was amazing. A mix of fresh-brewed coffee and herbs filled the air. People lingered around barrels of fresh fruit and vegetables. I walked the aisles, selecting warm baked bread and items for my veggie omelet.

When I returned home, Gage was in the shower. I set my reusable bags on the counter and started the coffee as I prepared breakfast. Within a few minutes, Gage appeared in a set of fresh, comfortable clothes and a wet head.

"Good morning, naughty nurse." I smiled as he greeted me with a kiss on the head. "Smells amazing. Whatcha cooking?" He stuck his nose over the sizzling frying pan on the stove.

"Veggie omelets, with warm bread and fresh fruit from the farmers' market," I announced as I whipped the eggs.

"Yum. You went to the farmers' market already? I'm impressed. I was knocked out. That massage of yours put my ass in a coma."

Gage ran his fingers through his wet hair. He was sexy with wet bedroom hair. Yet, I still was stewing on the foil packets I found last night.

"So, Gage, tell me about your New York trip," I encouraged.

"Oh, New York is New York. Fucking crazy." He sipped his coffee. I set up our plates and sat down at the breakfast counter with him.

"Crazy, huh?" I repeated.

"I had meetings with record executives. Producers and labels," he said as he dug into his veggie omelet with a smile.

"I didn't realize you had a place there as well."

"I do. I'll take you one day. I was clearing out some old things from the New York pad. One of my employees is going to be crashing there until we sign this new act. Matter of fact, if this band works out, I'd love for you to create an album cover for them."

I perked up. "Really? I would love that. I need a new project. My internship as a social media gal is up and I'm kind of bored. So, you were cleaning out your pad, huh?" I longed for more information.

"Uh, yeah, I brought home some things." Gage grabbed for a napkin.

Guess that's it, I thought to myself. Either he's bullshitting, knowing I saw the condoms, or he's telling the truth and I'm blowing this thing out of proportion in my head. I need to give him the benefit of my doubt. But three pads? Wow, a single man's dream. My intuition was nudging me but I'm ignoring it for now.

"I have an idea," Gage interrupted my destructive train of thought.

"Yes?" I bounced back.

"I want to take you shopping at North Park and buy you something in return for the massage and breakfast." He smiled like a child at Christmas.

"You do?" I was confused. I wasn't a puppy; there was no need to reward me every time I did something nice for him. "It's a give and take, Gage," I assured him. "I enjoy the massage and stuff. I do not need a treat for doing that."

"Nonsense," he cut in. "Get changed, your farmers' market attire is not suitable for a jewelry store and lunch at the Palm."

Wow. All the men I've dated thought lunch at Chick-fil-A was fancy. This is a nice treat. I need to enjoy the attention. Nova would die if she knew I was headed to the jewelry store at North Park. I know she has a wishlist filed away somewhere. When Mr. Right comes along he can honor her list. I'll need to text her when we're on our way.

That evening, when we arrived back home, Gage went straight to his office to check emails. I dropped my shopping bags in the entry and looked around the penthouse. I then glanced down at the shiny new bracelet on my wrist and smiled. This is exactly what Mother and Nova had in mind for me.

*

The next day I woke to rustling from the closet. "Hey there. Whatcha digging for?" I rubbed my eyes, trying to focus on Gage in the closet. I had no idea if he had even been to bed.

"Hey babe," he greeted me. "I have to jet to Miami for a bit. I have a few things to attend to. I emailed a project for you to consider taking on. A logo that needs cleaning up. Enjoy the penthouse. I should be back in a few days."

I moaned. "You just got back from New York, boo." I was saddened that I'd be alone once again. Gage stopped packing, sat on the bed, and apologized.

"This is how it is, babe. When a meeting or something arises, I need to go. Plus, I need to check on the Miami pad. Call your crazy girlfriend over for a slumber party or something. Show off your new bracelet."

I pulled my arm out of the comforter and glanced at the dangling new piece of jewelry I'd earned. "I do appreciate the gift, Gage. I would like to spend more time with you," I pouted.

"You will. Give me a bit of space to do my thing and then we'll plan for you to thaw out in sunny South Florida." He took my hand and gently kissed it. He then returned to his packing.

Within the hour, Gage was packed, showered, and called for the car downstairs. I was just finishing my morning coffee and he was gone.

A few days passed and I became the stirring house mouse. The logo project he emailed over was pretty basic work. I had it cleaned up and sent off in the first forty-eight hours of Gage's absence. I then picked up the phone and dialed Nova.

"Hey, Rapunzel," she answered. "How is the tower? Lonely over there?"

"Yes, I am, girl. He was here. I massaged him, cooked for him, blew him, and he was off to Miami."

"Loco girl!" she chimed in.

"I did get something shiny for being a naughty nurse, though. I used our Halloween costumes to give a therapeutic massage and the best hand job ever." I laughed.

"Sluuuuut!" Nova shouted. "That's a girl! So what now? Do you hide in the tower and wait for his return?" I rolled my eyes. "I can hear you rolling your eyes, Alex," Nova scolded me. "How about a girl's night out?" Nova offered.

"I'd love that. What kind of trouble can we get into? I'm kind of low in the finance department. Gage only tossed me one logo bone, which doesn't pay much."

"That's not what I'm hearing, girl. He threw you a couple of bones, which is why you shopped at North Park." I could sniff the jealousy through my cell. "Are you up for Vanity?" Nova asked.

I hesitated and then said, "I am."

"Gage would kill you if he found out. This is his way to keep a hold on you. If he throws you a bone, as you say, a logo every once in a while, then you become dependent on him. The logo is to shut you up. He actually wants you to depend on him financially. It's kind of controlling, if you ask me."

"You told me to roll with it, Nova," I snapped back.

"Girl, have fun in the tower. Enjoy the gifts. In the meantime, let's stash some cash for an emergency."

I sighed. "What kind of relationship am I entering if I have to plan my emergency escape? This blows."

"No, Alex. You blow. Keep him happy and get everything you want."

"Okay, mother." I stopped Nova's speech. "Pick me up at eight, we're heading to Vanity." I swallowed hard.

"Yay!" Nova cheered over the phone. "Eight o'clock, my love."

Nova hung up. Fuck it. Nova is right, I need my Plan B. If Mr. Heston comes home with another suitcase chock full of condoms, then I'm out of here. Serves him right for bailing again. I'm going to take it out on a few Vanity customers.

*

That night at Vanity, I never felt so exhilarated. This must be some kind of twisted game between Gage and me. I know he's off being a bad boy, so I sneaked out to play bad girl. He has his secrets, then I'll have mine.

I dressed extra slutty for my shift. I borrowed Nova's red mini-dress and red fuck-me heels. I added lashes to my makeup routine and busted out the red lipstick. The pervert of a manager that hired me stuck his head in the dressing room. He granted his approval by howling and licking his lips. Ew. I guess this look was working—I needed to showcase it on stage and see who bites.

Then I heard, "Angel, up next." I headed towards the

stage. I made my way through the second smoky dressing room. I passed all the beautiful entertainers once again.

"Hey, girl! Love the red," one beautiful spray-tanned girl hollered from the corner. I waved. Another girl looked me up and down and rolled her eyes. I got more dirty looks than smiles because the competition was fierce on the weekends at Vanity. There were so many women for the customers to choose from, so you had to look your centerfold best. Another insecure new stripper waved as I passed her locker.

I arrived at the stage. I heard the Nine Inch Nails song start: *You Are the Perfect Drug*. I knew that was my cue. I always had anxiety before stepping on stage. Good thing the stage lighting blurred out the view of the room of hungry wolves. You need to look above their heads and get lost in the music.

I stepped out of the curtain and onto the familiar stage. My four minutes of fame had arrived. I slowly walked to the sticky and shiny stripper pole and leaned up against it. I tossed my head back, put my hand to my chest, and slid down the fixture. I unleashed my breasts from the tight red dress. I heard "Woo-hoo" from the crowd. I rolled my head around counter-clockwise and licked my lips.

I noticed a few bills falling like confetti and landing in front of me. I smiled and let go of the pole. I opened my legs, exposing my red panties. I grazed my fingers across them in a teasing manner. I closed my legs and took the doggy-style position, gyrating my hips in the air. I then rolled onto my back. I pulled the rest of my dress down over my hips, down my legs, and kicked it to the side of the stage with my right heel. More money confetti fell over my bare stomach as I gyrated my hips.

I rolled onto my knees to greet the customer standing at center stage. I pushed both of my breasts together to create cleavage. I shimmied them in front of his face. More hoots came from the audience. It gave me more motivation to grab my nipples and pluck them outward one by one as the customer licked his lips. I laid down with my back on the cold stage and spread my legs once more. I opened and closed them a few times to tease the patrons. I rolled to my side and steadied myself back up on my high heels. The crowd clapped. I smiled and made my way to the exit as the song ended.

As I left the stage, a floor man with a silver wine bucket stepped out after me and collected all my earnings. All that money belongs to me, not Gage. I stepped back into the dressing room.

As the night rolled on, I kept tagging along with Nova.

"Girl, you sure are making money tonight. I haven't seen you this motivated in a long while. Gage needs to run off a little more often so I can have you all to myself." Nova laughed as she leaned back on the velvet chair, sipping her wine with ease.

"I kind of miss him. He can be a neurotic prick but it's still new and exciting. Is that strange?" I asked.

"Not at all, girl. He's rich, handsome, and he doesn't follow you around like a lost puppy dog. He actually has his own life and adores having you in it. Run with it, Alex. See how it all plays out." She smiled at me, checked her watch, and surveyed the room for our next dollar.

"He does like to treat me with goodies I'm not accustomed to having. Mother swoons over him. But it always seems he's keeping me at arm's length. I want more."

"You, my dear, are confusing sex with a real relationship. I don't think either of you want a real relationship. You want Trent."

"What?" I lost my breath for a second, embarrassed.

"It's okay. 'Money pants' is only a distraction. You feel more comfortable with Trent. He's more your level, meaning he gets your creative side. But bitch, you need to step out of the band box and experience something new for once. Date a real man with a real career who loves to show you the finer things in life because he can. Just go with the money flow. Wait. Why don't you surprise Gage? Yeah, count your garter, head to the airport, and take a flight to Miami, senorita!" Nova started pulling at my garter stashed with cash.

"Stop it, you crazy hooker," I yelled at her, pushing her hand away, laughing. "You are right, Nova. I need to get my act together and embrace this relationship. My heart is trying to steer me away, but it's because it's something new. Fuck it, I'm cashing out for the night. I'll head back to Gage's—I mean home—and pack a bag." I finished my wine, slammed the glass on the table, and jumped up with excitement. I then kissed Nova. "Love you, girl. I'll call you when I land," I said. I was off to the dressing room with newfound excitement.

When I arrived back at the penthouse, I scurried around as I packed my bag. I checked for flights, showered, and set my alarm for the next morning. I was doing it, and then a moment of panic washed over me. What if someone else was with Gage? What if he gets pissed that I showed up? What if he hates surprises? I don't even know if this man likes surprises. What a shame. I guess I'll find out.

I turned over in bed, switched off the bedside lamp,

and took a few deep breaths to calm myself. I glanced down at the bag on the floor. The garter was sitting on top of it, with all my money rolled and rubber-banded together.

Well, if Gage gets upset that I showed up, I'll get a room on the beach and take a few days to collect myself. I have enough money. I'll be fine, I reassured myself as I breathed out once more and closed my eyes.

The next morning, I jumped out of bed and headed to the kitchen to brew my coffee. I needed to feed Ernie, leave a note for the house cleaner to care for him, and book my taxi. I was starting to get excited. Miami would be a nice change of scenery. I was feeling kind of cooped up in my tower anyway, as Nova would say. I headed towards the bathroom and turned on the shower.

CHAPTER ELEVEN

MIAMI

All during the flight, I couldn't stop fidgeting. "How long is this damn flight?" I mumbled to myself. The man with the oversized Hawaiian print shirt sitting next to me cleared his throat. He turned the page of his copy of *The New York Times*.

I rolled my eyes as I looked out the tiny airplane window. There was nothing but blue sky and white fluffy clouds out there. The pilot startled me by interrupting with his descent announcements. My stomach turned for a moment. I sighed in relief as I wiped the dampness off my upper lip.

Another taxi dropped me off at the address I found on one of Gage's pieces of mail. I hoped he wouldn't be too pissed at me for showing up unannounced like this. I stood there, admiring a set of colorful beachfront condos. I debated getting a hotel for the night instead. Last night's earnings from Vanity were very generous. I could afford a hotel if Gage tossed me out.

Or what if I interrupted him and another woman? Gage seems somewhat private. Ugh. I breathed out once more to avoid a downward spiral, then walked up to the condo front door and dialed Gage's number.

"Hey there, Alexandria, are you missing me?" Gage answered.

"I am," I responded. "I did send you a little care package to your condo down there in sunny Florida."

I could hear him grin through my cell. "Ah, well that was thoughtful. I haven't received my mail yet. How did you send it?"

"Airmail, Mr. Heston. Check your front door. Maybe it was left outside." I smiled back into the phone, feeling a wave of nervousness wash over me.

"Hang on, then. I'll head towards the door," Gage said.

"I'll hang," I replied. I could hear flip-flops coming downstairs from the inside of the unit. Gage opened the door with the cell phone up against his ear, wearing nothing but his swim trunks and his flip-flops. I smiled as I breathed in a hint of cocoa butter.

"Wow, what a care package!" Gage hung up the phone as he gestured for me to enter the condo.

"Airmail dropped me off. Well, actually American Airlines and Frank's taxi cab, but it's all the same. Are you surprised? Is it a bad time?" My words were a bit shaky as I asked.

"Aw, Alexandria, I love the surprise. I wish you would have told me so I could prepare better. I have a few things to do but you are welcome to stay as long as you like. Make yourself comfortable." He smiled as he grabbed my suitcase and headed up the stairs into the main living room. I followed him up the stairs, admiring his oiled-up physique the whole way. Upon arriving at the top of the stairway, I looked up to see nothing but glass. There was nothing but pure blue sky and heavenly Atlantic Ocean.

"What a view!" I squealed.

"Yes, it is. Can I get you something to drink? Would you like to head out to the beach for a bit? What do you feel like doing?" Gage asked while he made his way to the kitchen.

"I feel like doing you. That's why I'm here." I laughed. I couldn't believe the words spilled out but after seeing him in just a swimsuit, I was pretty turned on. Gage came back into the living room, handing me an iced tea.

"Doing me, huh?" He smiled as I accepted the drink. "Right this way, my little care package."

Gage grabbed my hand, grabbed his coconut oil, and walked out onto the balcony. A breeze blew my hair back as I closed my eyes and inhaled the salt air. Gage adjusted and flattened out a beach chair on the balcony. He then walked towards me and pulled my cotton dress right over my head and tossed it aside. I gasped for a quick breath. He then took his coconut oil, opened the bottle, and poured a generous amount into the palm of his hand.

"Um, I love that smell," I egged on.

"I love the oil all over you."

Gage started to rub oil from my shoulders, over my breasts and down to my sex. I could feel the sun warm up my body as the oil glistened in its beams. He then placed one of his oiled fingers inside of me and began to slowly finger fuck me. My knees went weak. My breath was short. I felt amazing.

As my knees buckled, Gage guided me down to the beach chair. I laid on my back and spread my legs over each arm of the chair as Gage bent down and rubbed oil along his thick cock. He then pulled the cock out as long and as stiff as he could make it and entered me. Oh, this felt amazing. He started to thrust and thrust as I lay on my back looking up towards the blue sky. I then came very hard and knew at that moment I made the right decision to surprise him in Miami.

When we finished making love on the balcony, Gage got up and, yes, headed straight to the shower. I, on the other hand, sipped my iced tea and laid back on the recliner to continue to sunbathe nude. It felt so freeing to soak up the sun naked on his private balcony.

After a moment, Gage reappeared.

"Hey, doll. I have a few phone calls to make. I'll be in my office if you need me. Enjoy the sun and we'll get dinner in a little while." Gage turned away and headed toward the office. I returned to enjoying my moment in the sun. I closed my eyes and drifted off to sleep.

A few raindrops woke me from my nap. The afternoon thunderstorms were rolling in. I sat up, grabbed my iced tea and my dress, and headed indoors. I heard Gage on the phone and did not want to disturb him, so I found the bathroom and cleaned myself up. I guess we were grabbing dinner somewhere? Oh, how perfect. Gage and I having a romantic dinner for two, candlelit beach-side.

I selected another dress to wear, a black, form-fitting

ensemble with a pair of black heels. I laid everything out and hopped into the shower. When I finished cleaning up, I put one of Gage's tee shirts on, sat on his bed, and dialed Nova.

"Ola, Senorita Rae," Nova answered in her best Spanglish.

"Ola," I responded. "I'm in sunny South Florida, girl, soaking up the rays and getting fucked on beach chairs." I started to laugh as I reclined in Gage's comfortable king-size bed.

"El slut-o you!" Nova scolded me. "I'm proud of you, my li'l sexy Senorita. How was the flight, his reaction? Details!" Nova egged on.

"Flight was fucking nerve-racking, but my arrival was well accepted. His place is stupid beautiful. You should see this view, girl."

Nova hissed on the phone. "I hate you, but I'm proud of you, girl. It's balls cold in Dallas. Maybe I'll fly in and thaw out with you and that sexy beach chair you are bragging about," Nova said.

"That would rock, girl, but he seemed a little too surprised when I showed up. Give it some time before you show up, too." I got quiet on the phone and Nova could sense it.

"Well, do you have plans tonight?" Nova tried to cover up the silent airwaves.

"Yeah, we're heading to dinner in a bit; I hope it's just us. I'd like a little time alone with him, a romantic dinner. He can fuck for sure, girl, but not a touchy-feely lover. Does that sound strange?" I sounded a bit disappointed.

"Girl, give him a bit. It's the first flush; you may need to break him down bit by bit. Chip by chip. If he is worth it, then stick around a bit. Try holding his hand at dinner. Skootch close to him at the restaurant and see how he reacts."

I took a deep breath. "I do look good. I need to slip into my sexy black number."

"Oh, I know which number. The one we bought at North Park?" Nova's voice went up an octave.

"That's the one—he's made a comment or two about my Jane's Addiction tees or skirts being too short. I'll see if he drools or rolls his eyes."

"Okay, Alex. Text me the reaction."

"I will, girl. Gotta go. I love ya."

"Love ya too, beach bunny." Nova clicked off the line as I stared at the dress in front of me.

Why am I doubting a damn outfit? I look good. It's South Beach, for heaven's sake! I jumped off the bed and got ready.

Moments later, I lingered on the balcony, admiring the beautiful pink sunset. I could stay here forever, I thought to myself. Suddenly, I felt a hand on my waist. I smiled and turned around. Gage was all dressed for dinner. He had black-on-black pinstripe pants and a grey button-up shirt with fancy shoes to boot. I smiled, giving him the once-over with approving eyes.

"You look incredible," I complimented him.

He smiled, then asked if I was ready. Hum, no return compliment. He went to grab his cell and keys as I collected my cell and purse. We headed down the stairs to the garage below.

Reaching the silver Mercedes in the garage, Gage

opened the door for me. I nestled in, thinking of Nova. Nova would love the Mercedes. It was her stage name at Vanity. What were those girls up to tonight? Was I missing out on any of the exciting spenders?

The door suddenly slammed as my thoughts snapped back.

"You okay?" I asked Gage.

"We have one quick stop to make. There's a fabulous boutique on Ocean Drive I want to introduce you to. I have a revolving account with them. Let's go in and select something more appropriate for dinner tonight."

I was stunned. "I have a simple cocktail dress on. It's South Beach. I thought this was very appropriate." My disappointment and defiance showed.

"I let the short mini thing you've selected for WHIP's party go. And the New Year's dress—but now that we are about town as a couple, I'm going to put you into something more appropriate. I am a professional man; I have an image to uphold. I do not need to run into a client and have them think I rented you for the night."

I was shocked. "Are you saying I look like a hooker? Gage, it's a black mini dress." I tried arguing my way out but I knew he would win.

We pulled up in front of the little boutique on Ocean and made our way in. Gage selected a long, form-fitted skirt with a silk sleeveless shirt to complement. He even picked out a pair of heels.

"Toss those studded rock and roll band slut heels and try these Manolo Blahnik's on."

I did as I was told. "Let me hang on to the shoes. Nova will want them," I pouted.

The busty sales lady with overdone makeup cut the

tags off my outfit and scurried to the register. "Put this on your account, Mr. Heston?" she asked with a smile as she glanced over at me and suddenly lost her grin.

I rolled my eyes. I collected my studded rockstar shoes and slipped into the pair Gage selected. I walked over to the dressing room mirror and gave myself a once-over. I did look good. Polished. Mother would approve—but I was an emerging artist with a wild side. I felt out of my element. But, if it makes Mr. Heston happy, then I will oblige. I shuffled through my purse, pulled out the cell, and texted Nova.

At a boutique on Ocean Drive, in Manolo Blahnik's. She would understand.

Once we arrived at the swanky sushi joint on the ocean, I felt better. I wanted saké. I needed a drink.

The place was packed tonight. Dim lighting, candles, soft trance music. Perfect. Huge red sheers hung from the rafters, swaying in the ocean breeze. The place was stunning. The 'who's-who' of South Beach seemed to be dining this evening.

Gage shook several people's hands before we arrived at the hostess station.

"I have a reservation for three." Gage smiled at the pretty brunette with her hair pulled back in a slick bun. The hostess wore a tight dress that went all the way down to her ankles. She was sexy. Wait, three?

"Who's meeting us? I thought it was dinner for two?" I batted my lashes as Gage turned to look at me.

"Luke is meeting us. He was my dinner plan before the package was delivered at my door this afternoon." He smiled at me.

"I'm sorry to intrude, Gage. I had no idea." I felt small.

"Do not worry about it, Alexandria. Luke is my best friend. He'd love to meet you," Gage reassured me as we were directed to our oceanside table. The breeze was subtle and soothing. I took a breath in as Gage pulled my chair out and I sat down. He then took his seat at the other side of the table.

"Don't ya want to slide over here by me, sugar?" I asked, feeling the distance. Gage slid the chair a notch or two, but not like we were two peas in a pod. Then, Gage got this huge grin on his face. He stood up and shook the hand of this tall, slender, over-tanned man.

"Luke, how are you doing, buddy? This is Alexandria." Both men turned to look at me as I stuck out my hand.

"Nice to meet you," I greeted Luke with a fake smile.

"How are you doing, Alexandria?" he asked politely.

"I'm alright." I smiled once more.

"Southern girl, huh? " Luke glanced at Gage. "Where are you from, hun?"

Don't call me hun, I thought, but I replied, "Texas."

"I see." He glanced a second time at Gage. What are these googly eyes going on between them?

"I'm sorry to intrude on your plans, Luke. Thanks for having me here at dinner with you." I faked a smile once more.

"No problem, hun." There it was again. Ew.

The waitress showed up to take our order. When the saké arrived, I perked up. I needed a drink. Gage and Luke were lost in conversation. I decided to pour the saké and toast myself.

The waitress returned with our dinner soon after.

Everything looked amazing, sushi fresh from the ocean. I poked at my rolls as I smiled at Gage.

"Everything is amazing here," Gage said, directed at me.

"Looks good." I smiled as I picked up my chopsticks.

I then noticed Luke scoot a bit closer to Gage as the two of them pecked off one another's plate. Okay. I felt so dumb. Luke did not want me here. He did not even try to include me in any of their conversations. They were the two peas in a pod. Not me and Gage. Talking, eating off each others' plate. Fucking Bert and Ernie. I pouted to myself as I poured my third saké.

When dinner was over, we made our way out of the restaurant, the two peas still chatting like two damn schoolgirls as I lagged behind. Once we hit the valet station, I stepped up to Gage and squeezed his hand.

"Thank you for dinner. It was incredible." He squeezed my hand, then let it go to shuffle his pockets for a tip for the valet driver.

When the Mercedes pulled up in front, I reached my hand out to Luke.

"Nice to meet you, Luke." I smiled as he shook my hand.

"Pleasure was all mine, Texas." He smiled with those pearly whites. His teeth were way too white for that over-tanned skin of his.

Gage helped me into the car. Nothing was said the entire drive home. He listened to talk radio. For the first time in a while, I thought about Tyler. I missed our breakfast meetings at the Green Room. He'd laugh at my attire and about Bert and Ernie.

When we got back to the beach pad, I felt wiped. "You want to sit in the tub with me?" I asked Gage.

"Nah, I have some work to do."

Uh, utter decline. Oh well. I'll take the bath alone, then sit on the patio and text Ty.

After my long soak, I felt refreshed. I texted Ty from the balcony chair, which was still oiled up from this afternoon. Ty had nothing to say. No return text. What city were they in? I was bummed—I just felt I needed to hear his voice. I could stalk their social media page but I dismissed that thought and decided to check on Gage instead.

I headed towards Gage's office. I peeked my head in and he never looked up. He was staring at some boats online.

"Thinking of purchasing another new toy?" I startled him.

"Ha, you are my favorite toy. You keep me quite busy."

I rolled my eyes. "Hey, can I borrow your laptop while you're busy?" I asked sweetly. "I want to look something up, check on somebody." I left it at that. I changed my mind and decided to check up on WHIP after all.

"Sure. Take the one by the printer. Wireless password is MONEY." He smiled at me.

"Of course it is." I went over to the printer and snatched the laptop, then headed back out to the balcony. This weather is beautiful and balmy. I stood there, appreciating the moment, then sat on the beach recliner and started the computer up.

I hit the Internet Explorer button. Two pop-up chat

windows opened up. What the fuck is this? I searched for the 'x' to close the window. I then stopped myself and read the chat.

Hello handsome? Still up for drinks? one chat box alarmed me. Ew, what is this?

I read the second box. *I had a blast letting you smack my ass.*

"What!" I laughed out loud. This had to be a joke from sidekick Luke or something. Then I clicked the link the chats were coming from. The link directed me to an online dating profile for Gage. My heart sank. Okay, this could be something old. Who knows how he retained dates before the WHIP event. I swallowed hard. My face felt flush as I looked over my shoulder to make sure the profile man wasn't watching me. I read the two chats again. Um. The chats were sent two weeks ago! OMG. I was stunned. Is he lining up a Plan B for if I don't work out? Does he have one foot out the door? I clicked on each woman's profile and noticed they were both brunette, thin, and busty, one in Florida and one in New York. Wow. Guess he does like brunettes. Well, girls, I'm having an actual conversation with him in his beach house. These hussies are trying to rope him in through the fucking internet. I felt sick for a moment. Why isn't he happy with just me? I stewed on Gage's happiness for a moment. He did ask me to move in with him. Where are these girls living? This has to be an old profile with a few stalker chicks so I need to stop reading so much into it.

Brunettes, huh? I got an idea.

*

The next day, Gage had another meeting in Fort Lauderdale, which was about an hour north of his place. This window would give me time to muster up my surprise plan. I looked at myself in the mirror, counted my cash, and grabbed my flip-flops and bag. I went out to the street and made my way down Ocean Boulevard in the warm sun 'til I found the first hair salon. I went inside, looked around, and spotted the receptionist.

"Good morning, can I help you?" she asked.

"Yes, do you take walk-ins?" I smiled and felt flush. I was a little embarrassed that I did not make an appointment.

"We do not, hun, but Trevor had a cancellation. Let me ask if he'll take you."

I thanked her. She walked over to Trevor's station and asked him to fit me in. They chatted for a minute as I looked around, bobbing my head to annoying techno music.

The receptionist returned and said, "He'll take you. Can I get you anything to drink?"

I accepted wine. Three glasses later, I was feeling beautiful. Trevor made me the sexiest brunette on the beach. Well, at least I hoped that's what Gage would think. I stood up and stared into the mirror.

"You like it, sweetie?" Trevor asked as he fluffed the back of my head.

"I've only ever been blonde. I'm just in shock. We can make it blonde again at a later date, can't we?" I asked. Trevor sensed panic in my voice.

"Sure we can, sweetheart. You look fab. Your man will love the change. It makes your eyes stand out."

I smiled, knowing he was full of shit, over-tipped him, and headed back towards the beach pad. What did I do? I played that sentence over and over 'til I reached Gage's place. I went in, selected a sexy short sundress, and put myself together to surprise him.

A few hours later, Gage texted me and told me he was on his way back. I checked my hair and outfit for the hundredth time. I sprayed on more perfume. I was excited to surprise him. Piss off, little iChat girls. There's a new bombshell in town.

I heard the front door slam shut. It took me by surprise. I went to the staircase to meet Gage. He dropped his bag at the end of the staircase.

"What did you do with the other woman?" he said. He licked his lips. "You look sexy."

"I wanted to surprise you. Do you like it?"

"I like." He kissed me on the cheek, then grabbed my hand and pulled me to the bedroom. "We better be quick, my girlfriend might find us," Gage whispered in my ear as he ran his fingers through my dark locks.

It was worth it. I had his attention. Gage pulled at my sheer dress, giving it a slight tear as he rolled it up from the bottom to my waist. I leaned in for a kiss. He grabbed my waist and spun me around. He then bent me over the oversized king bed and pushed my legs open. I lost my breath in surprise. Gage unbuckled his belt and restrained my wrists together above my head with it. He then pulled down his dress pants. As I heard them hit the floor, I tried to pull my legs together, but Gage wouldn't let them budge. He stood between my legs, pants down. He licked his fingers and inserted them into me from behind. Ah. I closed my eyes. He thrusted a few times. With his other hand, he grabbed my hair.

"You like, Alexandria?" he asked as he pushed his fingers in and out of my pussy. All I could say was, "Ah."

Gage grabbed his hard cock, stroked it a few times, then inserted it into me. I could not move from the restraints and his body weight. I pushed upwards in motion with him. After only a minute or two, Gage pulled out, moaned, and came all over my ass and back. I continued to lie there with hot cum dripping down me.

Gage moaned once more to himself as he walked to the bathroom to collect a towel. I laid there, wrists tied, hot cum on me and my vagina a little more stretched. He returned and wiped up his excitement, then unrestrained me and rolled me over. I rubbed my wrists and caught the towel he tossed at me as he headed to the shower. I guess he liked the change.

"You didn't even notice my pussy," I yelled to him as I made my way to the bathroom. "I colored it as well. Carpet matches the curtains," I laughed as I wet a second rag under the running water in the sink.

"Felt like I was cheating on my girl. What a thrill, Alexandria. Loved the surprise."

I smiled and walked over to the shower to join Gage. I stepped into the water. He kissed me on the head and stepped out, grabbing for his towel.

"Don't you want to wash off the excitement from my back for me, Mr. Heston?" I asked, disappointed.

"I'll get us something to drink. You clean up and I'll join you on the balcony."

Another solo shower.

It was refreshing to shower and hang out on the balcony, enjoying the ocean breeze once again. Gage set out a bottle of wine and two glasses on the patio table, but he had a phone call to take. I went ahead and poured each of us a glass of wine while I waited for his return.

Ah, this is a pretty good slice of heaven here at the beach. I felt more at peace. I wish I could share this with Nova, Tyler, and Trent, though. We would have a fucking ball. Music would be playing. Ty would be telling us wild stories of him on the road. It would be wonderful. I smiled, thinking of my friends.

Then I felt a little lonely. Gage is great and all. I seem to be reeling him in, little by little. However, this relationship seems like work to capture his attention. I moved in with him, I flew to Miami to make time with him, I dyed my hair to turn him on. I. I. I. ...I felt stupid.

I wished he would linger in the tub with me, like Trent did one evening after my Vanity shift. Gage doesn't even know about Vanity. He'd kill me. Trent gets my creative side and Gage is accepting of it...to a point.

Hmm. What am I stewing about? Do I miss Trent? I'm not alone, but I feel lonely with Gage. Why won't the asshole kiss me with a bit of passion, like Trent? Instead he flips me over on my stomach, pulls my hair, and ejaculates all over my back. Ugh. I sighed as I stared at the waves crashing on the sand. I then felt a presence behind me.

"What are you contemplating about, my dark beauty? By the way, I like your hair dark. The blonde seemed to capture too much attention. I wasn't comfortable with that."

Wow, was that an 'ass-backwards' compliment or what? I smiled and handed him his glass of wine.

"What were you thinking about, Alexandria?" Gage asked for a second time.

I took a deep breath. "Well, first, I truly love this view of the ocean. I get lost in my thoughts, staring at it. And second," With a nod, Gage encouraged me to go on, "Well, I miss Tyler." I felt my stomach turn. "You told me when I moved into the penthouse with you that you would make sure that I see him and the guys from the band. I miss my friends." I felt sad as I took another sip of my wine.

"Look at you, Alexandria. You have a filthy rich boyfriend, a penthouse in Dallas, and a beach pad here in Miami. You also have many connections at your disposal for more projects."

I interjected, "What projects? You gave me one."

Gage continued, "Plus, you met Luke. You have my friends now. It's time to grow up. Little band boys aren't doing you justice. Maybe one day, you'll run the company with me."

I bit my tongue and stewed on that for a moment. The music business would be awesome to dive into, but I wouldn't run it. I'd be the trophy wife with dark hair and long dresses, entertaining clients at dinner parties. I see my whole future mapped out in front of me. I reached for the bottle of wine.

"Here, let me pour that for you." Gage refilled my glass and lifted his glass to toast me. "My beautiful Alexandria. A little stubborn, but she'll come around. To us." Gage clanked my wine glass but I didn't return the gesture.

When Gage noticed I didn't respond, he let out a sigh and slammed his glass on the table. "You want to see pretty boys? Fine, they'll be playing at the Miami Winter Music Conference in a few weeks. I'll set you up with passes and we'll make a weekend out of it." He stood up to leave the balcony.

Relieved, I yelled back towards the condo, "Thank you, Gage. I appreciate it."

Gage slithered away into his office and I sat there on the balcony, enjoying the waves and my thoughts of WHIP.

CHAPTER TWELVE

A few weeks breezed by. The winter music conference is coming up this weekend in Miami. I checked my cell to see when Nova was landing. I was so excited to see her. I missed her so much. Gage was in and out of Miami the past few weeks, so I had a lot of time to myself to stew about my friends. Nova could sense I was lonely. She didn't hesitate to accept the first-class ticket Gage bought for her to spend the weekend with me. I paced the balcony, watching the time crawl by as I awaited her arrival.

The doorbell suddenly rang, and I ran like a bat out of hell to greet my friend at the front door. I opened it, and the two of us just screamed. We grasped each other in the tightest hug we could stand.

"Ola, senorita!" Nova hollered. "Girl, the beach did you some good. You are so fucking tan, Mama. And brunette! What happened?"

I smiled and hugged her once more. "I had to make some changes to keep Gage's attention. Plus the tan. Well, all I do here is lie out. I'm promised a graphic gig but there is always some excuse why he can't grant me some work." I frowned.

"None of that! We have plenty of time to gossip about Mr. Heston and his controlling ways." Nova waved her hand at me. "I knew you were lonely so I brought you a surprise." She stepped outside the door for a moment and returned with a carrier in her hand.

"Ernie!" I squealed as I heard a meow from the cage. I immediately set the carrier down and opened the cage door. Ernie ran out. I scooped him up and kissed him all over as he purred. "Oh, Nova. I needed this. I need Ernie and I need you. Thank you." I started to tear up as I swayed with Ernie in my arms.

Nova smiled warmly at me, picked up her suitcase, and asked, "Where to, beach bunny? Show me my room." I squeezed Ernie once more, then carried him up the stairs, leading the way to the guest bedroom.

After settling her into her room, Nova and I decided to hit the beach for a few hours. We laid out on an oversized pink flamingo beach blanket and couldn't stop gabbing with one another.

"I sure missed you, Nova. I miss my friends."

"I know, girl, but this is an exciting chapter for you. Look at all Gage can give to you. You are very lucky. I'd dye my hair dark too, for a man like that. Say, when am I going to see him again? I'd like to thank him for the airline ticket." She rolled over onto her stomach to tan her backside. "This is heaven, girl. The beach is amazing. I feel so good, soaking up these hot rays. Dallas is still cold, girl. Yuk." Nova looked over at me. "You okay?"

I smiled. "I'm good. You will see him and Luke tonight at dinner." I rolled my eyes.

"Luke? Who's Luke, Alex?" Nova questioned me.

"Luke is Gage's supposedly best friend. They are two fucking peas in a pod. Damn Bert and Ernie." Nova howled at the Muppet reference. I went on. "Yes, these Muppets dine together all the fucking time. They gossip like two schoolgirls, and they eat off each other's damn plate! It's the strangest thing!"

Nova couldn't stop laughing. "Maybe you should dress up like Big Bird or something. He's a kinky fucker, isn't he?"

"Not really. Just dominant. We fuck, yes. No passion, no kissing, no snuggling. I massage him. I blow him. It goes on and on. Kind of strange, Nova."

"Sounds perfect to me. I'd massage and blow for this beach pad."

I rolled over to tan my backside as well and closed my eyes. "Nova, that's because you don't want a connection with someone. You want their PIN number." I laughed, but deep down I knew it was true. Sad, but Nova is pretty independent on her own. She uses men and moves on. I crave intimacy. "Can I be honest?" I felt an urge to confide some more in Nova.

"Yes, Alex, that's what I'm here for." She squinted her eyes to shield the sun as she waited to hear what I had to say.

"I miss Trent." There it is—the honest truth. I missed Trent.

"Girl, I knew it! The man in the band. It's okay, but remember that band man is on the road. Maybe you can have a fling tomorrow night at the show?" Nova purred.

I would love that, but I was too scared to run around on Gage. I dropped the subject and continued sunbathing.

*

Hours later, Nova and I were gussied up and ready to go to dinner with the Muppets.

"Nova, do I look okay?" I asked as I looked into the mirror. Nova was sitting Indian-style on the bathroom floor, fixing her makeup.

"I have no idea what the fuck you're wearing, but if it makes Gage happy tonight, wear it. I want no drama. I want to have a nice dinner and leave a good taste in his mouth for tomorrow night. I know he's letting you off the leash to see WHIP tomorrow. I don't want to rock the boat, Miss Little House on the Prairie," Nova laughed as she tugged on my sundress.

"It's a sexy, classy dress, Nova. Gage bought it for me," I defended my clothing option.

"It's fine, girl. He will definitely hate my attire tonight, but fuck it. I'm not his property. You are. Ha-ha."

"Piss off, Nova. Not cool."

Nova then stood up and hugged me to make everything all right again. We grabbed our purses and met Gage in the living room.

"Wow, you girls look amazing." He walked over to me and kissed my head.

"Awe," Nova approved.

"Shall we go?" Gage led us to the car. As I walked past the Mercedes logo on the vehicle, I gave it a tug and glanced at Nova. She laughed. I knew she caught my Vanity reference. I loved sharing that little secret with her. I at least have the upper hand on something in this relationship with Mr. Heston. While he had dating profiles and a vast amount of condoms in his suitcase, I had Vanity.

We arrived at the usual South Beach sushi restaurant Bert and Ernie loved to dine at. It's an ego trip for them, since the hostesses and waitresses fawn all over them, but whatever. I had Nova tonight. She was my rock. We were directed to our usual oceanfront table, where Luke was already waiting for us. Gage had Nova and me on each arm as we approached the table.

"Twin Texans tonight, Mr. Heston?" Luke grinned as he stood up to greet us.

"This is Nova, Alexandria's best friend. She will be dining with us tonight."

Luke put out his hand to greet Nova. Then the four of us settled in as Luke waved for the waitress to come over. Nova leaned into me.

"This view is amazing. Love the vibe here, girl," she giggled as she placed her hand on my lap and squeezed my leg. Gage noticed, gave me a dirty look, then went back to conversing with Luke.

Nova and I ordered edamame to start with our saké. Gage and Luke derailed into their own conversation once again. I nudged Nova's leg with mine as I looked over at the two of them.

"See what I mean? Not even here. At least I have you to entertain me tonight."

Nova licked her lips and grabbed my dress. "What do you got under this dress, little girl?" she whispered in my ear. "Tan pussy?" I laughed. Luke and Gage were so self-involved that they didn't even sense the flirting. "Why don't you dance with me?" Nova asked. She gulped her saké, stood up, and grabbed my hand. "Gentlemen, we are going to dance to this awful house music. We'll be back in a minute."

Gage nodded to let me know it was okay. I took her hand as we made our way to the dance floor. Ah, I felt free for a moment. I looked up at the red sheers flowing and then closed my eyes and took it all in as I swayed on the dance floor. I knew Luke would keep Gage occupied, so I could enjoy Nova. We danced our hearts out for at least five songs until Nova hollered in my ear.

"It's getting crowded. Let's hit the restroom." I agreed and grabbed her hand as she led the way. As soon as we made our way into the empty powder room, Nova locked the door and pushed me against it. "Now listen here, tan pussy." I laughed. "You have me tonight. I know bump on a log isn't very passionate, due to the kiss on the head he gave you earlier. I'll indulge you with a little passion."

Nova then leaned in and pressed her soft lips to mine. I opened my lips as she inserted her wet, sweet tongue into my mouth. She circled her tongue a few times, then pulled out and licked my lips. I lost my breath for a moment. She traced her tongue over the top lip, down to my bottom lip, giving it a slight bite. I could feel my bottom lip swell. She then slowly kissed me once more until someone trying to get into the room knocked on the door. We broke from our kiss. We both were startled from the knock and laughed. Nova reached behind me and unlocked the door.

"Thank you, Mercedes."

"You're welcome, Angel. Now that's out of the way, let's return to Sesame Street and see what those Muppets are up to." We both smiled at each other. I could taste a hint of sweet cinnamon left in my mouth from our kiss. I smiled and followed Nova back to the table.

Arriving back at the table, I could sense we weren't missed, due to the hostess sitting on Luke's lap. Gage was signing the bill.

"Are you dancing queens ready to go?" He didn't even look up as he asked the question. He continued to sign and slipped the hostess some money as she leaped off of Luke's lap and scurried away.

"We didn't even order our entrees, Gage," I pleaded to stay longer.

"Well, you girls were having a good time. I figured you were not hungry. Luke needs to get going, he has a date."

I rolled my eyes. "The hostess?" I asked.

Gage stood up and grabbed my arm. "Collect your purse and your friend. Do not embarrass me. We are going home," he ordered.

I rubbed my arm, picked up my purse, and looked at Nova. "Ready, girl?"

Nova gave me a sad look and nodded.

The car was silent as the three of us rode back to the beach pad. I felt embarrassed by the way Gage treated me at the restaurant in front of everyone. Arriving home, Nova followed me up the stairs. She went into the guest room, I went into the master, and each of us got out of our dinner attire. I felt a tear roll down my cheek as I changed into a comfy tee and gauze beach pants. I wiped my eyes, took a deep breath, and met Nova on the balcony.

"Are you hungry, girl? I could make us some eggs," I said.

Nova turned around and looked at me. "Maybe in a bit. Dude, where did that come from? Your arm okay? That wasn't cool," Nova said.

I sat on the recliner and pulled my knees into my chest. I had nothing to say about it. "I'm so ready to see Ty tomorrow," I said, changing the subject immediately.

"Me too," Nova agreed. "Is Gage tagging along?" she inquired.

"For a bit. He needs to speak with a couple of people from the label and the tour manager. But we'll be free to roam. I promise." I know I didn't sound convincing, but I tried.

*

The next morning I awoke to the ever-loving sounds of Ernie in my face.

"Morning, love bunny. You must be hungry." I petted Ernie for a moment, then sat upright, scratching my bruised arm. Anger washed over me for a minute as I recalled how Gage was an inconsiderate prick last night. I then huffed as I drew myself out of bed and headed to the kitchen to fetch cat food. When I entered the kitchen, Gage was standing there, drinking his coffee.

"Morning, Alexandria," he greeted me. I cringed for a moment. I pulled open the big stainless refrigerator door, beginning my search for cat food. I felt him come up behind me and kiss my head. "I said good morning," Gage repeated.

"Good morning," I grumbled back. Gage let out a sarcastic, "Hmm," then scurried back to his office. I was mad but I couldn't let it sour my day. I have Nova here with me, and we'll be seeing Tyler tonight. I got butterflies in my stomach, which energized me. I skipped back to Ernie to deliver breakfast.

After Ernie cleaned his plate, I returned to the kitchen to see Nova fumbling with the coffee maker.

"Girl, is this thing from outer space? Why is every gadget crazy big and crazy complicated to work?" Nova laughed as she started pushing random buttons on the coffee maker.

"Girl, you love crazy big gadgets. Don't be a hater."

Nova rolled her eyes and responded, "Mr. Heston better have a big gadget or I don't know what all the fuss is about with him. And his upper-class attitude."

I sighed. "Well, we'll be in the no-class zone tonight, baby."

We both screamed, "WHIP me, baby, tonight," as we laughed, slapping each other's ass.

"Take it easy," Gage reprimanded us as I stuck out my tongue to Nova. "You know, girls, we'll have to leave early to head out to the show tonight. I have a few hands to shake, then you birds can be free," Gage said as he set his coffee mug into the sink. "Alexandria, I'll set you up with passes. Do you need me to arrange a ride to pick you up?" Gage tried to sound sweet.

"Awe, G-man. Letting my girl off the leash for a bit tonight?" Nova teased Gage. "We'll be fine. We're going to watch the show, attend the after-party and see where it all takes us. Gage, I have a few friends of my own that I'd like Alex to meet. I'll take good care of her, I promise." Nova stuck her tongue back out at me. I blushed, feeling like I was asking Daddy for his approval.

"Sure, Nova. You have my cell if you need it. Alexandria, please come into my office. I'd like to have a word with you." I gulped, glanced at Nova, then followed Gage into his office like a puppy dog. I wanted to stay on his good side. I did not want to ruffle any feathers before this evening's excitement. I do adore Gage but this is important to me. I needed to see Ty. As I closed the door behind me, I felt a sense of panic.

"Alexandria." Gage startled me. I was staring off at the enormous picture window facing the water.

"Gage," I replied, as I focused my attention on him once more.

"First off, I'm sorry. I was abrupt with you last evening. Second, here are a few passes for you girls. Also, here is the number to the security team working the event, if anything goes awry. And here is some money. Use it to taxi around, whatever. Please be careful. I know how Nova can get." He gave me a stern look.

I walked towards the desk to collect everything. "I'll be okay, Gage. This isn't my first time going to the rodeo. I have been to concerts before." I smiled at him and he smiled back. I felt a wave of relief wash over me.

"Okay, beautiful. I'll be ready to go in a few hours."

I nodded, then scurried off to find Nova.

The screen doors entering the balcony were open and the breeze was stirring around the house. Ah, I love that fresh scent the ocean delivers. I stood there, inhaling for a moment as I began to calm down. Suddenly, I felt a pinch on my ass. Nova dashed by me, heading out to the balcony.

"Let's sunbathe a bit, to give us a healthy beach glow before our night begins," Nova hollered to me. She was setting up her beach towel to cover the recliner.

"I'm coming." I smiled and joined her on the balcony.

A few moments later, a shadow fell over my body,

jarring me awake. I opened my eyes to see Gage standing there.

"Hey," I said, shielding the sun from my eyes.

"Hey, I'm heading out for a bit. Get some sun, lunch, and be ready to go by four."

"Okay." I stood up and kissed him on the lips, then returned to the recliner. I knew a moment wouldn't pass until Nova had to chime in.

"Girl, are you feeling better? What was the chat about? Actually, I don't want to know, do I?" she said and then tossed her tanning oil at me.

"Hey." I picked up the oil and sniffed it. I loved the coconut scent—it smelled like vacation. "Yum. I do need to settle down." Nova got to her feet. "Where are you going, girl?" I pouted.

"Over to you, to settle you down. What did you bring to smoke?"

"Hey," I said.

Nova laughed. She dropped to her knees and crawled up to my recliner. She then shushed me as she spread open my legs. "Relax, girl. Lean your head back and relax," she said. She tugged at my bikini bottom and untied the right hip. I allowed the pantie to fall open. I let out a breath. Nova tickled my landing strip of pubic hair. I looked behind me to make sure Gage wasn't spying. Then, she moved her finger to massage my clit up and down a few strokes as I let out a few more deep breaths. Nova continued, "Heston has left the house. Relax and have a good orgasm for yourself. It'll flush last night's bullshit out and recharge you for tonight."

I did what I was told and let my spread legs loosen up as Nova began stroking my clit with her tongue. She sucked on it a few times before inserting her soft finger inside me. I groaned, feeling the hot sun on my body. Nova fingered me slowly as she sucked my sex. I let her softly lick and lick as I felt my sex throb. I was enjoying this as much as Nova. She moaned once and told me how making me wet was turning her on. She stroked a minute longer and I released all that negative energy as I came hard on her finger. Oh my God, I was in heaven.

A few seconds later Nova wiped her finger on my beach towel. I pulled her up to me and she kissed my lips.

There, Alex. Let that bastard go. Good times ahead tonight. She sipped her iced tea then returned to her recliner to sunbathe. I lied there, bikini bottom open, legs spread, soaking up the rays of the sun.

A few hours passed as Nova and I showered, ate, and got ourselves all gussied up for the evening.

"Thigh highs and smoky eyes!" Nova hollered as she stood in my bathroom doorway. We both smoked out our eyes. We put on trashy, form-fitting black dresses. We slipped into black fishnet stockings to round out the attire for the evening.

"Damn girl. We look hot," I approved of our selection as we both stood in front of the mirror in my bathroom, admiring one another. "I know I'll get the eye roll from Gage, but fuck it. Feels good to have my moment back in the sun. I want to look good for WHIP tonight."

I licked my lips as Nova replied, "You did have your moment in the sun this afternoon."

I blushed for a moment and said, "Girl, incredible work, I must say."

"Thank you, doll. Anytime, girl. Anytime," Nova said as she slipped on her other heel. We both were ready for our evening.

As the three of us walked to Gage's car, I could feel a hard stare burn right through me. Gage opened the passenger door and I slipped into the front seat. I no longer cared. He then opened the rear door to allow Nova to slip in. He said nothing more than "huh" as he shut her door.

"Remind me again. What is the attraction to this man?"

I looked at Nova in the mirror as I checked my makeup. "Well, our attire is not what Gage would have chosen for us, but he knows it's a girl's night out. So, he's keeping his opinion to a grunt," I said as I fussed with my eyelashes.

Gage got into the driver's seat and started up the car. The stereo was already on NPR or some snooze talk radio station.

"You mind if I put some tunes on, Gage, as we head over to the venue?"

Gage did not reply. I scanned the stations until I found the Killers. I turned up the volume.

Nova and I started shouting.

"Cause somebody told me that you had a boyfriend, who looked like a girlfriend, that I met in February..."

We were having a ball, and not going to give a fuck if Gage was in on it or not.

We finally pulled into the gate at the rear of the venue. Gage showed our passes. We were given a parking pass and directed where to go.

"Look at that swanky service," Nova purred. "Thank

you for the mad hookup, Gage. No way in hell was I strolling down Collins Avenue in stilettos."

Gage replied, "You girls are welcome. Just head into the venue with me. I'll meet with whomever and you guys make your way backstage."

I felt butterflies barreling in my stomach again. Tyler! The three of us got out of the car. Nova and I fixed each other's dresses, and we all headed towards the artists' entrance.

Gage began shaking hands the moment we entered the building.

"Nova, this venue is a lot bigger than the ones in Dallas," I said. I was excited but felt a bit nervous for the guys.

"This is good for them, stepping up into the big leagues. A few number one hits and holla! You're in," said Nova.

I agreed, nodding as I took in all the active stagehands moving about backstage. "Big leagues mean big egos," I said, smirking to the roadie as he rolled a road case right past us. Nova and I kept walking until she squealed, dropped her purse, and jumped into some older man's open arms. The two of them hugged, kissed, and exchanged compliments until I met up with them, carrying Nova's purse.

"Alex, this is Silver Fox. My Miami connection. The man about town. If you ever need anything? You need to know Silver Fox," said Nova. I extended my hand to the silver-haired, impeccably dressed, handsome man. He took my hand and kissed it.

"I've heard so much about you, Alex. Welcome to Miami," said Silver Fox. He did not look like he belonged at a WHIP concert. He looked like he stepped out of a Dos Equis commercial. "What is your plan, girls? I'm shaking a few hands, distributing some candy to the rockstars. Then, are we meeting at my place for an after-party?"

My eyes were wide as I watched Nova and Silver Fox make our plans for the evening. Candy, huh? Is this man a Miami drug lord? I don't want to know. As Nova and Fox ogled over one another, I looked around to see if Gage was anywhere. Huh? I guess he was letting me have a girl's night, without a chaperone. I was pleased.

"Okay, girl," Nova interrupted my thoughts. "Fox is going to do his business. We'll go meet up with WHIP, watch the show, then head to Fox's beach house for the after-party. No Gage. Bring the band boy," Nova teased, then turned and kissed Silver Fox on the lips as they solidified their plans. I was stuck on the last part of her plan: bring the band boy. I'm sure Tyler would tag along. If there was candy, there was Ty. Then, my heart dropped. Trent. I'm going to see Trent. I stood, chewing on that fascinating piece of info as roadies continued to roll by me. Suddenly, Nova grabbed my hand and pulled me into the direction of the elevator.

The steel doors closed to the elevator, reminding me of the Steel Door. I missed Dallas for just a moment. I felt out of place in such a big venue, with so many "important" people hovering around the band. I was getting used to the chicken heads, and now the vultures had set in. Everyone had a pass, a business card, a private number, and a fucking beach house. What the fuck happened? I was quiet as a group of us rode the elevator up to the suite.

No green room. They were suites. WTF. The elevator stopped. The steel doors opened and the crowd shuffled out. I grabbed ahold of Nova's hand and let her lead the way.

"I guess we follow the cattle?" Nova suggested.

"Moo," I responded as we headed towards another set of brass doors labeled "Grand Suite." This must be it. As the doors opened, I was taken aback by the beauty of the suite. It was definitely a step up from the grungy green rooms I was accustomed to from past WHIP shows.

"Who selected the color in this joint? Don't they know rockstars are dirty motherfuckers?" Nova whispered to me as I glanced around the room, taking it all in. Everything—I mean everything—was white with a gold accent. White, swanky leather couches and scattered ottomans took up most of the center space. Around the edges were gold tables loaded with white candles. Huge windows let in the light as the sun set between the palm trees. Huge sliding glass doors let guests out to an amazing terrace that gave you a front-row seat to Miami.

Ah, bliss. I was impressed. In the corner was a grand piano, white with gold trim. My starry eyes couldn't absorb much more without bursting. Then, I saw who was sitting on the white leather bench, playing that beautiful grand. Trent. He was playing *Overcome* by Live. It was perfect, subtle advertising that WHIP was in the Grand Suite tonight. My heart sank. I love that song, and I love him playing it more. It brought tears to my eyes. It's been months since I've seen Trent in the flesh. My legs wobbled a bit as I clutched Nova.

"Girl, this suite is amazing. Had no idea our boys were working so hard," Nova laughed. "Speaking of boys, Mr.

Boy Toy, Ty, is headed this way." Nova pushed me towards Tyler.

"Girrrrrl, my southern belle, I sure miss you!" Ty hollered as he swooped in, scooped me up, and began spinning me around.

"Let me take a look at you. Such a tall drink of water," I teased Ty. He stepped back and let me check him out. "Same ol' leather pants, I see. Y'all can't afford a personal shopper yet?"

Ty stepped back in towards me, kissed me on the lips, and then hugged me once more. "Alex, we have to powwow soon. I have so much to tell you. This tour is fucking grueling, but amazing at the same time, and...wait. What the fuck did you do to your hair?" Tyler ran his hands through my hair.

"Don't ask. Feeling like I needed a change." I was quick to defend myself.

"No, Ty. Ask her who the changes were for," Nova interrupted.

"*Cha-cha-changes...*" Ty started singing. He walked over to a nearby champagne bucket. He withdrew a bottle and poured himself another drink. "As long as you're happy, girl. You could be bald, and you'd still be sexy to me. Would you like a drink, baby girl?" he asked. He poured me a drink, and we toasted to changes.

The room seemed to be a bit warmer, unless it was my anxiety taking over. It felt like WHIP-ettes, journalists, and band members were everywhere. I lost my breath for a moment. I made my way through the crowd and onto the terrace, letting out a deep breath as soon as I reached fresh air.

As I let out some air to attempt to calm down, I heard,

"Hey Angel, nice of you to come to the show tonight."

Angel? I'm too far from Vanity to hear that stage name. I paused, then turned around, and found myself facing Trent.

"Hi, Trent. I just needed a moment to collect myself. Seeing Ty, drinking champagne. I'm a bit overwhelmed," I said.

Trent nodded as he set his wine glass down on the railing. "I know what you mean. This entire experience has been intense. It's everything we have ever wanted, and there is still more to come," he said with that beautiful grin that I missed. I was happy for him.

"You guys deserve all this success and more," I replied.

"It gets lonely, sometimes. And a bit exhausting, dealing with Tyler on a daily basis, but we're all adjusting."

I reached out my arms as Trent opened up his, and we embraced. Everything always felt calmer with Trent.

What is with Gage? I stewed for a moment. A fucking hug, a fucking bit of affection would do our relationship a world of difference. I quickly dismissed thoughts of Gage as I squeezed Trent once more.

Within moments of Trent and I reuniting, Tyler busted onto the terrace. He had a chicken head under one arm and a champagne bottle under his other arm.

"Awe, knock it off, you two love birds. Alex. My darling. Alex, I have a proposition for you. Would you and Miss Nova like to entertain our audience by dancing in our cage, on stage for the opening song?" Tyler asked as he sipped his champagne.

"There's a cage?" I laughed and looked over to Trent. He nodded his head. "Um, what do we get out of it?"

Tyler grinned that evil grin of his. "Baby, you get to be

up on stage with the hottest rock group out there right now."

I swallowed hard. "Did Nova agree to this?"

"That slut will do whatever you tell her to do. Anything for attention, she'll go for it. You guys look wicked sexy in your black dresses and thigh highs. We could not have planned it better," Ty said. He released the chicken head under his arm as he made his way over to me and kissed my head. "Thank you. It'll be a fucking blast," he howled, then was off to rejoin his adoring fans.

I turned towards Trent. "Guess I'm part of your show tonight," I said. My stomach spun for a moment.

"You'll be the main attraction. Ty will have some competition to deal with. You know that he does not like competition." Trent grabbed his wine glass and toasted to a fabulous show.

I excused myself, on a hunt for Nova to see if she would agree to this.

Twenty minutes later, the stage manager walked in and hollered to everyone that we were on in ten. I turned to Nova and squealed.

"You think Gage would mind if I was a part of the act tonight?" I asked, feeling myself panic.

"Why are you so worried about that man? You are young and beautiful. Now is the time to do what the fuck you want," Nova scolded me, fixing my smeared lip gloss.

"I know, but he doesn't even know about Vanity. I have so many secrets from him," I said, then bit my lip.

"Secrets? You guys have so many secrets between each other. I'm getting whiplash from all the deceitfulness between you two. Just have fun. Take my lead. It's one tune, so we'll sexy gyrate with one another, as if we were in Vanity. Let's do this for WHIP!" Nova looked me dead in the eyes and said, "Okay?"

"Okay," I answered, and began to feel excited. It's only one song. I'm going for it.

Nova and I walked hand-in-hand as we were led to the side of the stage. The huge metal cage was, to my relief, towards the back of the stage, behind the band. It was still centered, but behind the guys. This won't be so bad. It reminded me of the enormous birdcage I had to audition in for that smutty Vanity nightclub manager. Ew. I cringed at the thought of him licking his lips as he named me Angel. It's only for the opening tune. Then we're free to watch the rest of the show next to the hefty guy running the stage monitor console. Or we could join the crowd. My throat tightened up when Tyler grabbed my free hand. He pulled Nova and me into WHIP's group huddle.

"Guys, let's give them what they came for. These are our fans. This is for them. And girls? Opening tune is '*Whore Went Astray*,' so whore it up in the cage. Ooow!" Tyler screamed as he stuck his tongue out at me, and I smiled back.

All at once, the band cheered, "Whores and WHIP! Rock on!" The huddle broke apart and the room went black. I suddenly heard a roar coming from the fans. My heart jumped.

"Listen to that, girl!" I squealed to Nova. Dry ice smoke started to cover the stage. Dim lights led the pathway for the guys to head onto the stage and assume their position. "This must be our call as well," I said, clenching Nova's hand a little tighter. The two of us followed the band on stage and pulled ourselves into the cage. Red lights accented the metal platform the cage rested on. I withdrew my breath and swung my head and hair around as the drums started. *Bum Bum. Bum Bum.* I flipped my hair around once more and latched onto the metal bars to steady myself.

"Whores!" the crowd blurted out. *Bum Bum*, the drums went once more. The cage lit up and the crowd screamed.

"Let's play, Alex!" Nova hollered. I licked my lips as I held on to the metal bars. Nova pushed herself into me, licked my collar bone and up my neck. I purred and started swaying my hips to WHIP's music. Within seconds, Tyler grabbed the microphone and started belting out lyrics. I kept dancing as I watched the back of his head. He was erotic to watch. Pure David Bowie. He ran his fingers through his hair during the chorus. The girls all went weak in the knees. I then spun myself around and faced the backdrop curtain that had WHIP's album cover art hanging on a banner. I smiled with glee. I was proud to have designed that piece, and now this entire venue is looking at it and taking photos of it. Soon, it'll all be blasted via social media. My work is out there. I put something out there that people love. Knowing that gave me more energy to keep dancing in this ridiculous cage for these guys who loved my work. I spun back around to face Nova. The two of us put on the most seductive dance you could ask for. Within moments the song ended. Tyler complimented us by asking the crowd to scream for his WHORES. The crowd erupted. I grabbed ahold of the cage railing and guided myself out of the contraption. I walked past Trent, who gave me a wink, and headed backstage.

"What a fucking rush, girl!" I screamed to Nova. "Only a few moments, but we were a part of the show. How exhilarating!" I felt flushed, but I was on top of the world. I was on stage with my two best friends and my design. Even though Ty called me his whore, I had a blast!

"Let's clean up, grab a drink, and watch the rest of the show," Nova suggested. Just as I turned to head to the restroom to freshen up, I saw Gage standing there. My heart stopped.

"What the fuck was that, Alexandria?" Gage scolded me. I felt like I was six again. He grabbed my arm. "Excuse us, Nova," he said as he led us outside, onto the loading dock by all the tour buses. He spun me around and sternly asked, "What were you doing up there? You made a fool of yourself. You are supposed to be representing me, you are my girlfriend and..."

I cut him off. "I was doing Ty a favor. We were—"

Gage slapped my face. I was shocked as I held my throbbing cheek.

"Perfect song. You looked like a whore. How do you think that makes me look, Alexandria?" Gage demanded. I bit my lip and held back the tears. "Now, apologize to me and I'll let it go. Go back to your friends and mind your fucking manners. I'll see you tonight at home." Gage shook his head then placed his hand on the small of my back. He led me back into the venue.

Nova was still standing by the monitors when I returned. "You okay, girl?"

"I'm fine. Gage wanted to see what our plans were for the rest of the evening. He said he'll meet me at home."

"Umm, okay. Well, let's freshen up and watch the rest of WHIP's set." Nova gave me a look of pity, then sipped her drink and never said another word.

The show wrapped up. Everyone headed back to the Grand Suite to regroup and figure out the after-party plans. I was unusually quiet. I was stewing on Gage. I felt ashamed. I should not have been on stage with WHIP. Maybe I should go home to him. I'm burning all the trust between us. I'm scared I'm ruining something that is good for me. I need a grown-up relationship. I'm trying with Gage. I've worn the clothes he likes, excluding tonight's event. I've colored my hair because he thinks brunettes are more proper. He made it clear how he didn't like the attention that my blonde elicited. I also went to dinners and events with him, being personal and elegant.

I'm confused. I missed this part of my life. I missed my rock n' roll misfit friends. The artist within craves to have people like Tyler and Trent around. It inspires me. Well, I'll head to Silver Fox's house for the after-party. Then I'll need to be home at a decent hour to apologize to Gage. Once I put Nova back on a plane to Texas, things should go back to normal for the two of us. I let out a deep sigh, then scanned the room for Nova.

*

The band decided to join us over at the 'Man about Miami's' mansion. This was no beach pad like Fox led us to believe earlier. This is a fucking palace. I was sure I was in the wrong line of business. I walked in and, just like the Grand Suite, people were scattered everywhere. A local Miami DJ was spinning some tunes in the corner between the bar and the obnoxious pool that overlooked the ocean. Candles were lit. Topless girls roamed throughout the room, delivering alcohol or pills on a tray.

"Pick your poison," one well-endowed beauty offered to me.

"I'm good, sugar. Thank you," I said.

"Sugar?" she responded. "Honey, there's plenty of sugar, snow, whatever you may call it. By poolside, on the other trays." She pointed in the direction of the pool, where Tyler had already found a spot. He was snorting coke off the abdomen of a young pair of Latina girls. I shook my head.

"Thanks," I replied. As the girl scurried off, I made my way up the spiral staircase, absorbing all the amazing art that Fox had on display.

"Quite a collection, huh?" some shirtless man with a giant afro and gold chains scraping his bare chest asked me.

"I'm impressed. Don't know Fox very well, but so far I've noticed that he has impeccable taste," I said, smiling at the man.

"He sure can throw a party. Best-looking people in South Beach." He smiled, displaying one gold tooth among his perfectly straight teeth.

I laughed. "Guess I'm a South Beach babe for the evening," I said.

He nodded, looking my body up and down. "You sure are. Umm. You are—"

My laugh cut him off. I was starting to realize how uncomfortable this thug was making me feel. "Well, nice to meet you," I said, quickly ending our conversation.

"You didn't. I'm James. Nice to meet you." James lifted my hand, turned it over, and kissed my palm.

"I'm Alex, and I need to find my friend. Nice meeting

you, James," I said, rushing up the rest of the staircase.

I roamed in and out of rooms that all seemed to be occupied, searching for Nova. Where the fuck did she run off to? I went around a corner and down a low-lit corridor, towards a darkened room. I stopped in my tracks once I heard that familiar laugh. Nova. I called out her name and heard more giggling.

"Nova?" I called once more.

"In here, Alex," said Nova. I followed the voice through a door that led into Fox's master bedroom. There she was. My party girlfriend. She was spread out on Fox's bed, on her stomach. She was drunk. "Come in, whore." She laughed again. "Hey, Silver Fox. Don't you know you have the two famous WHIP whores in your bedroom?" she asked as Fox walked up to the bed and spread Nova's legs a bit wider. He tossed some coke on her ass like he was tossing flour around on a baking sheet. My eyes must have been huge when Fox turned to me, asking if I'd like a taste.

"No, I'm good," I replied, standing there. "Nova, honey. Are you okay?" I asked my drunk friend.

"I'm so good, Alex. This has been the best vacation I've had in a long-ass, time," she said. Nova was jumpy as Fox snorted a line down her ass cheek, then licked her opposing cheek. I felt like I should exit discreetly as I took a step back. "Don't go, girl. We're just getting started," Nova purred. Fox pulled out this butt plug with fringe, putting the entire object into his mouth to coat it with saliva. He then pulled it out and began to insert it into Nova's butt-hole. Nova moaned.

"You want to play, doll?" he asked me as I stared at Nova.

"You owe me, girl. I relaxed you this afternoon. Please

return the favor. I'm so horny, girl. This champagne coke cocktail is amazing," said Nova. I swallowed hard, then shut the door behind me.

"What should I do?" I asked. Fox got up off the bed and took my hand, leaving Nova spread with a butt plug in her ass. I took his hand. He walked me towards his dresser chest. Oversized mirrors hung on the wall above it. I looked in the mirror and saw candles flickering. I saw my best friend spread out on the oversized bed with an iron rod headboard. Fox disrupted my view as he stood behind me, holding a strap-on. I laughed. "Never wore one of those before. I always had the real thing," I said.

Fox smiled and said, "I have the real thing. I'm going to masturbate while you fuck Nova for me." My pupils must have dilated three sizes.

I took a swig of champagne from Fox's glass, then said, "Fuck it. Fuck Gage. We're fucking rockstars tonight!"

Fox laughed and said, "No, dear. You're fucking Nova tonight."

I am. What the fuck am I doing? I'm mad at Gage. So I rebel by fucking my friend with a strap-on? I'm insane. Certifiable. I took the strap-on, removed my dress, and slipped into the new ensemble—fishnets and a strap-on. I'm in porn heaven. I had to step into this vinyl pantie with a belt to keep it fastened. It won't slide down my hips due to the weight of this dick hanging. Pretty sizable dick, I must say. For a toy. Rubbery to touch, but pleasantly stiff.

"Does this accessory look good on me?" I asked Fox. He laughed as he turned up the music and slid into an adjacent chair. I could see from the corner of my eye that he was unfastening his belt. I ignored it. I crawled into bed, positioning myself behind Nova. Nova was swaying her hips.

"Come on, Alex. I want something bigger than this butt plug," she said. I laughed and pulled the plug out of her rectum. I then reached over to the bedside table and grabbed her champagne. I took a sip, drizzled some over my strap-on, then bent over to Nova and kissed her with my champagne-filled mouth. Champagne dripped from her mouth and down her neck as she moaned. "Please fuck me. Fox won't fuck me. He never fucks anyone. He gets off watching. Don't fret. He'll leave you be," she said.

I swallowed more champagne, then tossed the glass. I felt warm and sexy. I took the champagne-drenched dildo. I opened Nova's slippery pussy and inserted the strap-on. She moaned as I slowly but forcefully fucked her. I felt dominant. Is this what it feels like for a man when he's fucking a woman? I fucked her doggy-style as Fox sat in the chair, quietly stroking his cock. I was turning him on as well. I went in and out of Nova a few more times until she came hard, screaming, "Oh, girl, this is fucking amazing!" I pulled out and Nova collapsed on the bed. I then saw Fox cumming all over himself as he stroked to finish his orgasm as well.

Wow, I was exhausted. I stepped back, stepped out of the strap-on, and grabbed Fox's shirt on the floor. I then walked to the bed, spread Nova open as she lay on her back, and wiped off her excitement. She sat up and kissed me hard.

"Girl, that felt amazing. You gave it to me like a man!" she said. We both laughed. I continued to lay a good while with Nova on the bed 'til her high started to come down.

"Where's your dress, Nova? Let's go get some breakfast. I'm famished," I said.

Fox walked us down the stairs arm-and-arm. We were

all glowing. As Nova was saying her goodbyes to Fox, I headed towards the pool to see Tyler once more.

"Baby girl!" Ty shouted as he watched me strut over to him in the pool. I crouched down poolside and rubbed my hands through his hair.

"You drowned rat. Are you having a good time, rockstar?" I said, smiling at my intoxicated friend.

"The chicken heads are taking care of me," he replied.

"I see that," I said as I noticed a few other women had joined the pool party, all swimming nude. It looked like the set of *Boogie Nights*. I huffed a moment. "Ty, are you heading back to the hotel soon?" I asked, a bit worried. "I'm heading out to get food, and then heading back to Gage's with Nova."

Tyler rolled his eyes. "I'll go with you girls. I can have chicken heads anytime, in any city. But I'm in Miami with my best friend. So I'll take off with y'all," he said. He kissed the girls goodnight and stepped out of the pool, naked. I handed him a random towel. He covered himself up and went to fetch the bassist to tag along with us. I guess Trent never showed.

"Are any other band members leaving with us?" I asked Tyler.

"No, it's cool. Just the two of us came to the after-party. The other dudes stayed behind."

"Okay," I responded. I wrapped my hand around Ty's waist as Nova wrapped hers around the bass player's. We headed out of Fox's pad, down to the all-night café down the road.

"This reminds me of the Green Room in D-town, baby girl. I miss our powwows after our late-night parties and band practices. Don't you?" Tyler said. He was still amped up as he lit his cigarette and played with the assorted jellies on the table. I smiled as I reviewed the plastic menu we were handed when we were seated.

"I'm famished," Nova said, leaning back into the cold, orange booth. "What an evening, guys. I danced, I partied, I got laid. Who's the rockstar here?" Nova flashed a naughty grin to me, and, of course, Tyler picked up on it right away.

"Sorry I called you girls whores on stage, but you played the part well. You fucking grabbed the attention of our fans, and they loved it!" Tyler swirled his spoon in his coffee. "Who fucked you, Nova?" He started fishing.

"Never mind that," I interrupted.

"No, I want to know."

"It's between us girls." I gave Nova a look to drop it.

"Yes, it was between us girls," Nova agreed.

"You sluuuuts," Tyler scolded. "Well, I was laid before the show, after the show, and got blown at the pool at Fox's pad. I sure like that crazy motherfucker. He sure can throw a party. He disappeared, though," said Tyler, and I started to laugh.

"Here's your eggs, frontman." I pushed a dish over to Ty as the waitress served our table. I was beaming as I sat there staring at Tyler and his eggs. "I'm so proud of you," I said as I smiled at Ty.

"Thank you, I'm loving every moment of this, Alex, every fuckin' moment."

I nodded. "You found it. You found your way into this crazy world. You're doing it, rockstar." I blew him a kiss.

"You will too girl, your design is a hit, tonight you were WHIP's infamous whore for the show—I mean what else do you want?"

I laughed then rubbed my cheek as it still had a slight sting to it. I never mentioned the slap to Tyler; he would not stand for it. "I miss you, Ty."

"I love you, Alex, it means the world to me that you were here tonight...really, it did."

I held back my emotions as I knew after breakfast I would be saying goodbye once more.

After breakfast, we all said our goodbyes. WHIP was heading out that afternoon to resume the east coast tour. I was taking Nova back to the airport later in the day, and then I'd be all alone again. I wondered what Gage had planned for us, if he wasn't still cross with me.

The taxi parked in front of Gage's beach house and waited as Nova and I dragged ourselves out of the car. We looked like a couple of hussies, strutting the walk of shame as we rolled into the house. Fishnets torn and uneven, dresses all wrinkled, smoky eyes smeared. We were a sight, for sure. When we made our way up the front stairs towards the kitchen, I hollered out, "Hello?" and got no response. Nova went straight to the guest room and collapsed on the bed. I went to the master bath to wash off the night. I was bushed. I started peeling off my clothing. I stood there, looking in the bath mirror. Through the reflection, I noticed two dozen roses lying on the bed comforter. I felt guilty. Or maybe Gage felt guilty. Either way, guilt was consuming our breathing space. I walked over to the beautiful red roses, picked up the card, and opened it.

"Beautiful Alexandria. Let's wash last evening's episode.

Please have dinner with me on my boat tonight." His boat? I tried to recollect a boat. Whatever. At least he was trying to apologize, even though I'm sure he believes I brought on this episode. I'm too exhausted to mull over an episode right now. Shower, then bed.

CHAPTER THIRTEEN

A few hours later, I awoke with a major fucking headache. I made my way into the kitchen to start afternoon coffee and feed Ernie.

"Where's prince charming?" Nova asked, pulling herself up onto a barstool.

"I'm not sure. He comes and goes. And I don't pry. But he did leave roses in the bedroom for me, and invited me to dinner on his boat this evening."

Nova rolled her eyes and said, "Hand me a mug, girl. It's your funeral. Why are you keeping this toxic relationship going with him?"

"It's not toxic. I'm in a grown-up relationship now. I didn't consider his feelings. Or how it would look when I chose to dance on stage last night," I said, pouting a bit as I grabbed a coffee mug for myself. I was making excuses for Gage's behavior.

"Consider his feelings? Gag. Girl, he should be proud he has a wild, beautiful, creative girlfriend. I'm sure you're taking care of his every need. It's all about what it looks like to Gage, not happiness. Just the outer shell. What it looks like to everyone else, not you guys," Nova said. She was right. "I completely misjudged him," Nova confessed.

"I know! He's in the music industry, for Christ's sake. You'd think he'd be a bit edgier," I blared out loud. Nova nodded in agreement. "Well, I'll see how the evening goes and tell you all about it tomorrow. We'll have our coffee. I'll call his driving service, and I'll send you back to Texas in style. I wish you could stay longer, though."

"Me, too," Nova agreed. "But I need to get back to making money. Check on the condo, and check on my regulars. If I disappear for too long, the 'Vanity vultures' will come out and steal my customers. They are my bread and butter, girl," Nova said as she rubbed her fingers together, making the money sign. I understood.

After coffee, I went into the laundry room. I threw on a sundress I had hung in there to dry, flip-flops, and my sunglasses. Nova and I headed to the airport, where I said my goodbyes for the second time that day. I was sad.

"Girl, if you need me, if you need to come back to Texas and start fresh, you can room with me. We'll figure it out together," she said, kissing my head as I pulled her in closer and hugged her tightly.

"Thank you. I love you. Travel safe, and I'll call you tomorrow," I said. Nova agreed and made her way into the airport. I got back into the town car, rolled the window down, and waved as the driver pulled away.

Later that evening, Gage was still not home. I started my routine to get ready for our dinner. I went into the closet to select something appropriate and it looked like Gage had done that for me. There was a beautiful new dress hanging there with a note attached. It read, *"Leave the fishnets at home."*

I laughed. Duly noted. He was not a fan of the fishnets. I then went to grab my robe and noticed my closet was bare. Wait. I panicked. All my personal clothing—short dresses, rock tees, you name it—were missing. I didn't notice it earlier because I had grabbed my sundress from the laundry room. What the hell happened to my threads? I ran over to the bedside table to grab my cell and feverishly texted Gage. *We've been robbed. Clothes nabbers hit up my closet!* I waited. Then, *ding*, a return text.

Nabbers donated old threads. Shopping spree soon to update you with a more appropriate wardrobe, Gage replied.

I was pissed. I know my Aerosmith concert tee wasn't glamorous, but it had a story behind it. It was sentimental to me. All my cocktail dresses were gone. Only a few pieces hung in garment bags from that snotty boutique we visited when I first arrived in Miami.

"Not cool!" I fucking screamed. Ernie meowed, jumped off the bed, and ran out of the room. Okay, maybe he has good intentions. Or maybe he's a fucking control freak. He likes to dress his doll how he wants to, not allowing her to showcase her own individuality. I paused and took in a deep breath, then pulled the dress off the hanger. "Guess you are it tonight, unless I show up nude," I said to the dress as I changed for dinner.

✶

I arrived all put together for Gage at his boat. The marina, in and of itself, was breathtaking. All the pelicans and seagulls, floating freely about, soothed me. My spirits lifted as I found the dock, where another one of Gage's toys was parked.

"Step aboard, Alexandria," Gage said and smiled, extending his hand. I accepted it to get on board.

"Music business is good for you, Mr. Heston. Impressive," I said.

Gage nodded as I looked around the galley. "You look beautiful. Thank you for wearing that dress," he said, handing me a glass of white wine.

"It was the only item in the closet. I could have gone for option number two, which was nude, but I didn't want to piss you off," I said, and then gulped my wine. I tried not to make eye contact.

"Listen, Alexandria. You are beautiful, and I want to dress you with beautiful things. Is that so bad?" asked Gage. I felt guilty. There it is again. The common denominator with this relationship: guilt.

"It's very nice of you, but you didn't have to chuck my clothes," I responded, pouting in a low voice.

"Grow up and learn to accept my gifts. I'm trying here, Alexandria. Now, let's not argue about clothing. Let us have a nice dinner and enjoy one another, before I leave tomorrow."

"Leave?" I questioned him.

"I have work up north to attend to. I don't want to discuss it," Gage said. He refilled my glass, then headed up to the second level of the boat, where our table was set for dinner. He never wants to discuss anything. Ugh. I was frustrated but hungry, so I dropped the conversation and followed him up to the second floor.

"This can be all yours, you know. I'd love to share my things with you," Gage said and toasted me. He spun around the top deck of the boat. I smiled. I mean, isn't this what every girl wants? All the money you could imagine. A penthouse in the city. A beach house and a fucking boat? Not to mention a new wardrobe. I decided right then and there to knock off the shenanigans and try with Gage, despite his outbursts. "Alexandria, it's nice to have you all to myself. I told you, I don't share well. I'm glad the band is out of the way and on the road. The crazy girlfriend is shipped back to Texas. And I have just you." He homed in on me like a hawk and kissed my lips. "Well, you and your damn cat."

"Hey!" I was quick to defend. "Ernie isn't bothering anyone." I was defensive about my pet.

"I'm teasing, Alexandria. Relax. Here. Sit down, and let's enjoy our meal," Gage said. He pulled out my chair and I settled in, adoring the feast displayed in front of me.

Gage and I finished our seafood dinner. I leaned back in my chair, taking in the soft music playing, feeling the water we floated upon.

"What an amazing evening. The dinner was delicious. I'm really enjoying the scenery and the music. Would you like to dance with me, Gage?" After a few glasses of wine, I felt sexy. Staring at this gorgeous man across from me, on this amazing vessel, was driving me nuts. I wanted to dance.

"Dance?" he responded. "I don't dance." He shifted his weight in his chair, letting me know a dance was out of the question. His cell phone rang. "This is Gage," he took the call, standing and walking to the other side of the deck. I leaned back, dismissing the intrusion, and chewed on the "I don't dance" comment for a bit. Dismissing it all, I returned to admiring the seagulls, pecking away at something on the deck. I then overheard Gage say that he needed to go, that he was entertaining friends. He turned down the ringer and headed back to our dinner table.

"Entertaining friends? You mean girlfriend?"

Gage put up his hand and said, "Stop."

I mumbled "Friend" under my breath.

"Are you ready for dessert?" Gage asked.

I stared at the floor, mulling over his "Entertaining friends" comment. "Sure," I responded.

"Well." Gage stood up and reached out his hand. "Dessert is downstairs." I took his hand and followed him to his bedroom.

The master bedroom on the boat was for the master. It was stunning. Everything was maroon and marbled out. I'm sick of being impressed with all his stuff.

"Elegant," I commented as I looked around. Gage turned up one of the speakers in the room and turned towards me, starting to undress. He removed his white button-down shirt and his belt. I stood there, admiring the dessert menu on display. "Can I have anything on the menu?" I asked as I licked my lips, watching him peel away his clothing.

"Well, I fed you dinner. Now I'll feed you dessert. Open your mouth, Alexandria," Gage said. He grabbed my hair and lowered me to my knees. I obliged, even though I thought we would make love. It was a romantic evening, after all. Blow jobs are quick and dirty. I wanted a little more passion. "Open up," Gage said, a bit forceful this time. I opened my mouth and he shoved in his endowed hard cock. "You take this all, Alexandria. You've been a bad girl. You need to please me, so I can forgive you and all your bullshit this weekend."

"Uuuuh," I moaned as he pushed my head into his crotch, and I sucked him off. He came rather quickly. He then stepped away to grab a towel, and I leaned back on the floor, against the bed, humiliated. "I wanted to make love, Gage. Have any dessert left?" I hollered towards the bathroom.

"All that cum was icing, just for you, baby. I was your piece of cake." Okay...? "Aren't you tired from all the partying with your friends? Why don't you lie back and rest? The car service will bring you back to the house in the morning. We'll have coffee on the deck, before I take off." Ooh, coffee before he leaves. I'm stoked.

"Sounds good," I responded. Gage stepped over me and headed into another room made up to be his third office. "Good night!" I hollered.

"Rest well," he responded.

I scooped myself off the floor and headed towards his bath to rinse my mouth, pee, and grab one of his tees to sleep in. Once I crawled into bed, I felt a wave of exhaustion wash over me. I thought about Tyler, Trent, Nova, and my evening with them all as I drifted off into a deep sleep.

✽

Morning arrived in the usual Miami manner. The endless sun waking you up, refreshing you. I felt much better after some rest. I sat up and looked around. No Gage. Guess he's up and at it already this morning. I needed a moment to focus. I pulled myself out of bed and headed upstairs to find coffee.

"Did you rest well?" Gage asked, typing away on his laptop.

"Do you ever rest?" I responded as I made my way to the coffee maker.

Gage gave a subtle laugh. "I work," he said, and returned to typing.

"I see that. Last night's dinner was nice. Thank you," I said.

He looked up at me while I stood there in his t-shirt, sipping my coffee. "Nice bed attire," he commented. "I'm glad you liked it. Drink your coffee, grab your dress, and I'll have the driver waiting in thirty minutes to pick you up." I agreed, nodding my head. As I turned towards the steps to head back to the bedroom to gather my things, Gage grabbed my arm to stop me. "Hey, I was upset with how you looked and acted the other night. I don't give a flying fuck about Nova. I'm not in this relationship with Nova. So, I'm giving you a warning. This is not an unconditional love, Alexandria. It's based on certain conditions. You want to be my wife someday? You must play the role of girlfriend and lover just right. If this running-around-with-the-band phase isn't out of your system yet, you need to let me know right now." Gage still had a hold on my arm.

I got a bit defensive. "That 'band phase,' as you call it, are my friends, Gage. They are in my life, and they're important to me." I pulled my arm away as some of my coffee spilled onto the stairway.

"Based on certain conditions, Alexandria. I'm gone for a few days. You have plenty of time to get your act together. So we can move forward."

I huffed for a moment and shook my head without saying a word. Gage kissed my head and told me once more to gather my things.

*

The beach house was quiet as I roamed around it, feeling like a stranger in Gage's house. He told me he wanted to marry me. He told me his things were mine. But how come I feel like I cannot breathe? I'm experiencing anxiety like never before. Maybe I miss Texas. Maybe I miss my friends. I felt all alone in this place. As my throat started to close, I looked around the house. I suddenly grabbed my cell and my flip-flops. I flew out the door and headed to the beach. I needed fresh air. I needed open space to breathe. Just as I exhaled, my cell rang.

"Hello?" I answered, a bit out of breath.

"Alexandria, honey. Are you alright?" asked Mother.

"Yes, Mother. I'm walking towards the beach."

"Oh, how nice. That man is so good to you," she said. As she praised Gage, I felt my throat starting to close up again.

"How are you, Mother?" I interrupted, hoping she'd drop the conversation about Gage. I wanted to kick him off her pedestal.

"I'm fabulous, sugar. Your Father is well. We were just concerned about you. We wanted to see if Mr. Heston proposed yet?" I could hear her laugh and hope on the other end of the line.

"No, Mr. Wonderful has not proposed quite yet. Unsure I would accept the proposal. We're working out the kinks between us." I could feel Mother rolling her eyes.

"Well, if you know what's good for you, you'll take care of that man. He has everything you could ever want and need. Aside from money, Alexandria. He's very handsome. You go on and be a good girl now." I sighed as Mother reprimanded me over the phone.

"I'm trying, Mother. Look, it's hard to hear you. I'm outside by the water," I lied.

"Okay, then. You call me next week. I want a full report. Alexandria?"

"Yes, Mother," I responded.

"Don't make me worry about you."

"Okay, Mother. I love you."

"Uh-huh," Mother responded, and we both hung up.

"AHHHHHHH!" I screamed, startling the beachgoers around me. I ignored the crowd, found a palm tree in the sand, and parked my butt right under it.

A few hours had passed, and the sun was starting to set. The sky was many shades of orange, pink, and blue. Miami Beach was beautiful. The warm, salty air was intoxicating. It soothed me. I felt refreshed as I stood up and gathered my flip-flops. I needed to make my way back to Gage's.

After a long shower, I slipped into a white silk robe that Gage had purchased for me. I poured myself a glass of wine and headed out to the balcony to look at the stars. I hadn't heard from Gage all afternoon. I wondered how his business trip was going. I opened my cell to text him. I needed to text something sweet so he would forgive me. *Hey, this beach bunny is lonely without you.* I hit send, then sat back on the recliner, sipping my wine and staring at the stars in the sky. A few moments later, I received a return text.

Alone time is good for you. You need to muddle over things. I'll call you in the morning. Sleep tight. G.

Muddle my foot. I shut the cell and sipped more wine.

*

The next few days were quiet. I was starting to get bored. Gage needed to feed me another project, not just have roses delivered. It was a thoughtful gesture to show that I was on his mind, but I needed more. I ran along the beach every morning, cleaned the house, and attended to the cat. Ernie did help keep things in a routine for me. He made this place seem less lonely. After scooping the litter box, I decided to lay on the bed with Ernie and continue to mull. My cell phone rang. I saw Trent's name flash across my screen. The butterflies were awakened as I answered.

"Good afternoon, rockstar," I answered.

"Ha, ha," he answered. I heard his deep, beautiful laugh on the other end. "How are you, Alex? It's been a few weeks since we've spoken, so I thought I would check on you. Is it okay for you to talk?" Trent inquired.

"Oh, yes. I'm alone. How's the road? How are my boys?"

Trent smiled through the phone. I could imagine that intoxicating grin, just for me. "The road is lonely. Tour is amazing. Boys are somewhat behaving," he said. "Tyler is a wild one, though. This man has got to be Jim Morrison reincarnated."

I laughed and said, "Still in the dirty leather pants, I see."

Trent laughed as well and said, "Gross pants, but he eats pills at every meal, downing it with liquor. It's pretty intense."

"Well, I guess if he's playing the role, he needs to earn an Oscar for it. Ty's pretty tough. He's always been a partier. How about you?" I wanted to hear more about Trent anyway. Drunken stories of Ty bore me.

"I've been writing a lot on the road. I've been thinking a lot, too."

"Oh, yeah? About what?" I inquired.

"How big this all is going to get, and how I wished I had someone to share it all with," he answered.

"Well, you got me. I'll listen to your ideas. You can call me daily, to give me the play-by-play of everything WHIP is doing. Okay?" I asked.

Trent agreed. "That sounds good. Are you holding up okay?" He sounded sincere.

"I am," I said, paused, and continued, "I will be, I guess. Gage and Miami are a bit too intense for me. Nova is a bit wild. The last visit with her rocked the relationship boat for Gage and me. But it'll pass. I've had the place to myself, and I'm getting rather bored."

"I'm sorry to hear that," Trent said.

"I'll be fine. Do you have any projects for me? My creativity needs a shot in the ass. I miss drawing. Gage thinks it's a bullshit hobby, and doesn't want the mess in his place. So I've been drawing with my computer. Hey, I saw my design hanging on the stage at your show, and that really lit my fire!" I was excited to share my gratitude with Trent for selecting my design for WHIP's album cover.

"You are a really good artist. Don't let anyone tell you it's a bullshit hobby. Paint, write, draw until your heart's content. Creativity is what feeds you. Uncreative people don't understand that. They dismiss it all as a waste of time. But for us, the ones with the old souls, we need it to stay alive," he said. I agreed completely.

Trent and I continued to talk for what felt like an eternity. We couldn't control the passion and excitement that flooded out of us. We needed each other. I was lonely in Miami and he was lonely out on the road.

As my cell battery began to die, I said goodbye and promised to call tomorrow. I felt so much better as I plugged in my phone to recharge for the next call. I know my cell buzzed a few times during the conversation with Trent, but I dismissed it. I was not in the mood to check in with Gage. I'll return his call after another glass of wine. I don't want the two of us arguing that I did not accept his call. I'd finish my wine while thinking of an excuse for why I didn't pick up. I seem to do that a lot lately. I make excuses and tell white lies to Gage more often than not. But I felt I could be completely honest with Trent without any judgment, without any recourse. What's the deal? I just stewed.

*

The next few days were quiet without Gage. I had endless conversations with Trent. I felt like we were growing closer, as Gage and I seemed to drift apart.

I was talking with Trent one evening as he read me some newly written lyrics. He also sang a few WHIP melodies through the phone which made me feel beautiful. I was getting the personal attention I craved from Trent with no distractions.

"Alex, I wrote a poem that I think you and I could identify with. You with Gage and me with my Father." I fell silent. Trent ruffled a piece of paper over the phone and started to read. "It's called *'Kept inside.'*"

"Good title," I said while listening intensely.

"What can I think, how should I feel? Living like it's unnoticed is too hard and unreal. It's not me, push it aside. Guilty feelings you cannot forget nor hide. Not wanting to be hurt, I don't know whom to tell? Stress and misery has been putting me through hell." Trent paused. "Do you like it? I just started it."

"I like it," I replied. "Trent, I do not know what I got myself into here with Gage, but can I leave it at just that for now?" Trent agreed.

I didn't want to cough up any details about my and Gage's abusive relationship I was tangled in. All I really wanted was to escape with Trent for a little while and listen to his music and poetry. I might have needed this space to explore myself and find out what is truly good for me—not Mother, not Gage, not even Tyler, but me.

Gage checked in on occasion, but the conversations were brief, cold, and to the point. I'm expecting him to return tonight. I needed to clean up the place, shower, and put my face on for his arrival. I was told we were having a quiet dinner tonight. Then, there was some sort of barbecue this weekend, for the Fourth of July holiday. I don't like how Gage tries to push his friends on me. I'm uncomfortable in his "who's-who" crowd. But I agreed, so I'll be polite and do my part. Thinking of tomorrow's gala with his friends, I headed over to the wine rack. I wanted to make sure we were plenty stocked in that department. I'll need wine to get through any event with Gage's crowd.

The evening arrived quicker than I had hoped, but I was ready to see Gage. He'll appreciate the dress I've selected from my new wardrobe. I glanced over my selection once more in the mirror before grabbing my purse. I rushed down the stairs to greet Gage. The driver pulled up in front of the house. God forbid that Gage would get into a taxi cab. He stayed in the vehicle a moment, finishing up a phone call as I stood in the entry to greet him. I saw him look at me through the window, then look away to wrap up his phone call. I felt stupid as he glanced away. He then stepped out of the car, tipped the driver that unloaded his suitcase, and walked up to me, kissing me on the cheek.

"Good evening, Alexandria," he greeted me. He was in his usual business attire—a perfectly coordinated outfit selected by some busty suit sales lady. I gave her props, because he did look fine. I looked him up and down and greeted him back with a smile. "Hungry, pretty lady?" he asked me.

"I sure am. A man in a pinstripe suit on the menu?" I

answered. He smiled. I know he enjoyed the flirting; it kept his ego in check.

"We're meeting Luke for sushi in a bit. Are you ready to go?"

I pouted for a moment. "I haven't seen you in weeks, Gage. I thought a candle-lit dinner for two would be just what we need, after being apart for so long," I said. I let out a deep, disappointed sigh.

"I'm sorry, doll. I already made plans with him. It'll be nice. The three of us at our usual restaurant. Then, I promise you'll have me all to yourself for the rest of the evening."

I agreed as we set his suitcases in the entry, locked up the house, and jumped in his car to meet Luke. The car was quiet as we listened to talk radio once again. I pouted, dreading seeing obnoxious Luke. But I sucked it up. When we arrived, Luke was at our usual table by the water, a drink in his hand.

"Old-Fashioned for the handsome businessman," Luke ordered for Gage. "And a small saké for the southern belle." Luke stood up and shook Gage's hand, then they gave each other a man hug. I was greeted with a sarcastic smile. I know he hates me. Luke is insecure, and we fight each other for Gage's attention. Tonight, though, I do not have the energy. I sat back, enjoying the ocean breeze, sipping saké. Bert and Ernie can have each other.

Dinner dragged on. While the two Muppets shared food and conversation, I drank saké and secretly wished Trent was here with me instead of Gage. We would be laughing and holding hands. I was caught daydreaming when Gage tapped on my leg.

"Hey, are you ready to go?"

Startled, I finished my drink. I quickly ate my last piece of ginger to get rid of the sushi taste and responded, "Sure," as I stood up. I then gave a half-assed smile to Luke, turned, and headed towards the valet.

When Gage and I returned home, we were both quiet. I made my way to the bedroom to change.

"Wait," he hollered after me. "How about a nice massage to wind down the evening?"

Okay? I always give massages. Is he offering to return the favor this time?

"I'll grab the massage oil and meet you in the bedroom," I said. I got a sudden burst of energy. I fetched the oil like a good girlfriend and met him in the bedroom. Gage walked up to me, already in his underwear briefs. "Wow, you shed that suit fast," I said as I set the massage oil on the nightstand.

"I couldn't wait any longer to have you put your hands on me. You looked beautiful tonight." There he goes with flattery to get what he wants, and I always cave.

"Lie down, handsome. Let me rub all the stress away," I said. He smiled, giving me inspiration to rub him down. As I massaged Gage, I drifted off thinking of Trent. The guilt didn't startle me back into the moment as it usually did. I stroked upward and downward on Gage's back as he moaned his appreciation. It was soothing to me as well.

I worked Gage over from the back to the front. When I reached his penis, he saluted an okay to pleasure him. I was enjoying it. I slowly ran my hands up and down his shaft, making myself wet. I then threw my leg over Gage and saddled on top of him. He inserted his oiled dick inside me. I closed my eyes, fantasizing of Trent when we made love in my loft in Dallas, the first night we met. I imagined

Trent pulling his shirt over his head and exposing his inked chest. Then as I leaned against him, he slid his hands down my pants and gently fingered me. I continued to squeeze Gage's dick with my pussy as I imagined fucking Trent and not Gage. I worked it more thoroughly than when I used my hand moments ago. I continued thinking about pulling Trent's silky, long black locks as he breathed in my ear. Then we kissed so passionately that I lost my breath just tasting him while he made love to me. I kept fantasizing as I took my time sliding myself up and down Gage's throbbing cock, which was unusual for the two of us. I then came so hard that I think I shocked him with my enjoyment. Of course, he would take all the credit. He'd pat himself on the back. But I whispered, "Thank you, Trent," as Gage got out of bed to go clean himself up.

CHAPTER FOURTEEN

The next morning, Gage was up and about, getting things ready for his Fourth of July party. I rolled over on my back and let him scurry about as I replayed last night's massage in my head. Gage did have a beautiful cock, but my desire was building for Trent. I miss his embrace, especially the one he gave me when I came home from Vanity, completely wiped out. He just makes everything better. Gage startled me as he hollered into the bedroom that the coffee was brewing. I huffed for a moment, then headed towards the kitchen to retrieve cat food and caffeine. Daydreaming was over for the moment.

*

Later that day, the BBQ was set up on the balcony. The beer bottles were displayed in tubs of ice. Reggae music played in the background. I was in the kitchen, preparing a salad, as guests started to arrive. I didn't know anyone, maybe an associate or two of Gage's, but that was it. So I made sure I looked pretty. I wore my white gauze sundress, a white two-piece string bikini underneath, and my cork wedge sandals to match. I felt pretty. Which was good because, knowing Luke, there will be some women's competition at this picnic. I need to let these bitches know that Mr. Heston was spoken for. I chuckled to myself as Gage walked into the kitchen.

"Thank you for helping me prepare some of these side dishes. I hope you'll like my friends and colleagues. I know they'll adore you," he said. He kissed my head as he took the salad tongs out of my hands, smacking my butt with them. He thanked me once more for the massage. I felt like my good girlfriend's deed was complete. I grabbed a beer and headed out to the balcony to introduce myself.

After everyone settled in and ate, we waited for the sun to set. We were all going to walk over to the beach and watch fireworks. I excused myself. I went on a hunt for my cell phone to check my messages. Nova had texted that she was in New York City with a client of hers. Tyler had texted that he was with the guys in Arizona, partying in the desert, tripping on something.

Lastly, I saw a message from Trent. Trent texted that he wasn't tripping in the desert. He went home to Louisiana for the weekend. He was working on stuff in the studio and would meet up with WHIP in Atlanta. I guess all my friends were good. I know my parents were attending their usual golf outing at the country club. I'll call Mother tomorrow to listen to the latest gossip. I sat back on the vanity stool in the bathroom, kind of bummed that everyone was good without me. I shouldn't be jealous. I'm at a party that I needed to enjoy. Then Gage peeked his head around the corner and asked, "How's my girl?"

"Drunk. Checking my messages. Are we ready to head

over to the beach?"

Gage responded, "Yes. Please fix yourself up and get rid of the beer. It looks trashy. Meet me in the living room when you are ready." He flashed a stern look, for me and the beer. I gave him a salute.

"Aye, aye, Captain," I called out as he walked out of the bathroom. I did as I was told. I fixed my hair and makeup, put my cell away, ditched the beer, and brushed my teeth. I then made my way to the living room. Everyone was filing down the staircase to head to the beach. And yes, with beers in hand.

"It's a party. What the fuck, Gage?" I mumbled to myself, following the herd to the beach. Gage and Luke set down a few coolers and beach blankets. I stopped to remove my wedge sandals and put my feet into the warm sand. "Ahh, heaven," I said. I smiled at one of Gage's party guests. He gave me an off-putting look, then walked away. "Okay," I said. I then made my way to one of the blankets, grabbing a corner to park my butt as everyone else made themselves comfy. Gage, of course, was sitting with Luke and two blondes on one of the blankets. I waved to him as he continued acting like he was engulfed in whatever story the bimbo was telling. I didn't know her. In fact, I didn't know any of his girlfriends. He loves to give me a hard time about Tyler, but he seems to befriend every hostess, waitress, personal assistant, and boutique sales lady. The list goes on and on. I was tired of the act I had to put on around his friends. They always acted like they were better than I was. They would make a snide remark from time to time, which irked me. I turned around on my corner of the blanket and watched the fireworks display. I wish I was leaning back into the arms of some loving man. Not squishing my cheek on a corner of a beach blanket so it didn't get pinched by a crab.

When the fireworks ended, the crowd started to disperse and go their own ways. I helped with the beach blankets by shaking them out and folding them. I collected every one of them, then headed over to Luke's bimbo huddle. Dropping the blankets, I interrupted their conversation.

"Hey, guys. Y'all enjoy the show?" I asked. Everyone paused. The two girls gave me a dirty look as Luke introduced them. I blushed with embarrassment. Their names went right over my head.

Gage chimed in, "This is Alexandria." I felt like a third wheel.

"Are you heading back to the house?" I asked.

"Um, listen, Alexandria. I'm going to take Luke and his guests over to the marina. The girls would like to see my boat. I'll be home in an hour or so. You take the blankets back to the house. I'm sure you want some time to yourself. It's been a long day." Gage flashed another famous stern look down at me. I pouted, said my goodbyes, and excused myself. As I turned to make my way back home, I felt someone approach me. I turned as Gage grabbed my arm. "Does it give you pleasure to humiliate me? What is with the childish pouting? I'll only be a bit. So run along, and I'll see you at home." He then kissed my head, released my arm, and smiled at the girls and Luke. I gripped the beach blankets tighter as I made my way back to the house.

What the fuck? It's a holiday. Aren't boyfriends reserved for national holidays? I was working myself up.

Who the fuck were those two bimbos? He gave Nova and me a hard time about our thigh highs and smoky eyes. But those two can strut around my man in ugly print bikinis and booty shorts. And I'm supposed to be okay with that? I felt my throat close as tears started rolling down my cheeks. I went into the house and up the stairs. I plopped right on the bed and began sobbing.

"What am I doing?" I hollered out.

Ernie responded, "Meow."

"I hear you, Ern. Jump up here and give me some lovin'," I said. Ernie jumped up onto the bed with his motor running. I cried as I began petting him, feeling exhausted. I drifted off into a deep sleep.

A few hours later, Gage arrived home. He was tiptoeing around the house. I rolled over to see who was wrestling around the kitchen.

"Gage?" I called out.

"Go back to sleep. I'm just making a sandwich. I'll be in there in a bit," he said.

A sandwich? A fucking sandwich takes precedence over me. I slithered out of bed, pulled my sundress off, and headed for the shower.

Moments later, I was refreshed by the shower. I pulled my silk robe on and headed to the kitchen. "Did the girls enjoy the boat?" I asked.

"They are just friends, Alexandria. Don't start with that jealous shit," he said, pushing his empty plate aside.

"Jealous?" I laughed. "It's okay for you to have friends all over town, but I have a few friends in a rock band and you make me feel like I'm trash. You act like I'm running around with thieves and jailbirds!"

Gage rolled his eyes and said, "Don't be so dramatic. I'll let you be friends with WHIP."

"You'll let me?" I was getting pissed. "You wouldn't have even met me if it wasn't for WHIP!" I was getting defensive, too. "Just because they do not wear a suit and tie, you immediately dismiss them. They're artists, following their passion. What's wrong with that?" I was stirred up.

"I'm not arguing about your band friends at this hour of the night." Gage was getting angry himself.

"Why couldn't I go to the boat with everybody?"

"Is this what all your huffing and puffing is about, Alexandria? That you weren't invited to the boat? Grow up. You would have been bored. They were Luke's friends, and I was being polite. You didn't need to tag along." Gage pushed crumbs around in front of him on the counter as he avoided looking at me.

"Tag along?" I yelled back. "Yes, I would have been the fifth wheel with Luke and the two bimbos. It was just inconsiderate, Gage. You hurt my feelings. What happened on the boat?" I was fishing for a confession.

"Nothing happened on the boat. I'm not your friend. I'm not your party planner or babysitter. If you wanted to go, you should have gone. Now quit drilling me about my damn boat! I'm here now, aren't I?" Gage picked up his plate and threw it across the kitchen. Glass shattered everywhere.

"Nice," I said, staring at the broken pieces on the floor.

"Clean it up, Alexandria, and go to bed. I'm not dealing with a paranoid woman tonight. Dump your insecurity somewhere else. I'm taking a shower." Gage stood up and walked out of the room. I grabbed the broom and tended to his mess.

The whole evening, I tossed and turned, stewing in bed. What am I doing here? This man is a handful. He makes me feel guilty if I want to hang with Nova or Tyler. He makes me feel like I wasn't pretty enough, with my blonde hair and my eclectic wardrobe. I gave up my loft when he invited me to live in his penthouse thinking I would be safe and not alone. I left Axl in Texas. I had a few bullshit graphic design projects when he promised me more. I'm disappointed with how things are turning out. I feel like I can't breathe. We never make love. It's just sex, with no emotional attachment. And he hates my cat. This sucks. I pulled myself out of bed and dialed Fox. I don't know why, but I felt like I needed an outside, non-judgmental party to plead my case to.

"Well, if it isn't the lovely southern belle," Fox's raspy voice answered. "How are you, my dear?"

"Hi, Fox," I said. I felt an instant comfort level with this stranger. "I was just feeling sorry for myself, so I wanted to call and boo-hoo to you." I felt stupid for calling and dumping my trivial life problems on this grown man.

"Ah, honey, tell me what's eating you? Or should I say who has been eating you?" Fox laughed on the line.

"No one, you fucking pervert. Not since Nova muff dived on the balcony before WHIP's concert." I laughed as I recalled that juicy memory.

"Well, love, give me some details and I'll give you some advice. There is nothing I haven't been through, and no heartache that I haven't felt."

I took a deep breath and confessed to Fox everything Gage had put me through—WHIP, Dallas, Nova, on and on. It felt so good to get it all out there. To just hear myself talk about everything actually made me feel better. When I finished, Fox paused.

Then, he told me, "You are responsible for your own life, my dear. You have to take the reins on this relationship. Who has been there for you the most? What relationships do you value? Who makes you shine, sweetheart? I mean, who gives you the room to be comfortable in your own skin? Who lets you make mistakes? Who lets you live the life you want to live at this moment? I don't want to overstep my boundaries here, but Mr. Heston has his own set of rules. He likes you a certain way, if you behave a certain way, if you hang around a certain crowd and if you please him just right. I could go on and on, dear, but the answers are in these questions. Get a good night's rest, and tomorrow you'll have a fresher outlook on where to go from here. I know you don't have much money, and you don't have Axl, that made me laugh, but it'll work itself out. Grow some balls or borrow my big balls and take control of your life." Fox let out a deep breath. "Alex?"

"I'm here, Fox. Just digesting it all. Thank you for picking up the phone this late." I was grateful.

"I'll always pick up the phone for you. Get some rest and call me in a few days. Let me know how things are working out and if I can help with anything."

"Thank you again, Silver Fox. Good night."

I hung up the phone as I glanced around the room, making sure Gage wasn't eavesdropping. Fucking paranoia setting in. I needed to get a grip. I went out to the balcony to take in the evening air and think about Gage's web that I was entangled in.

*

The next morning, I woke refreshed, as Fox promised. I had some decisions to make and plans to attend to. Coffee was the first plan that needed tending to. I rolled out of an empty bed. Looks like Gage was up and about already. I grabbed my robe, slipped on my Dallas cowboy slippers, petted Ernie, and made my way to the kitchen.

"Good morning, Alexandria." Gage greeted me with a smile. "How are you feeling? Rest well?" I was confused. Ah. I'm assuming he was pissed last night, the way he tossed his dish across the room. But I wasn't starting any bullshit this morning.

I replied, "Yeah, I slept like a rock." I did. Therapy hour with Fox made me feel much better. "What are your plans today?" I kindly asked.

"Well, I thought you and I would take the boat out for a bit. Get you some sun," he said.

Oh, it's my turn to go to the boat. I was so tempted to ask if we'd be met by two bimbos upon our arrival. But I didn't. I played nice.

"Sure. Let me feed Ernie, slap on sunscreen, and we'll head out," I said.

Gage smiled as he got up off the barstool and made his way over to me. I stopped mid-pour as he approached me from behind at the coffee station.

"I'll be ready in half an hour," Gage said, slightly kissing my neck as I set down the coffee pot. I turned towards him. He leaned down and kissed my lips softly. Then he pulled at the tie on my robe, swinging it open. I was shocked by the affectionate display he was putting on. He kissed my neck once more. He moved the robe out of the way and pushed me against the cold stainless counter. He then pulled on my satin panties and shoved them down to the floor. Surprised by the morning passion, I went along with it. Gage kissed me as he untied his pajama bottoms and pulled out his erect cock to greet me.

"Good morning," I said, gripping his hard cock. It was beautiful, and he was very much endowed. Why can't I treat myself with this beautiful penis? After all, it's mine for the time being. I stroked his cock a few times as he moaned in appreciation. Then, he grabbed my hand as I released him, and he spread my legs. He licked his fingers and wet my pussy with his saliva. I moaned a bit. I was turned on. Still pissed at him, but I'll take it out on his cock for the time being. He then stroked himself a few more times before entering me.

"Ohhhh," I moaned as he slid deeper into me, lifting me off the ground as he pushed himself in. His throbbing cock made me so wet. Even though he was deep, it felt so good that I wanted him deeper inside me. Gage pushed and slid in and out of me, until I came so hard.

I was losing my energy from the hard orgasm as he continued to fuck me. Within moments, he pulled out and came all over my leg. I laughed with exhaustion. Gage smiled as he let go of his dick, grabbed a dish towel, and tended to our excitement. I reached for my mug and sipped some coffee. Gage then excused himself and headed for the shower. I closed my robe, sat on the barstool, and finished my coffee. I'm going to enjoy today.

After a day of sunbathing and boating, I felt refreshed. I was sitting in the car with Gage, reminiscing about my day. The morning romp, sunbathing in the nude, scanning through social media, checking on WHIP. Then suddenly, I was inspired.

"Hey Gage, do you know of an art supply store in this area?" I was excited.

"Sure, what do you need?" he replied with curiosity.

"Well, I know you're headed out of town again for the week. So, I wanted to pick up some supplies to keep me occupied. I just thought of something I'd like to paint for a girl I know. Olivia," I said. I was pleased with the thought. Painting Tyler, on stage, holding his microphone for his little groupie girlfriend. She would get a kick out of it.

"Sure, it's right around the corner," Gage said, then was distracted by a phone call. When we pulled into the art supply store, I got instant butterflies in my stomach. Welcome back, passion. Gage parked the car, handed me money, and waved me off as he tended to his phone call. It didn't bother me. I grabbed the cash and headed in.

When we arrived home, Gage went into the bedroom to pack for his trip. I went to the spare room to set up my supplies. I threw on one of Gage's old tees and a cotton pair of underwear. I put on a Foo Fighters CD and got out my pencil to sketch Tyler. Olivia would appreciate this. She's always been kind to me.

I reached for my cell phone and texted her. *I'm working on a surprise for you, girl.* I then went back to sketching. I was completely in my zone when Gage popped his head into the room.

"Hey, how's the painting coming along?"

I continued to sketch. Without looking up at him, I responded, "Good, still in the sketch phase." I continued to draw.

"Who's the sketch of?" He was curious. "Your favorite boyfriend?" He laughed as he sipped his drink.

"Not my boyfriend. You wouldn't want a picture of you sketched unless it was from Andy Warhol. I'm no one, so I'm sketching a friend for a friend." I sat back on my knees, admiring my work laid out in front of me. Gage looked over my shoulder.

"It is your fucking boyfriend!" He cursed as dobs of alcohol splashed from his glass onto my painting.

"Hey!" I protected my work. "Not my boyfriend!" I defended once more.

As Gage headed to his office, he called back, "It looks like shit."

It did not. I continued to work, not finishing until about midnight. I missed dinner. Oh well, I needed to paint. It was therapy for me. As I stood up and stretched, I looked over the canvas once more with appreciation. I grabbed my cell. I snapped a photo of my painting of Tyler, gripping the microphone and singing his heart out, and sent it to Olivia.

What do you think, girl? I texted, with the photo attached.

I got a response immediately: *OMG, I love it. We sure miss you on the road, girl. Be good down there in Miami, sun bunny.*

I laughed as I read her text, then responded, *Miss you, too, WHIP-ette. Safe travels.* I then headed out towards the kitchen. I poured myself a glass of wine to drink on the balcony while I basked in the glow of my awesome new art piece. What a thrill.

*

The next morning Ernie and I rolled over to a half-empty bed. Gage took off early this morning and didn't even say goodbye. I laid there, thinking how childish he could be. Was he jealous of a painting of a rockstar? He's so lame. I know this won't be the end of it. Somehow Gage always seems to go through the trash every time we argue. Even if you think you resolved an issue, it'll come up and be thrown back at you later. Gage dumpster dives.

I was not going to let it dampen my mood. I painted. I was excited. I hopped out of bed and headed to the spare room to check out my work. I needed to make sure it dried nicely. As I walked into the spare room, I saw that my painting had been kicked across the floor, with a shoe print over the face.

"What the fuck!" I hollered. "Can I not enjoy anything without his approval first? What did that fucking bastard do?" I was livid. I picked up the picture. The footprint had dried on the canvas. He must have done this after I went to bed late last night. How childish. What is going on here? I sat on the floor in utter shock. I was sad. That was a good piece. How disappointing. My cell phone rang. I pushed myself off the floor and went to fetch my phone, where I left it last night. It was on the table, on the balcony, next to my empty glass of wine. When I reached the table, I saw that it was Gage calling. I tossed the glass across the balcony as I opened my cell.

"Good morning, jealous bird," I answered.

"Excuse me?" Gage was laughing. He seemed a bit distracted with some other voices in the background.

"Are you in New York?" I asked.

"I just got here, babe. Wait, hold on a moment for me, Alexandria," he said.

I tapped my foot on the floor, waiting for him to return to the line as he talked to someone. It sure sounded like Luke. What the hell was Luke doing in New York? Plus, I never get invited to travel, but it sounded like Bert was there to party with Ernie in the city. I then heard a girl's laughter in the background. Oh, maybe it's a Muppet parade. The whole Muppet gang is in New York. I was fuming.

Gage then got back on the line and said, "Hey. Sorry about that, Alexandria. I'm here. Hello?"

"I'm here, Gage," I responded.

"Listen, I didn't want to wake you this morning. You looked so peaceful sleeping. You wore yourself out sunning and painting. So, I split before dawn. I'm headed to the apartment now. I'll check on you later," he said. More laughter filled the background. I shook my head as we both hung up. He ruined my painting. Not cool.

I gotta get the fuck out of here. I'm so over this. I need a plan and I need money. I headed to the kitchen for coffee. I was in much need of caffeine to construct my exit strategy. This was it. No more toxic, twisted games between us. No more being who I'm NOT for this insecure demon. I'm getting my plan together...today.

CHAPTER FIFTEEN

After two cups of coffee, I was back on level ground. I grabbed my cell and called Fox.

"Good morning, beautiful. What can I do for you? I still have my morning boner," Fox said.

"Don't make me laugh. I'm in a foul mood this morning," I chastised him.

"Ha-ha. What did HE do now? Please don't make excuses for him," he said.

I paused. Then I told Fox how wonderful the sex was with Gage, and sunbathing on the boat. And how I thought things were turning around, until Gage put a huge footprint on it all.

"He's an asshole, Alex," he said.

I agreed and said, "Fox, I need some cash. How can I make some quick, under-the-table cash? I've only worked at one club in Dallas called Vanity, but the Miami strip club scene is a little out of my comfort zone."

"Well, doll, you called the right place. I have a swinger couple that is having a party this week and they're always in need of talent at their events."

"Talent?" I asked.

"Yeah. A few beautiful gals and guys to work the room of their party. Dance on the floor, do a little striptease show, shit like that. Nothing you couldn't handle. I'd be there. Or you could wear your thigh highs and g-string, and serve drinks topless for a couple of hours?"

I thought to myself for a moment, then said, "Okay. I'm in. I mean, I can serve drinks at the swinger party, but that's it. I'm not sleeping or blowing anyone. Or even lap dancing for anyone. I need my go-to girl, Nova, to pull that shit off. So, I'll cocktail. Thank you, Fox," I said. I was excited.

"Hey, doll, it's a few grand Thursday night. I'll pick you up at nine and we'll take care of business."

I felt relieved. I said goodbye and hung up the phone. I'll work the party. Gage will be in New York with the Muppet Gang, so he won't be here to distract me. Some extra cash will give me some freedom to make my next move to leave.

*

Thursday showed up quicker than I anticipated. The week was quiet. I hadn't heard much from Gage except for the occasional doorbell ringing, alerting me of another flower delivery.

I seem to have this constant stomachache. Something is telling me that he is up to no good, but I'm ignoring it. I don't have time to stew. I have to get gussied up for the evening. Fox will be here by nine o'clock. I need to bring my A-game to this party.

Right on time, the man I've confided in has come through for me. I was so grateful to see the black Cadillac as it pulled up. That sharp-dressed man got out and opened the back door for me. I grabbed my bag and locked the door to the beach house. As I stepped into the back seat, Miss Nova was sitting in there.

"Yeehaw, bitch!" Nova hollered out. "I'm so here to party with you!"

I laughed as I hugged her, and asked, "What are you doing here?" I was shocked but relieved. I didn't have to work this event solo.

"Fox called, told me about your dilemma. I took a few days off from Vanity and decided to fly in and join you. Are you surprised?" Nova asked.

"Yes, I'm surprised. I didn't realize how much I would miss you until you were gone, mama!" I said and hugged her once more.

"Okay, ladies. Let's have a good time tonight, make a little money, and get laid," Fox chimed in. The two of us laughed like we were naughty schoolgirls.

"This is going to be fun," I agreed with Fox.

"Well, Alex," said Nova, "I brought you a cocktail dress, since yours is sitting in some thrift store bin. I can't believe Gage got rid of all your threads, girl. And look at that ugly ensemble you are wearing. What the fuck is that?" Nova pulled on my sundress.

"Don't start, girl. I don't want to even think about him tonight. I want to have a good time. Besides, we are going to be topless serving cocktails; no one will care what I showed up in. Just as long as it's lying on the floor somewhere," I said. I stuck my tongue out at her. Then I clutched her hand, to show that I was appreciative that she was here with me.

A few moments later, the three of us pulled into the driveway of another fabulous beach house on Star Island.

"Wow, Fox, this home is amazing!" I shouted, rolling down the window to admire the home with awe.

"Now, girls. I'm a guest here. I'm not working the event, but I will keep an eye on you two. I will introduce you to the couple throwing the party. You'll shimmy down to your panties and cocktail tray. And make your way around the house. Any questions?" Fox asked, smiling as he looked at the two of us in his rear-view mirror.

"We are good, Daddy!" Nova shouted as she leaned up to Fox and kissed his cheek. I closed my eyes for a minute and took a deep breath.

Nova and I were linked arm-in-arm with Fox as the three of us made our entrance. The door opened, and the hostess greeted us with a playful smile.

"Hello, Fox. Who are your friends?" The hostess kissed Fox on the lips, then stepped back to have a look at Nova and me. She was tan, with long, silky black hair. Thin, wearing a form-fitted sheer dress, holding a cigarette and a glass of wine.

"This is Mercedes and Angel." Fox nodded at each of us as he made the introductions. I was happy that we were using stage names tonight. Who knows what kind of guests will be invited to a swingers' party?

"Pleasure to meet you, girls." The beautiful hostess smiled at us with great approval.

"Okay, girls. You are in. Head to the back bedroom and leave your things there. Then meet with the bartender out by the pool, and he'll give you instructions." Fox pointed to the back bedroom. "My work is done here. Now show me where the drugs and sluts are!" Fox laughed as he took the hostess's arm and walked away.

I looked at Nova and asked, "Are you ready, Mercedes?"

She laughed as she scanned the room, and said, "I'm so ready."

This home was impeccable. Expensive beach furnishings and tons of windows, with an amazing view of the water. One perk of living in Miami is everything is surrounded by water. The lights were dim. The music was subtle and erotic. Nova and I made our way through the crowded main room. Each of us wore our black thigh highs, black G-string panties, and black high heels. Boobs were on display. I didn't mind having my breasts out, especially when you looked around the room and everyone seemed to be nude. I actually blended in.

"These guests are gorgeous!" Nova hip-bumped me. "I'm getting laid tonight. There is so much X here, it's incredible. This music alone is turning me on!" She laughed.

"Everything turns you on, Nova. You are such a—"

We both screamed in unison, "Sluuuuut!" Then we laughed.

"I'll head to the pool area. You work in the main room. We'll meet in the middle," I said, making our plan with Nova. We went our separate ways. Once I stepped out into the pool area, I was taken aback once again by the stunning view. "This puts Playboy's pool Grata to shame," I mumbled under my breath as I began mingling with the guests. Everybody was on X. Pairs of people were spread about the pool area. Either they were in deep flirtatious conversation, making out, dancing, or fucking. No one paid attention to the cocktail waitresses. I roamed about the party, serving alcohol, X, and a smile. The hostess would introduce me to friends and colleagues of hers from time to time. Some would make an offer to have sex with me, but I would pleasantly decline.

After a few hours, Fox found me and asked, "How are you holding up, doll? Some party, huh? I'm telling you, this is Miami's A-list here. This is much better than going to the local swinger bar. You have to fill out all the paperwork outside on some bench, before entering the club. Kinda kills the mojo, huh?" Fox laughed as he tossed back the remains of his drink.

"Need a refill, sir?" I asked politely. Fox laughed as he brushed the cold glass against my tits. "Hey now," I scolded him.

"You need a break, doll? Are your dogs barking? How about you and I head inside, find a couch to park our asses on, and I'll rub your feet for a bit?" He smiled at me.

"Awe, that sounds perfect. But wait. Do you have a foot fetish? What am I getting myself into?" I laughed as I set my tray down at the bartender station, took Fox's hand, and went into the main room.

"There are a few chaises in that corner," Fox pointed out. There were a few gold velvet chaises to the left of the room, where one wasn't occupied by a couple.

"Lead the way, Fox," I said as I let him lead me to the chair. We settled in on the velvet piece of furniture. It was large enough to accommodate both of us. Fox sat one way, and I sat on the opposite end, flinging my legs onto his lap. Fox purred as he removed my heel and started to massage my foot. Either it was the X, the view, or his foot fetish, but I could feel his cock stiffen underneath my leg. He rubbed with more intensity. I leaned back and gazed up at the enormous chandeliers hanging from the ceiling. I then closed my eyes as the foot massage started to relax me, and I tuned into the seductive trance music. It kind of sounded like something WHIP would create. Ah, for a moment there, I wished Trent was here. I recalled the evening he came over to the loft and massaged me. Then we made incredible love that night. Wow, how that man can turn me on by just smiling at me. I was lost in the moment when Fox nudged me.

"Hey, doll, look who's making friends," he said. He grabbed ahold of my other foot and began the same rub routine on it. I turned my head and saw Nova kissing some handsome stranger on an opposing chaise.

"You are such a voyeur, Fox. Maybe we shouldn't watch," I said, trying to shame him a bit.

"Of course we should. We are at a nudist swinger event on X. This is exactly what we are supposed to do. If they wanted privacy, they would have occupied an extra bedroom or left the premises. I am into voyeurism. Remember when I sat in the room and watched you and Nova?"

I rolled my eyes and said, "Yes, I remember that. But that was between friends." I was a little embarrassed, as I recalled the WHIP after-party. My friend is really a slut. "I just worry about her, Fox," I said, being honest with a man on drugs, watching my friend get fondled.

"She's a big girl. We are right here. She wants this man to fuck her so bad. Let's not take that from her." I started to pull my foot away as Fox gripped it harder. "Shh. Watch," he said.

I turned and watched Nova. She was so beautiful. I

envied her confidence in her sexuality. That was one gift I didn't get blessed with. She's the strutting cat, and I'm the scared mouse, dangling from her lips. I let it go and watched her. The strange man received slow, passionate kisses from Nova. She leaned him back against the chaise and hovered over him. She dangled each breast into his mouth, and he licked each nipple affectionately. I was getting aroused watching as I rubbed my foot along Fox's hard cock. He sat quietly, rubbing my foot and stroking my thigh high.

Nova started to remove the man's jeans and underwear until he was spread nude along the velvet chair. Nova continued to thrust her tongue in and out of the man's mouth as he moaned. She then used his pre-cum to masturbate him, making him a bit harder, to her liking. Once he was hard and moistened, Nova sat on him, reverse cowgirl style. She slowly let his hard cock enter her. She moaned as he pushed deeper into her. She would be an incredible adult film star. Look how comfortable and sexy she is with this man. Years of working Vanity, I guess. She's always putting on some kind of sex show. She continued to fuck him harder, riding his lap. He then leaned forward. She dropped into a doggy-style position. He fucked her until he came, pulling out his large cock and cumming on her backside. I was officially aroused.

"Wow," I said quietly to Fox as he pulled out a cigarette and lit it. "Now I need a cigarette after that."

Fox laughed as I sat up and adjusted my thigh high. Nova let the man wipe her clean with his boxer shorts. Then he leaned back, lighting a cigarette to share with him.

"Who is that man?" I asked Fox.

"Some man she's been dating here in Miami. Every time she flew in, these two would be inseparable."

"Huh?" I responded, feeling better that she knew the man. This must be another little secret she hides from me. "A customer?" I asked.

"No. These two have been on and off again for quite some time. He wants to marry her, you know, but Nova is rebellious. She likes the man to chase and chase her. I don't feel she's ready to settle yet. Do you? She's a naughty girl. She doesn't want to give that up yet." Fox took another drag off his cigarette.

"Huh?" I responded once again. "He's handsome."

Fox ignored me. I whistled to gain Nova's attention. She took a drag from her cigarette and rolled her head in my direction. We locked eyes through the cloud of smoke. She smiled. My friend was happy. High but happy. I pointed to my watch. It was going on four AM, and I wanted to collect our money and head home. Nova nodded. She called over to me. She was going back to his place—the man she just had sex with. She would call me in the morning.

"It is morning," I said, then blew her a kiss. "Come on, Fox. Nova got laid. I need to get paid, and you need to go home."

Fox agreed. We got up and gathered our things. We said goodbye to the hostess and made our way home.

*

After Fox drove away, I stood in front of Gage's door. I felt tired and hungry but satisfied with how the evening went.

What a killer way to make some extra cash. I have the upper hand now. Serving drinks and hanging out with my pervy friends. I loved it. I took a moment to breathe in the fresh morning air before I headed in.

I turned the key, pushed open the door, and heard "Where the fuck were you tonight?" My heart pounded so hard I thought it would leap out of my chest, and onto the stairway in front of me. Gage asked again: "Where were you, Alexandria? I have been home for hours. I have been calling you for hours. Again, where were you?" He was drunk. I kicked off my heels and headed up the stairs to face him.

"I was at an intimate party with some friends. I thought you weren't due back until Saturday?" I asked kindly.

"Bullshit," he said, tossing the ice around his drink. He stood there, looking at me. "What friends? You have no friends here in Miami." He cleared his throat.

"You like that, don't you? No friends here. I'm all alone here. Well, for your information, Nova flew in to surprise me!" I barked back.

"That explains your attire. What are you dressed like that for? You look like a tramp," Gage scolded me once more.

"Well, I had no cocktail dress to wear. So, Nova gave me one of hers," I barely finished my reply when Gage lunged towards me and grabbed my arm. Shocked, I stumbled a bit and fell to the ground.

"Get up, Alexandria. You are headed for the shower, to wash off this mess," he said. He pulled my arm once more and dragged me to the shower. He then pinned me against the wall as he turned the showerhead on. He pulled my dress off, ripping it as it flew over my head, and scraped the fishnets down my legs.

"Ow, Gage. You are hurting me!" I started to fight him. As I fought Gage, he fought harder. My outfit was ripped and pulled off. The fishnets were dangling from my legs. He grabbed my hair and threw me into the shower. I slammed against the wall so hard I knew it would bruise, but I continued to push him.

"Don't fight me. I'm washing this evening off of you!" he yelled with his intoxicated breath. He then grabbed my head. He pushed me under the showerhead and soaked my hair. As I fought with soapy eyes, I slipped and hit the floor once again. He leaned down, grabbing a handful of hair. He banged my head against the floor, yelling, "Why do you do this to me? Wash yourself clean. I can't deal with you like this!" He then stood up. He threw soap and a rag at me and walked out of the bathroom.

I sat stunned under the flowing water. I couldn't cry. I was numb. What the fuck just happened? What the hell did I do? When the fuck did he get home? My mind went in circles as I steadied myself to get on my feet. I pulled off the rest of the thigh highs and stood under the rushing water. My head pounded and my back ached. I wiped away the eye makeup, the perfume, the smoke in my hair, and washed it all down the drain. After a few minutes, I shut off the water and reached for the towel. As I stepped in front of the mirror with my dripping hair, I stood there in shock. My back was welting up. My eye had already begun to bruise. I had scratches down my leg from the thigh highs being removed unwillingly. I panicked for a moment, holding back the tears that were beginning to surface. My whole body stung as I stood there. Gage walked back in and handed me my robe.

"Put this on. We'll talk in the morning. I'm tired from my travels," he said. He turned and walked out of the bathroom as I stood there, dripping in fear.

The next morning, I felt like I had a hangover, even though I didn't have an ounce to drink at the swingers' party. I just served drinks. My head hurt, my back ached. I laid there, feeling nothing. Everything from last night's event was tucked away within me somehow and I couldn't release it. I was afraid to exhale. It might hurt. I sensed Gage was still home. I pondered if I should attempt to face him, or continue to pretend to sleep and see how the morning unfolds.

My cat surfaced from under the comforter and greeted me with his butterfly kisses. I tried to smile back at Ernie, but my bruised face couldn't handle that emotion right now. As I looked around the room, I noticed my bag on the floor with my cell phone next to it. I immediately sat up and leaned to grab my bag. I wanted to make sure my money was still inside. If he found the money, that might cause a second scene. I dug through the bag and, to my relief, the money was still stowed away in the inside pocket. Gage would have had to dig to find it, but I know he could care less about my bag. I then reached for the cell and flipped it open to check my missed calls. There were thirty fucking missed calls from Gage last night. One voicemail from Nova. And one voicemail from Olivia.

Hmm? Psycho phoned me thirty damn times during the party. Nova probably was giving me an update on her secret beau. But Olivia? I wondered what she wanted. I typed in my password and listened to my messages. I heard Olivia's terrified voice on the other end. I got chills.

"*Alex, girl, it's Olivia. You need to call me. Tyler is in Atlanta General.*" Olivia was sobbing and said, "*He overdosed tonight. The band is here with me and you need to call me back!*" Click. There was silence on the line and I dropped the phone.

Oh my God. What should I do? I sat there panicking for a quick moment. Then I slid to the floor and reached for my cell once more. Nova. I'll call Nova. I dialed her, my hands shaking as I held the phone to my ear.

"Hey girl, I was just about to call you. I got some messages about Tyler. You know he overdosed last night after their set in Atlanta?"

I interrupted and said, "Yes. Olivia left me a message late last night. I just got it now. We need to get to Atlanta, stat!" I could feel panic rising within me once again and said, "Your beau has a car we can borrow?" I bit my lip, waiting to see if Nova could line us up a ride.

"Hold on, girl. I'll ask him," she responded. I was in agony waiting. I needed to change, grab my purse, feed Ernie, and flee to Georgia. "Alex?" Nova returned to the line. "He said we could have his Range Rover. I'll be there in twenty minutes."

"Good," I said. I exhaled for a second, then hung up the phone. I jumped up and scurried about, grabbing Capri pants and a button-up sweater. I then slipped on a pair of flats. I went to the mirror to brush my hair into a bun. After brushing my teeth, I caught a glimpse of my swollen face and let it go. My friend needed me. Tyler was priority now. I ignored the pain. I grabbed my bag and headed to the kitchen to feed Ernie.

Gage was sitting on the balcony. He hollered, "What's all the rushing about? Where are you headed off to? We need to have a chat, Alexandria," he said. He still seemed bitter.

"I don't have time for a fucking chat, Gage. Nova's on her way over. I'm heading to Atlanta!"

"Atlanta?" Gage interrupted me.

"Yes, Atlanta. Tyler is in the hospital and he needs me."

"Wait, what happened? Rockstar partied a little too hard?" Gage laughed.

"I'm not doing this right now. Yes, he overdosed," I said, feeding Ernie and pouring coffee into a to-go cup.

"Great. That asshole is going to cost me money and tour dates." I threw my spoon into the sink, making a loud clanking noise.

"Cost you money? That's all you're fucking worried about? You're unbelievable. My best friend is lying in ICU and you don't give a fuck about him or me, do you?" He exhausted me.

Gage walked into the kitchen, grabbed my arm, and said, "Of course I care, but business is business. And WHIP is my business. Shall I take you to Atlanta? I could charter a plane," Gage tried to be sincere, but I saw right through it. He wanted to tag along to check on the band. And make sure I didn't run off with them.

"No," I barked back. I corrected my tone and restated, "No, thank you. Nova and I will drive. I'll call you later." I heard Nova beep the horn to alert me that she was outside. "I gotta go, Gage," I said. I kissed Ernie on the head while he chowed on his breakfast, grabbed my coffee, and ran downstairs to meet Nova.

I hopped into the hunter-green Range Rover and let out a scream of frustration.

"You ready, girl?" Nova asked, putting the vehicle in drive. She glanced at the bruise on my face and said nothing except, "I see Gage is back."

I ignored the comment and said, "Let's roll. Do you have directions?"

"All set. My man set the GPS up for us. So, your job is to look out for cops on the Interstate. It's about nine hours, but I can get us there in seven!"

I laughed and said, "This is unbelievable, Nova. I had a feeling something would happen on this tour."

"I know, Alex. But Ty is Ty. He'll play sexy frontman rockstar as well as he can. Fucking Jim Morrison, eh? Don't worry. He'll be okay. He's in good hands," Nova said. She tried to comfort me, but I remained numb. I couldn't feel anything. I couldn't feel the bruises or the heartache. Just confusion. I was fucking scared for my friend. I sipped my coffee and watched the trees go by as Nova flew up Interstate 95.

Eight hours later, we arrived at Atlanta General Hospital. The whole day seemed to be a blur. I texted Olivia and asked for the room number Tyler was in. She and a few guys from WHIP stepped out to get a bite to eat, which was good. I wanted a moment alone with Ty. Nova said she would walk with me to the room, then she'd go get coffee for us. I was grateful.

We stepped out of the elevator onto the chilly ICU floor and headed to Tyler's room. My whole body stiffened. My legs felt like noodles. I reached the door and peeked inside.

My heart sank. I saw my best friend lying in a metal-framed hospital bed. He was surrounded by sterile hospital monitoring equipment. He was hooked up to IV fluids. He looked as thin as a rail. He was awake but didn't even hear me approach him. He was staring out the window, a tear rolling down his cheek.

"Ty?" I whispered.

He rolled his head towards me and smiled. "Alex, I fucked up."

I smiled back to reassure him it was okay and said, "It's alright, Morrison."

"They pumped my stomach. I don't even remember last night's set, girl. I guess I collapsed and the EMTs had to resuscitate me. Now I'm awake and hooked up to all this shit," Tyler said. He glanced at the IV pole, then looked back at me.

"You look skinny, Ty. I've missed you," I said.

"What a wild ride it's been. I've just exhausted myself. I guess we're taking a few dates off the schedule, so I can recoup. Trent is taking me to his house in Louisiana, after they release me," Tyler said. He released a pitiful sigh.

"Trent? That man is so good," I said. I smiled once more to let Ty know that was the right thing to do. "You need rest. Maybe you'll write a good song about all this in your down time. Kind of like Nikki Sixx and the *Dr. Feelgood* album." Tyler laughed. "Good to see you smile," I said as I sat down on his cold hospital bed and squeezed his hand.

"You, Alex. You look like shit."

"Thanks," I responded to his brutal comment.

"What has that man done to you?" I shifted my weight. Gage was something I did not want to talk about. "I'm sorry I wasn't there, Alex. Sorry I've been caught up being a rockstar when you've needed me," Tyler said. He was sad for me as he squeezed my hand and stroked my bruised cheek.

"I'm okay. I'm a tough girl. Let's get you healthy, then we'll address my drama," I said. I looked down in shame.

"You're a brunette in ugly clothes. You look tired and stressed. You're my best friend and I love you, Alex. Aside from the ugly getup I still see a beautiful, creative Texas girl in there. Is he worth it?" Tyler asked.

I said nothing at first. I was so full of emotions that I had no idea how to release them. I had no idea which one to address first. "I don't know anymore, Tyler. I love you. Please eat today. The gang will be back in a bit. You are surrounded by friends. You are loved. Breathe out and settle down," I said. I tried to encourage Tyler as his eyes started to look heavy. I knew he needed to rest.

Nova popped her head in and said, "Hey, Ty. Road a bit too much for ya? You fucking asshole. You are such a rockstar."

I interrupted and said, "Leave him alone, Nova. Let's step out for a bit. He needs to rest."

The two of us hugged Tyler, then made our way out toward the lobby to discuss plans. As we approached, I could sense everybody feeling sorry for me. Olivia hugged me first. Then the other guys kissed my cheek and stepped away. Trent squeezed my hand and I got a lump in my throat.

"Excuse me, I need air," I said. I turned away and headed for the stairwell. Trent followed me and pushed the heavy door open to give us some privacy. The door slammed and echoed so loud that I jumped.

"It's okay, Alex. It was just the door. Tyler is so happy you are here. He was asking about you last night. You are his rock, you know."

"I've been a terrible friend. How did the drugs get so bad?" I questioned Trent.

"No one knew. Ty was being Ty. We'll get him back to my place and get him some help. He needs to rest and heal," said Trent.

I stood there with my arms crossed, mulling over everything. I had a hell of a twenty-four hours. I was exhausted. Trent walked up to me, uncrossed my arms, and pulled me into his embrace. My bruised back made me shudder as Trent pulled back.

"You okay?" he asked.

I looked up at him and started sobbing. It was uncontrollable sobbing. He gently put his arms back around me and swayed with me as I cried. I was releasing everything. The party, Gage, Tyler. I was releasing everything into Trent. He was the only one that would understand my release of emotion. He then lifted my head, wiped my tears, and looked at me with those beautiful dark eyes. I don't know what overcame me, but I reached up to him and kissed him so passionately. Kissing him released it all. I knew I would be okay. He returned my kiss with just as much passion and intensity. I pulled away from our embrace. I sat down on the concrete stair, staring at the wall in front of me. Trent sat down next to me and held my hand. We didn't speak another word.

Moments later, we rejoined our friends in the lobby and discussed our plans. I felt better. It was good that Trent was taking Ty home for a bit to heal. He is such a good egg. He made plans with everyone. For a moment I was happy. I then looked over at Nova, who was fiddling with a non-lit cigarette. I saw her eyes light up like saucers. I laughed, then turned to look at what she was staring at.

There in the doorway of the lobby stood Gage. My stomach dropped. He scanned the room, then proceeded to walk right up to me and kiss my head. "I didn't hear from you. I wanted to make sure you were alright," Gage said. The whole gang grew silent. They protectively watched Gage and me.

"I'm okay, Gage. We haven't been here long. I already checked on Tyler," I said. I gulped, then looked at Trent. Trent flashed a concerned look. Gage then walked away. He began to give the band a timeline on the tour, how he's going to handle the headlines, and so on. I stood there, watching him. He was so kind and dapper when I first met him at the WHIP CD release party. But now look at him—controlling and toxic. I didn't say another word. I watched Gage control the conversation. He made sure Nova would get Tyler back to Trent's house. He had a plane nearby to take the two of us back to Miami. I walked over to Nova and hugged her. I waved to the band and headed back towards Tyler's room to say one last goodbye.

When I entered Tyler's hospital room, he was still in the same position. He was awake and staring out the window.

"Hey," I said, startling him.

"Hey back," Tyler said. He rolled over to face me. "Mr. Record Label Man was in here, checking up on his investment."

I rolled my eyes and said, "I'm so sorry, Ty."

"Don't be, sugar," he calmed me. "He's was a big part of WHIP's success but now he's about to get fucking fired.

Bastard is all hat, no fuckin cattle. I'm furious with him and his behavior. We need a band meeting—I'll handle all the label stuff later when I'm at Trent's resting. Will you be okay? I'm assuming he wasn't here to check up on me, but to check up on you."

I nodded my head and said, "I'll be okay." I kissed his lips and told him that I loved him very much. "Please call me when you get settled. I really miss you, Ty."

"I miss you, too, Texas. We need to shoot the bull over all this." He smiled at me and my eyes teared up. I kissed him once more. Gage then popped his head into the room.

"Ready, Alexandria?" he asked.

"I'm coming," I said. I slowly got off the hospital bed and waved a subtle goodbye to Tyler.

The entire plane ride, Gage and I didn't say one word to each other. When we reached the beach house, I went straight up the stairs, scooped up Ernie, and flopped on the bed.

"Dinner?" Gage called to me.

"No," I replied. I closed my eyes and drifted off to sleep.

CHAPTER SIXTEEN

The next week Gage and I went about our routine. We pretty much stayed out of each other's way. I hid the money from the swingers' party. Gage never brought that night back up. I was completely walking on eggshells at the house, but Gage seemed fine. I guess this is what he thinks a good relationship is. Eggshells. It all came down to eggshells. I knew he was getting ready for another trip, because the suitcase was out once again. I was happy to see him go. I wanted time alone. I needed privacy to figure out what to do, without him lurking around every corner. I made sure not to rock the boat. I went about our business as usual, and obedient as ever.

"He'll be gone for one week," I kept telling myself over and over.

I secretly spoke to Tyler from time to time, to check on his mental health and see what the band was planning to do. I also missed Trent. I longed for his embrace. He was taking such good care of Ty. I was grateful for that.

I felt so alone in Miami. I was realizing how uncomfortable I was in my own skin. I was depressed. All my drawings were stashed away in the garage. I had no interest in them anymore. I was officially a house mouse. I was bored.

Gage left in the usual manner, slipping out the door before I awoke. I was relieved. I couldn't fake another tearful goodbye. I sat up in bed and took my time greeting the day. I had the place to myself. I could call all my friends in a bit and talk openly. I could try to figure out what the fuck to do. I took a deep breath. I then decided to get up and go for a run on the beach. That was what I was going to do. A good run on the beach will clear my head. A perfect plan.

After my morning run, I felt exhilarated. My endorphins were running on high as I reached the front door of Gage's house. There, at the door once again, sat several boxes from the flower delivery man. I kicked them aside as I put my key in the door.

    I paused for a moment. I turned around. I felt sorry for the flowers. I picked each box up, one by one, and carried them up the stairs. There were twelve damn boxes. I opened them all up, and put each one on display throughout the house. Each one had a corny card attached, with some *"I'm thinking of you"* bullshit written on it. I hated flowers. Especially roses. The official "I'm sorry I fucked up" flower that I was so tired of receiving and caring for. Vases were all over the place. The scent of roses filled the air and made me quite nauseous. I brushed it off and went for a cold bottle of water in the kitchen.

    I stood there, drinking my water. I stared at the flowers.

"Ugly fucking things," I said. I was working myself up. I had twelve dozen roses in my face, displayed in ugly vases that Mr. Heston picked out. I hate his taste. I hate the clothes he bought me. I hate my dark hair. I hate this fucking beach house. I hate him.

"Ahhhhh!" I screamed, throwing my water bottle across the room. That felt good. I needed to let that out. I then walked over to the mop in the laundry room so I could clean up the water. As I reached for it, I had a sadistic thought. I grabbed the mop head and twisted it off the stick. I gripped the stick in my hand. I walked out of the laundry room and headed back towards the flowers. I paused, looked around in frustration, and started swinging.

"I hate fucking roses!" I screamed. I bashed every single one of the vases. Ernie went running into the bedroom. I continued releasing my anger. Glass, petals, and water flew everywhere! I didn't care at all. It was exhilarating! I bashed and bashed until the entire room was littered in pieces of flowers and bits of glass. What a release! I then stepped through the mess, squishing petals into the floor, until I reached the balcony.

I stepped out onto the balcony and screamed, "I'M DONE! I've had enough Miami!" I started to laugh at the mess I'd made and felt revived. It was my 'AH-HA' moment. No more excuses.

I was finally leaving Gage.

Suddenly, a red truck pulled up, below on the street. I leaned over the balcony to check it out, watching it park.

"Axl?" I said to myself. "Axl!!!" I screamed. Both doors

of the truck opened and out jumped Austin, Tyler, and Trent. I screamed, "Yeehaw! Up here, bitches!"

The boys looked up at me, shielding their eyes from the sun. I ran through the house and down the stairs to greet them. I opened the door and jumped straight into Trent's arms. He spun me around.

"Oh my god!" I screamed as I spun. After he let me down, I went over and hugged Austin and Tyler. "What are y'all doing here?" I put both of my hands on my head. I was dizzy with excitement.

"We came to rescue you, sugar!" Tyler said as he kissed me on the head. "And look," he said. He reached into Axl and grabbed a bag off the front seat. He started pulling items out.

"Box of hair color!" I laughed. He unrolled a tee shirt. "WHIP tee," I laughed once more.

"Jeans and your converse shoes that were left in Axl," Tyler said as he tapped on the bag. I grabbed the shoes. Tyler screamed, "Let's color your hair! Burn those god-awful clothes! Grab Ernie and head the fuck back to Texas!"

I mouthed "Texas" as tears streamed down my face.

While Austin made his way into the house to fetch Ernie and Tyler followed, Trent turned to me and hugged me once more.

"I'm here, Alex," he whispered, kissing my head. "I'm never leaving you alone again. Trying to keep you and the band separate did not work for either one of us. You are part of the band, because you are a part of me. Let's take you home." I raised my head to look up at him. He leaned in to kiss me. I returned the kiss while laughing through my tears. I then paused, stepped back, and took a long look at Trent. This felt right—no eggshells.

Suddenly, we both heard, "What the fuck happened in here!?" I grinned, knowing just what Tyler was talking about. Trent gave me a concerned look. We both looked up towards the balcony as roses began showering us.

END

ABOUT ATMOSPHERE PRESS

Atmosphere Press is an independent, full-service publisher for excellent books in all genres and for all audiences. Learn more about what we do at atmospherepress.com.

We encourage you to check out some of Atmosphere's latest releases, which are available at Amazon.com and via order from your local bookstore:

Twisted Silver Spoons, a novel by Karen M. Wicks

Queen of Crows, a novel by S.L. Wilton

The Summer Festival is Murder, a novel by Jill M. Lyon

The Past We Step Into, stories by Richard Scharine

The Museum of an Extinct Race, a novel by Jonathan Hale Rosen

Swimming with the Angels, a novel by Colin Kersey

Island of Dead Gods, a novel by Verena Mahlow

Cloakers, a novel by Alexandra Lapointe

Twins Daze, a novel by Jerry Petersen

Embargo on Hope, a novel by Justin Doyle

Abaddon Illusion, a novel by Lindsey Bakken

Blackland: A Utopian Novel, by Richard A. Jones

The Jesus Nut, a novel by John Prather

The Embers of Tradition, a novel by Chukwudum Okeke

Saints and Martyrs: A Novel, by Aaron Roe

When I Am Ashes, a novel by Amber Rose

ABOUT THE AUTHOR

Jacqueline always had a love for creativity, whether it was writing poetry, lyrics, or painting mixed media art. She earned a degree in Music Sound Engineering through ARTI, worked live music venues, and even sold her own line of punk rock swag.

After touring for a decade, she started to long for life at home. With her love of cats, she pursued her Animal Science degree through the University of Texas and became CVA certified through the Texas Veterinary Medical Association.

Today, Jacqueline is proud to hold the lead surgical technician position at a 'feline only' hospital as she continues to write, participate in art shows, and root for her Dallas Cowboys.

She resides in South Florida with her husband and two cats- very grateful for this balance in her life.

Made in the USA
Columbia, SC
02 April 2022